ALSO BY

ALICIA GIMÉNEZ-BARTLETT

Dog Day

PRIME TIME
SUSPECT

Alicia Giménez-Bartlett

PRIME TIME SUSPECT

*Translated from the Spanish
by Nicholas Caistor*

Europa
editions

Europa Editions
116 East 16th Street
New York, N.Y. 10003
www.europaeditions.com
info@europaeditions.com

This book is a work of fiction. Any references to historical events,
real people, or real locales are used fictitiously

Copyright © 2000 by Alicia Giménez-Bartlett
First Publication 2007 by Europa Editions

Translation by Nicholas Caistor
Original Title: *Muertos de papel*
Translation copyright © 2007 by Europa Editions

All rights reserved, including the right of reproduction
in whole or in part in any form

Library of Congress Cataloging in Publication Data is available
ISBN 978-1-933372-31-0

Giménez-Bartlett, Alicia
Prime Time Suspect

Book design by Emanuele Ragnisco
www.mekkanografici.com

Printed in Italy
Arti Grafiche La Moderna – Rome

CONTENTS

PRIME TIME SUSPECT

1.

That morning I was in a melancholy mood. The dense clouds that had been gathering for hours finally seemed about to burst. It was so humid my hair stuck to my scalp in clumps. Suddenly I had a vivid, awful glimpse of the impression I must make on others: a woman in her forties, getting ready for work, with nothing worth remembering from the day before. I sighed. Why on earth was I so concerned about the effect I might produce on somebody else? I don't usually bother with that kind of thing: in the end it gets boring, or drives you mad. Basically, we're all varying combinations of what we actually are and what we'd dearly love to be. We are . . . a mishmash of states of mind and states of health, an amalgam of genetics and biography, of emotional sensibility and nutrition. A Swede who breakfasts on *smorgasbord* is never going to be the same as someone from Valencia who's crazy about *paella*. You can't compare the gaze of a woman of experience to that of a youngster fresh from the nest. Nor would a hypothetical daughter of Mae West have the same character profile as an even more hypothetical daughter of Mother Teresa.

My state of mind was beginning to annoy me. If I was in such a crisis of melancholy for no other reason than the weather, why didn't I look for something more intellectually stimulating? I've never considered myself particularly stupid, and always thought myself sufficiently concerned about the fate of the human race to avoid getting hung up on trivial matters. But that particular morning, any higher reasoning seemed destined to spin out of control. There was only one car speeding round the racetrack of my mind: the sad impression I would make on anyone who saw me.

I only realized later that this had been a premonition. When I saw this clearly, I wanted to tell the whole world I had got the first inkling of what was going on. But nothing is more futile than proclaiming yourself a Cassandra, particularly if you're a woman. People are used to us foreseeing problems and get tired of listening to us and judging our predictions against what actually happens. I admit, it's a pain always being the bearer of bad tidings. I also admit there is little scientific evidence for intuitions, and not much support from books either, but in practice it's been proven to exist. And it's the only way I can explain how my mood that melancholy morning was confirmed shortly afterwards by a very unusual case. A case in which image, appearance, and influence on other people, as well as the reputation of a celebrity, were at the heart of the affair. A murder that raised more dust than a Touareg in the desert.

Garzón rudely interrupted my thoughts. When he came into my office and saw me staring out of the window, he harrumphed in a way that could have meant anything. We had not worked together for a while, but he was always finding an excuse to consult some file or other in my lair. This gave him the chance to have a chat, or even the opportunity for the two of us to go and have a coffee together. As I already mentioned, that particular day dawned gloomily: it seemed to have put everyone in a bad mood. When I saw how the weather was also affecting my colleague, I tried to lighten his mood:

"How are you today, Fermín?"

"Not good," he growled. "I've got a headache."

"Have you tried aspirin?"

"Yes," he said weakly.

"And . . . ?"

"If I say I've got a headache that means it didn't do any good, doesn't it?"

His mood wasn't just cloudy; it was downright tempestuous. I was fed up with being sympathetic and getting nothing in return, so I snapped:

"How about a lobotomy, do you think that would work?"

He slammed the drawer shut that he had been ferreting in and turned towards me.

"Very funny, Inspector. In fact, that's about the funniest thing I've ever heard you say in all the time we've known each other. But if you're interested, there's no call to feel jolly."

"Why's that?"

"We've just been handed a case on the rebound."

"What's that?"

"What you heard. The chief inspector wants to see us in his office in an hour for a meeting. But gossip travels quicker than a trail of gunpowder, and I already know what he wants to talk to us about."

"The rebound case."

"Exactly."

"And where has this case rebounded from?"

"From Inspector Moliner and his partner, sergeant Rodríguez."

I whistled. Moliner and Rodríguez had a reputation for dealing with the most difficult cases, the ones that needed a good dose of diplomacy, and an even bigger one of caution. Let's just say that they took on any case that had a public dimension, one that could end up in the press.

"And why has it rebounded from them, if the rumor mill grinds that fine?"

"Because they're needed on another case. Apparently one that it's strictly forbidden to talk about."

"Which means of course there are all the more rumors circulating."

"Absolutely. Apparently it's a murder: a young society woman has been killed, and everything points to the fact that she was someone important's lover."

"Jesus!"

"And that's why the case has been handed to Moliner and Rodríguez, while the one they were busy with has been passed on to you and me."

"If those two were involved, it can't be that bad. They're the ace detectives, after all. What kind of case is it?"

"No idea."

"Fantastic! You've no idea about the only thing you are authorized to know."

"You never hear rumors about things that are not meant to be hidden."

"How long were they on the case?"

"Only a couple of days."

"Then I don't understand why you're so upset about taking it on. We'll still be in time to do it our way."

"Yes, but you know how I hate getting involved in things that other people have already had their paws on."

"That's known as virginity syndrome, typical of people with lots of prejudices—for example, men who are past it."

I was trying to provoke Garzón, but at the same time I appreciated his concerns. Not being there at the start of an investigation often complicates things. It might just be a feeling, but once a case has set off in a given direction, it's hard to question whether that was the best way to go about it, and harder still, almost impossible, to go back to the beginning and start from scratch. It may well be that detective work is not creative, which means there is only one course of action to follow—the direction the clues lead in. But that would be like saying all of us detectives are the same, that there's not the slightest ounce of individual choice in our methods. Could I allow myself to think so negatively when I was about to embark on a case, on such a melancholy morning, and with my hair sticking to me with the damp? Definitely not. As we made our way towards Chief Inspector Coronas's office, I wanted to believe that we were going to put the artist's signature, the designer label, or at least the craftswoman's mark on our next case. And it proved to be so. It would be no exaggeration to say that we branded our initials in fire on a case which brought us fame, if not fortune, among our police colleagues. A lot more fame than we would have liked.

"Do you know what a son of a bitch is?" Chief Inspector Coronas asked by way of introduction.

While Garzón answered seamlessly, "Of course," I launched into a speech less likely to please.

"Well, I'm not sure. In fact, it's odd, but most of the ways people insult men seem to end up insulting women too. Why, Chief Inspector, should the fact that a man is an evil shit have to involve his mother, for example?"

Coronas raised his hand to stop my dialectical speeding in its tracks.

"Let's not get things out of proportion, Petra. It's just an expression. Do you know what a son of a bitch is?"

"Yes."

"Good. Now we're getting somewhere. What you have to investigate is the murder of a son of a bitch. He was found dead in his own home two days ago. He'd been shot, and, according to the autopsy report, someone then cut his throat. A case of unbelievable savagery."

"That's how sons of bitches usually die," declared the sergeant.

Yet again, although it did not seem prudent to mention it, I did not agree. It's public knowledge that sons of bitches do not always get the death they deserve. I've even noticed that authentic, pure-blooded sons of bitches have an alarming tendency to survive against all the odds; I'd even dare say, to lead long and happy lives.

"He was murdered at midnight. They used the old trick of the fake pizza-delivery boy to get into his apartment. A very clean job, given the circumstances. Few signs of a struggle, although the guy does seem to have put up a fight: a lamp and a glass were found on the floor. Not much more. No prints. No trails to follow so far. There's a not very conclusive witness report. A female neighbor says she saw a well-dressed man running away from the front door of the building. She admits she could not identify him, because she lives on the fourth floor and could not see him properly. It's a case for very competent people, ones with lots of imagination and experience."

"Like Moliner and Rodríguez," Garzón said slyly.

"They've got other fish to fry," the chief inspector said without reacting. "But if you think this case isn't worthy of you, I can always offer you a drunken street brawl that needs clearing up."

"No, Chief, don't get me wrong. I simply meant I hoped to be able to live up to such eminent predecessors. And I guess that Inspector Petra feels the same."

"If you've got anything to say about the other two, I prefer you say it to their faces. They're waiting for you right now in the next office, killing time."

Not a very good choice of metaphor given the circumstances, and I wasn't too happy about Garzón's sarcastic remark either. Particularly as our colleagues Moliner and Rodríguez never boasted about being our star detectives, and if they did have a high regard for themselves, that was because they were real cops. Does that mean I think Garzón and I are just playing at it? No, but for some reason I see us as normal people who, during work hours, do our job as best we can. That's not the case with Moliner and Rodríguez. When life was breathed into their clay on the day of creation, they were cast as policemen. No one can look as cool and yet stern as they do in their jackets, nobody can worm things out of suspects the way they can, or inspire respect just by coming into a room. And as for the way they speak and the slang they use, I've asked myself a thousand times what makes them sound like Humphrey Bogart in a starring role, while I can never achieve the same effect however hard I try. Here's looking at you, kids. If two policemen were to be kept as standards in iridium-platinum in the Musée de Sèvres, they would be Moliner and Rodríguez; if Noah had included human professions as well as animal species on his ark, Moliner and Rodríguez would have been the ones to represent the police.

"So Coronas said he was a son of a bitch, did he?" Moliner laughed at the start of our meeting. "Well, he's not far wrong. What do you two think?"

"What do you mean?" I asked. I hadn't understood a word.

"You must know who the victim is. I'm sure you've heard of him: it's Ernesto Valdés."

"No!" said Garzón, shaken to the core.

"Yes!" exclaimed Rodríguez, delighted to be the first with the news.

"So how come there's been nothing in the press?"

"Look, Fermín, you know we can delay things like this for a while. But it'll soon explode! I'm sorry you'll be the ones . . . "

I cut in rudely.

"Wait a minute: so all three of you know who this Ernesto Valdés is?"

All eyes turned in my direction, as if they were asking themselves who had let E.T. into the meeting. Moliner took the lead.

"Yes, Petra, you know: Ernesto Valdés, the number one gossip-column reporter."

"As it happens, I don't know," I said, relieved that at least I hadn't shown my ignorance of a transcendental philosopher.

Rodríguez started teasing me:

"Do you ever watch TV, or read the newspapers . . . Perhaps you glance at magazines at your hairdresser?"

"She only reads weighty tomes and listens to Chopin," said Garzón, joining in the merriment.

Probably as a concession to my rank and sex, Moliner cut short the revelry.

"I'm surprised you don't know him, because Ernesto Valdés's fame goes far beyond the gossip columns. He's one of those aggressive, ruthless journalists whose programs or articles are always being talked about. He deals with scandals: secret weddings, divorces, celebrity spats, you know the kind of thing."

"Is he the guy who practically insults everyone he interviews?"

"That's him. He works in television and on a couple of magazines."

"What did they shoot him with?" the sergeant wanted to know.

"A nine-millimeter semiautomatic. A very precise shot to the temple. Must have been a professional."

"Would a hit man have stopped to cut his throat afterwards?"

"Sometimes they're asked to do complicated things."

"Was he shot first?"

"That's what the autopsy suggests."

"Then whoever did it took a risk sticking around and finishing him off with a knife."

"But if he was hired to exact revenge . . . "

"Is that your hypothesis?"

"To be honest, we didn't get as far as a hypothesis, although there are more than enough people whom he offended. Revenge is a strong possibility."

"I can imagine."

"Perhaps not. He published articles without permission.

And compromising photos. He's been mixed up in all kinds of intimate affairs. He was a man . . . how shall I put it? A man who was somewhat amoral in the pursuit of his profession."

"You can say that again," said Rodríguez.

"But no crime is ever justified," Moliner concluded with an ironic grin.

"How did the witness describe the man she saw running away?"

"Tall, well-dressed, athletic build and firm stride. She couldn't be more precise, so you'll have to be very careful and treat her statement cautiously."

"How far had you got in your investigation?"

"Not far. We got the autopsy results, the ballistics report, and the statement from this hypothetical witness. We were just starting out."

"What about the victim's private life?"

"He lived on his own. Divorced seven years ago. Has a seventeen-year old daughter who lives with her mother. He apparently doesn't have any close friends, or any friends at all. He was completely dedicated to his work."

"Have you questioned his ex-wife?"

"Not yet."

"Were you looking more towards his professional life?"

"I'm afraid we were, and that makes things even more complicated. Anyway, welcome to the world of sequins and glamour! Do you have an evening gown, Petra?"

"I spend my evenings in pajamas."

"And you, Fermín, have you got a dinner jacket?"

"No, I always get takeout."

Moliner laughed loudly. He gave the impression he was relieved to be handing us the hot potato, and he probably was. I was still not sure whether getting the case on the rebound was bad or good. It was too soon to say. We were getting in early enough for lots of things to still happen: the appearance of fresh witnesses, last-minute betrayals . . . The third day after a murder is still a blank sheet and you can write what you like on it. I didn't envy Moliner and Rodríguez. Their victim had been found dead a month earlier, but it was only after it looked like she may have been someone important's girlfriend that the case was taken from another pair and handed to Moliner. A hot potato for them, too.

"What do you reckon?" Garzón seemed to be reading my mind once we were alone.

"Nothing special. But we need to get moving."

"A courtesy visit to start with?"

"Even without an invitation."

On the few occasions I had seen Valdés on television, I had thought he looked very shifty. I was so struck by his character that I found it almost impossible to separate out his physical appearance. I had only a vague memory of his features: weasel eyes, a slightly hooked nose, a scrawny moustache, and the mouth of an old fishwife who never stops maligning people. There was no doubt he was repulsive, and, in fact, death had done him at least one favor: it had given him some dignity. In his drawer at the mortuary, as he emerged from the plastic bag like a chrysalis, he even looked human. We could clearly see the bullet hole in his left temple and the slit across his throat that the police surgeons had stitched up so skillfully. His bloodless face bore no expression.

"Mouth shut at last," Fermín said.

"For ever and ever, amen."

"The question is: did they kill him to shut him up?"

"Or was he killed because he talked too much?"

"True, the shot is so precise it seems as if it was meant to dissuade him—if he's dead, he won't be able to talk. But slitting his throat looks like an act of revenge."

"So there are two possible motives, Fermín. Although personally I wouldn't rule out some private reason either."

"That's always a wise approach."

"Do you think he would mind if we searched his house?"

"I've been told there's not much left there. Rodríguez took what papers he had in his drawer back to the police station, and the old goat never used a computer."

"No matter. I want to see how he lived. Have you got Moliner and Rodríguez's report?"

"Right here."

"Good, let's go and check it against reality, then."

I may well be too fond of clichés, but the fact is that I expected to find something very different when we entered Valdés's sealed apartment. I don't know how to put it exactly, but I was imagining a kind of cross between something out of an American thriller and a sordid tenement building. I could not have been more mistaken. The bloodsucker journalist's den was decorated with all the delicacy of a newlywed. Curtains that matched the settee, cream-colored walls, subdued carpets, enormous bows on the armchairs, and silk tassels dangling everywhere. If the saying "The home reveals its owner" has any truth to it, there was something here that did not fit. Either this was not Ernesto Valdés's home, or our larrikin had a hidden side to him.

"What do you think of this décor?"

Garzón shrugged and said offhandedly:

"A bit chichi, isn't it?"

"Too fussy to be true. And besides, it's all brand-new. As if the place had just been made over."

"Is that important?"

"It could indicate a sudden change in Valdés's life."

My colleague looked at me doubtfully. I asked him:

"What would make you change your curtains at home, Fermín?"

"I never have. I still have the ones you suggested when I rented my place."

"O.K., let's leave aside your particular case: when would someone change them?"

He stood there thinking about this as if I had asked him something as complicated as an algebra equation.

"Well . . . " he eventually muttered, "well, I suppose I'd change them if the moths had got at them."

"Oh, Fermín, you're impossible!"

"Why?"

"Apart from anything else, because in this day and age moths don't attack curtains like kamikaze pilots, and because you're answer isn't what I was looking for! Although it does make my point. You would only change your curtains in an emergency, right?"

"I guess so."

"And you'd only change the entire décor of your apartment if there'd been an earthquake."

"I don't see what you're driving at."

"What I'm driving at is there must have been a convincing reason for a divorced man who's up to his ears in a demanding job to fill his living room with exquisite touches like this."

"A woman?"

"Possibly—a woman he was planning to live with. What do you think of my hypothesis?"

"I think it's something I would never have thought of in a million years."

"And also that I shouldn't have dreamt it up in another million?"

"To tell you the truth, Inspector, the idea of following a line of investigation just because someone has decided to change his furniture seems to me a little . . . frivolous."

"Right! But you forget that when frivolity isn't at the very heart of things, it's often behind them. Are you following me?"

"Ever since I learned that moths are yet another endangered species, I haven't been able to take a thing in."

"Do you know the difference between a female and a male moth?"

"Please, Inspector, have pity on me! Can we get back to the details of the case?"

"Mothballs."

On our way back to the station after leaving the apartment, I went on playing at being one of Molière's *femmes savantes,* just to annoy Garzón. I liked getting up his nose from time to time. If I didn't, we would have got on so well that we would never have argued, and he would soon have become bored. Besides, he allowed me to get away with it, and I liked that a lot. There is no greater proof for a woman that her attempts at seduction have succeeded than when a man—be it her father, friend, husband, or work colleague—not only puts up with her little jokes but actually seems to enjoy them.

The papers from Valdés's apartment were on my office desk, part of quite a thick file. When we looked at them closely, we found only the routine documents any ordinary citizen might have: bills, insurance policies, bank statements and counterfoils, previous years' tax returns, credit interest statements, legal documents . . . nothing that was either odd or particularly relevant. Moliner and Rodríguez had already run a careful check on all his phone calls. Everything as expected: calls to his two workplaces, to television stations and magazines, orders for take-out food, the occasional call to his ex-wife . . . Our predecessors had found nothing that could arouse our suspicions. Nor was there anything suspicious in his bank accounts. They looked healthy and stable. According to the notes scribbled in Moliner's handwriting, they had compared the amounts paid in with Valdés's income from all his different jobs, and they tallied. A model citizen? Most people are, which meant we should not jump to any conclusions.

I decided to pursue my frivolous line of investigation, and

searched among the bills for any that might be for a furniture or household goods store. I didn't find that, exactly, but did find an invoice from an interior designer: "Juan Mallofré. Stylist and Designer. Complete design service." Valdés owed him three million. His studio was in Bonanova. I asked the still doubtful Garzón to check among Valdés's outgoings for the amount that he had apparently owed the designer only a month earlier. While he was reluctantly obeying orders, I opened an envelope that contained something our predecessors had noted as an important document: Valdés's diary. But the fact that nobody had removed it from his apartment—or, more to the point, the fact that the murderer had not removed it—seemed to indicate we were not going to discover the motive for the crime hidden in those pages full of names and telephone numbers written in minuscule handwriting.

When Garzón reappeared I told him what I had been thinking. He was quick to draw conclusions:

"In other words, he wasn't killed by someone trying to stop him giving out information. That makes the hypothesis of revenge more likely. That is, unless the murderer knew perfectly well there was nothing implicating him in that dairy."

"What could there be of interest in the diary of someone who doesn't even have a computer so that everything he does remains confidential?"

"But remember it might have been a hit man, and they can be pretty dumb. Perhaps he was paid to kill him, and he didn't notice anything else. What if that diary were stuffed with crucial information?"

"I very much doubt it, but tell me, Fermín, how much do you know about the underworld of paid assassins?"

He replied half-heartedly.

"It's not my specialty. But look, Inspector, it's not here."

"What isn't?"

"Valdés didn't take three million out of the bank in the past month, and he didn't sign any check for that amount, either in the name of Mallofré or to the bearer."

"Don't you find that interesting?"

"Perhaps he hasn't paid it."

"We ought to find out. But now we're heading somewhere else."

"Where's that?"

"To see his ex-wife."

"Do you think she'll be upset about his death?"

"Would you be?"

"I don't think so. If I were Valdés's ex-wife, I reckon I'd be toasting with champagne."

"Don't be so sure. Did you see how much he was paying her in alimony?"

"A lot. It beats mc: how can someone earn so much just for stirring up the mud?"

"That's where gold nuggets are found, isn't it?"

"As far as I can tell, they're found everywhere except for police stations! Could you spend three million just like that to change living-room furniture?"

"Not even if I'd come under attack from a whole army of crazed moths!"

Garzón scowled at me, but when I burst out laughing, he soon joined in.

Valdés's ex-wife lived in San Cugat, in a house with a garden that was part of a luxury estate. Two Labradors licked our hands as we went in. The former señora Valdés was a tall, attractive woman with a look of long-suffering or bad temper etched permanently on her face. Yet she received us cordially enough. It seemed as though she had been expecting our visit, and saw it as a nuisance she would have to put up with. She looked at us completely indifferently, without the slightest spark of curiosity in her eyes.

The room she saw us into was decorated in a style of conventional luxury. She offered us coffee and sat with us, apparently keener to listen than to speak. We had already checked that the person who would inherit Valdés's not very substantial possessions was their daughter, Raquel. There was no life insurance taken out on her behalf, so there seemed little point in taking that tack in our questioning. His former wife did not at first sight seem to be a suspect who might have killed him to get direct financial benefit from his death. Did she perhaps hate him? Had the relationship between the two of them become impossible after their divorce, was Valdés pestering her? She smiled scornfully at my battery of questions.

"No, Ernesto never pestered me. He was always a perfect gentleman."

Garzón and I waited for her to add something more, but all she did was light a cigarette. Then she smiled a mechanical smile lacking all expression, a professional kind of gesture. I surmised that if she did have a job, one of her duties must be to smile a lot.

"Do you work, Marta?"

"Yes. Public relations for a jewelry store."

"But your husband always paid you alimony."

"That went to my daughter. Immediately following our divorce I appeared as beneficiary because the bank considered my daughter underage. It was never changed, perhaps through an oversight, but it was Raquel who got the money."

There was another silence, which apparently did not make her feel uncomfortable.

"Did you have any problems with señor Valdés in all these years?"

"No, I've already told you, he was a perfect gentleman."

"What does that mean?"

"It means he paid regularly, he called occasionally to ask after our daughter . . . We didn't split up hating each other. There was no great tragedy. The fact is . . . "

"What?"

"The fact is, I understand less why I married him than why we separated. We could have gone on as we were for ages."

"Might I ask what happened?"

She blew out smoke, as though to minimize the importance of what she was about to say.

"Well, I don't know, he got more and more involved in his work, and besides . . . this might seem cruel, but we never really belonged to the same social class. My father was a lawyer; his was a barber. These things don't seem important at the beginning, but after a while . . . "

I could imagine what Garzón must be thinking.

"But there was no ill-feeling between the two of you."

"No, the peccadilloes of youth should be seen for what they are."

Garzón spoke, in a voice as neutral as hers.

"Were you aware of the details of your ex-husband's daily life?"

She shook her head in such a way that her highlighted hair waved from side to side.

"I preferred not to know too much. I saw him occasionally on television."

"Did you hear your daughter make any comment about whether Ernesto Valdés was in any sort of trouble, or if he was going around with anyone new recently?"

"No, I have no idea about that. Ernesto saw our daughter only seldom. I don't know anything about the people he spent time with."

"Is your daughter at home?"

For the first time, I caught her bitter or scornful smile tighten.

"No, she isn't. I thought it was better for her to continue going to school as though everything were normal."

"We'll need to speak to her."

She crossed and uncrossed her legs, sheathed in a pair of black velvet pants. I noticed her shiny, beautiful tan boots.

"Yes, I suppose you will. She's upset: after all, it's her father who has been killed."

"I'm afraid it's essential."

"Come back tomorrow then."

She showed us to the door with the same lack of emotion that characterized everything she did. It occurred to me that the forced smile on her face was simply a sign of boredom. The aseptic atmosphere of the whole estate only served to reinforce my impression. A few young mothers were wheeling their offspring in prams or unloading their shopping. I tried to imagine what life must be like for those women in what, when all is said and done, was nothing more than an upscale bedroom barrio. Their husbands away all the time; everyone the same. Lengthy mornings punctuated only by the occasional cup of coffee. Afternoons with the sun slowly setting, bringing the children home from school . . . television . . .

"She doesn't look like the sort of woman who would commit a crime of passion, does she?" Garzón commented when we were back in the car.

"If she ever knew what passion was, she must have forgotten it by now."

"What could she have seen in someone like Valdés?"

"My dear Fermín, time goes by, and not only produces wounds but great changes."

"That's enough of your philosophizing. What on earth do you mean?"

"Well, I bet that when they met Valdés was fresh out of journalism school, all combative and crazy about the Revolution of the Carnations in Portugal."

"Sure, and she was a lawyer's daughter with a head full of romantic ideas."

"Something like that."

"And the only thing left is that she's still a lawyer's daughter."

"And Valdés's body."

"Right, and the coroner has given permission for him to be buried. This afternoon, I think."

"We ought to pay a visit to the cemetery then."

"What for?"

"I don't know, just to nose around."

Nosing around at Valdés's funeral did not provide us with much new information, although it did give us a few clues about his private life. For example, we could see that he had very few friends, even among his work colleagues. The only people who attended were his boss, a couple of female reporters, and a tiny number of his associates. His ex-wife and their daughter were also there. His daughter was the only one who shed any tears. In every sense it was a very cold occasion, and we waited outside the cemetery for it to finish.

"I wouldn't like to go like that," I said.

"Once I've gone, I couldn't care less what the final ceremony is like," the sergeant put in. "If they want to cremate me, that's fine! If they prefer a posh funeral, that's fine by me too. And if they wanted to cut me in pieces and feed me to the lions at the zoo, I have no objections either."

"Don't be so crass, Fermín!"

"I'm serious! Once I'm in the next world, why should I care?"

"What about your last wishes, the final chance to assert your personality?"

"I couldn't give a stuff about personalities; and, besides, nobody pays any attention to last wishes, do they?"

"You may be right."

We saw Valdés's ex-wife and daughter coming out of the cemetery. I went over to them.

"I know this isn't the moment, but I'd like to know when we could talk to your daughter."

The older woman looked at me in a way that made it plain she deplored my lack of tact.

"Tomorrow at five. That's when her classes finish."

Garzón was surprised at the tough way I had approached her.

"I want her to realize that we'll be sticking close to her from now on," I explained.

"And will we?"

"I'm not sure yet. At any rate, everyone has seen us now."

"Is that why we came?"

"Let's just say it was a general warning."

"'Watch out, the cops are on your trail'?"

"Something like that."

"I'd love to think we were on the trail of the killer, even if it's three days old."

"Who knows, perhaps we are!"

The shop run by Juan Mallofré, stylist and designer, must not have received too many visits from the police. The receptionist who attended us did not even seem to realize what our profession was. Garzón repeated it for her, and added that we were from the homicide squad, in order for it to sink into her befuddled mind. Her first reaction when she finally understood was to hide us from the sight of the customers thronging the store, as if we were a pair of old-fashioned umbrella stands that showed the place up.

"Take a seat," she murmured, pointing to the most distant corner. "I'll go and inform señor Mallofré at once."

"We prefer to look around," I replied calmly, dragging off Garzón to look at all the pieces of furniture displayed in an enormous room.

The sergeant stared at the living rooms and dining rooms,

the fake windows with their curtains, the elegant standard lamps, as though we were surrounded by science-fiction creatures that might attack at any moment.

"Don't you like them?" I inquired.

"I'm not sure," he said doubtfully, peering at an elephant-shaped table base. "I don't think I could ever get used to living somewhere with so many . . . obstacles."

"Me neither," I admitted.

"Thank heavens, I thought I didn't like it because I'm cheap!"

"Not at all," I said, lowering my voice. "This is all garish and basically conventional."

"For people with more money than taste?"

"For people who like to think they have taste."

The receptionist was staring at us as though she were afraid we might steal one of their mastodons.

"Take a look at that for a bunk bed!" Garzón said, rather more loudly than necessary. But the bed was something else: four Moorish slaves showing off their powerful muscles as they raised the corners of a baroque four-poster bed.

"What do you think of that, Inspector? If I wanted to get that monstrosity into my bedroom I'd have to knock a wall down. What do you think it's for?"

"I don't understand the question."

"I mean that with all those guys in turbans and so many curtains, it must be for something more than going to sleep in."

"Perhaps it's to give you inspiration," I said slyly.

Behind our backs, a voice said:

"Hi, how are we today?"

Mallofré was the kind of artist-salesman who treated his clients as though they were lifelong friends. As he showed us into his office he behaved so naturally, and seemed so in control of the situation, that I began to grow suspicious. Was he so worried about our visit that he had to make such an effort to hide it?

"Señor Mallofré, we're here because of the death of Ernesto Valdés."

"Yes, isn't it dreadful? I read about it in this morning's newspaper."

"You may have read about it today, but in fact he was killed some time ago. Long enough for us to have seen from his private papers that he was a client of yours. That's correct, isn't it?"

"He was a very well-known, popular man."

I was taken aback by this evasive comment.

"He was a client of yours, wasn't he?"

"Yes, yes, I knew him; he came here several times."

Garzón raised his eyebrows at me. He wanted to take over.

"Señor Mallofré, among Valdés's papers we found an invoice from your design studio. An invoice for three million pesetas. It's dated very recently, so I suppose you remember it."

I saw that the designer was sweating, and suddenly finding it difficult to breathe.

"Of course! I decorated his living room. I'm very pleased with the result. The style was very simple, but charming."

"Did Valdés pay for it?"

He gave a false, theatrical laugh that sounded more like a shriek of terror.

"Do the police pay murder victims' debts then?"

Garzón went on relentlessly.

"We can't find any check made out to you in his bank statements, or any outgoing that corresponds to the same total or date."

Disconcerted, Mallofré turned to me. His cool, calculated façade had slipped.

"Inspector, my clients are important people who earn lots of money and make a great contribution to the public coffers. I myself always pay my taxes down to the last cent. But if on occasion . . . I mean, that if they say they would like to . . . "

I understood.

"Don't worry, we're not tax inspectors."

"I wouldn't like a silly little thing . . . "

"Rest assured, we won't pass anything on. We're interested in something else. Valdés paid you under the counter, didn't he?"

"He insisted on it. He said he had some money he couldn't account for, and I . . . well, three million isn't that much anyway."

Garzón took out his notebook and started to write in it. My next question surprised Mallofré, who looked up at me.

"How many times did you meet Valdés?"

"I don't really know, two or three I think. Probably three times—twice in his apartment, and once back here."

"Was he alone when you saw him?"

Garzón showed his surprise openly, raising his eyebrows at me.

Mallofré was somewhat taken aback as well. He replied:

"No, he was with a woman. I suppose it must have been his wife."

"What did she look like?"

The interior designer started to relax, and to behave in the way he thought a witness was supposed to behave.

"Medium height, thirty-something, short hair, brunette . . . A very normal sort of woman."

"What made you think she was his wife?"

"Oh, Inspector, I don't know . . . she chose the colors, the furniture . . . she knew a lot about decoration! Styles, makes, fashions . . . I remember being surprised, it's quite unusual."

"Did he treat her as though she was his wife?"

"Well, to tell you the truth, he was constantly taking calls on his cell phone. He kept leaving the room."

"Did Valdés use her name at all?"

"I didn't notice. But tell me, wasn't señor Valdés married?"

"He lived on his own. He was divorced."

Mallofré looked intrigued.

"In that case . . . "

I escaped his growing curiosity by standing up and rushing out. That's usually the best way to do it: a swift "thank you" and then a no-nonsense "goodbye."

"I suspect we've got lots to do," said Fermín.

"What do we go for, money or love?"

"Money, of course!"

"Shall I ask for an investigation of his accounts?"

"Yes, and a thorough one."

Inspector Sanguesa, our financial wizard, promised to pull out all the stops. Apparently it was relatively easy to identify accounts held by Valdés in other banks, but harder to uncover any front companies he might have set up. It would take only a few days to find out where he had his investments, although the Swiss banks might take a bit longer. What with one thing and another, we wouldn't have a complete picture for over a month. One minute the investigation had been moving along rapidly, and the next we had come to a complete stop. The financial information was crucial. Unless new and unexpected revelations came to light, we would just have to wait, carrying on day by day and, above all, being patient. The promise of a quick resolution to the case was evaporating into thin air. I'll never understand why we police always think it'll happen, when it so rarely does. Garzón insisted we should press on, that it was possible for us to make considerable progress in the next few days. I didn't want to contradict him: the leads we had to follow seemed to me so slender that doing anything was better than nothing. But I was tired. I often forgot that my partner had energy and vitality enough for two. Garzón hardly seemed to age. He had no psychological hang-ups. When he got up in the morning, he dedicated himself to the present as if the past had vanished overnight, and the future extended to the next twenty-four hours. A personality like his is nothing less than heaven-sent. The complete opposite of how I am. I forever drag my load of memories, contradictions, mistakes, and frustrations along with me. And it takes a lot of effort to get moving. Everything else suffers. I find it even harder to take on the future. To me it always seems like a panorama laden with doubts ready to come crashing down around me at any minute. Yet Garzón was right to say we should press on as quickly as possible. Up to now, this seemed like a perfectly ordinary murder case. Increasingly obvious shady deals, a family situation complete with ex-wife and daughter, even a mysterious lady lurking in the shadows. All of which fitted a typical upper-middle-class sort of crime. But that did not mean to say things would stay the same if we found we had to investigate Valdés's professional world. Gossip bordering on the gutter press, and celebrity magazines: what was that world like? I must confess I didn't have the slightest idea, but it seemed to me it must be a cesspool, where people floundered about, surrounded by an awful stench. If that was where the investigation led us, beyond Valdés's immediate family, we were in trouble. I couldn't be sure that Garzón's desire for a quick solution to the case sprang from the same suspicion as I had that things could become very complicated, but he must have seen the problem as well. What on earth did the pair of us know about the love life or the scandals of the famous? And it was not just a matter of our lack of knowledge of a specific world, but the problem of how complicated the investigation could become if we found ourselves involved with all these different characters. Just thinking about it made me shudder. Was I getting ahead of myself? If I had asked Garzón, I'm sure he would have said I was; but I had no intention of asking him. That's the trouble with optimists: you have to be very careful with them. I crossed my fingers for luck, less and less convinced that we had a clear path in front of us.

The next day we had to question Raquel, Valdés's daughter. Our best hope of getting anywhere was if she had information about her father's private life. But we were out of luck. Raquel took after her mother; she was just as cold and lacking in emotion. She hid behind her beautiful dark eyes all the time and left our questions unanswered. "Did your father talk to you abut his job?" "No." "Did he confide in you?" "No." "Did he ever say someone had threatened him?" "No." No, no, a thousand times no. Why were we wasting our time like this? I thought, and told her so in no uncertain terms. Curiously, losing my temper provoked a reaction and she began talking more sincerely.

"I'm sorry if you're wasting your time. It's not because I don't want to tell you anything. The fact is, I've never known much about my father. I preferred not to. Every time he tried to tell me something personal or about his work, I cut him short. In the end he just kept quiet."

"Might I know why you felt like that?"

She stared up at the ceiling, obviously upset by my question. I thought she was not going to answer, but eventually she looked at me again, and asked:

"Did you like my father's programs?"

She had caught me out. I hesitated:

"Well . . . I have to admit, I didn't watch them very often."

"I did," Garzón admitted.

"And what did you think of them?"

"They were a load of crap," he said without a moment's thought.

"There you are then, there's nothing more to say. I used to have Sunday lunch with him occasionally because he was my father. We would meet and spend some time together, and avoid any arguments. I never wanted to get mixed up in all that dirty business."

"Was his private life dirty business too?"

"I haven't the faintest idea. He never even mentioned it."

I decided to cut short an interview that was going nowhere.

"Thank you, Raquel, you can go now."

For some reason I could not fathom, she seemed surprised I was dismissing her so abruptly. A hint of guilty embarrassment crept into her expression. She apologized.

"I assure you, I don't know anything more."

"Yes, that's fine. You can go."

She did not budge.

"It's just that I'm sure it looks as though I'm here, unaffected by my father's death, and don't want to help."

I tried to use her reaction to my advantage.

"Isn't that how it is?"

"Of course it isn't! But what can I do? I suppose he must have said something, but sometimes what he said made no sense at all."

"Like what for example?"

"Like . . . recently he said he had met a fantastic woman and that his life was about to change."

A pair of floodgates crashed open in my mind. Garzón fixed his gaze on the young girl like an eagle spotting a lamb. In his usual subtle way, he asked:

"Who was she?"

"I swear, I don't know anything more."

I brought my chair closer to hers, suggesting an intimacy I had not thought necessary until now.

"Raquel. You do realize that anything you remember could be useful to us, don't you?"

She hesitated, still not grasping the importance of what she had just revealed to us.

"Are you saying that because of the girl? Look, that wasn't the first time my father came out with something like that. Sometimes he would swear he was going to get married again, have another family . . . Then he would never mention it again."

"Did he tell you anything specific about this woman: her

name, what she looked like, what her job was, how old she was?"

"No. All he said was that he had met her, and that his life was going to change."

"Did he talk about refurbishing his apartment?"

She looked at me as though I were speaking double Dutch. "What?"

"Haven't you been to his place recently?"

"I've never been to his place!" she protested.

"So he didn't tell you he had changed all his living-room furniture?"

Her face took on an air of lofty disdain. She stood up, and when she spoke, there was scorn in her voice:

"Look, I don't know what kind of relationship you think I had with my father, but I can assure you it was not a normal father-daughter one. As I've told you, we had lunch together some Sundays. That's all. I don't know anything about him decorating his apartment, and I'm not interested. Can I leave now?"

I nodded, keeping my eyes on the papers on my desk so that I did not have to meet her gaze. When we were on our own, Garzón exploded.

"What a little madam! You think she's going to be so snooty about her inheritance?"

"Perhaps she isn't going to get it all. Perhaps somebody has already got their hands on some of her crafty father's secret riches."

"You mean the mystery woman? Where does she get us?"

"That's not the real question. The real question is: what can get us to her?"

"The accounts Sanguesa uncovers?"

I threw my pen onto the desk. I had had enough.

"I've been trying to avoid it, but . . . "

"What are you talking about?"

"Have you got a pair of gum boots, Fermín?"

By now completely lost, Garzón stared at me in amazement.

"Why do I need boots?"

"Because, unless I'm very much mistaken, we're going to have to wade into the cesspool of the gossip columns."

2.

I have always loved the idea of having breakfast in bed with the newspapers spread all over the covers. I suppose I must have seen it in some nineteen-fifties film, and ever since, all through my youth and adulthood, it has seemed to me the height of sophistication. That morning I indulged myself. I collected the papers from the doormat and made myself a huge, strong bowl of coffee. It was a free Saturday, one of those days when you don't even want to think about what needs doing, just in case a whole heap of messages and things you've been putting off suddenly reappear. But it's not easy to avoid your fate, especially when it concerns work, and so it was that I found myself staring at Ernesto Valdés's ugly mug on all the front pages. Although the news of his murder had appeared the day before, it was considered sensational enough to warrant more coverage. There was talk of Valdés's influence in the world of journalism, and of how he had imposed his idiosyncratic style in the world of gossip, dragging it down towards the gutter. As far as I could tell, Valdés had stopped treating the rich and famous with deference, and instead had criticized them ferociously, sometimes to the point of ridicule. His formula had hit the bull's-eye, especially on television, but it had its critics, particularly among the traditional magazines. They refused to join in his celebrity manhunt, because, when all was said and done, celebrities were the ones who provided their livelihoods. I found all of this really interesting: for once, it was journalists providing the police with information and not the other way round. I was particularly interested in an article that explained how this sort of column worked. Apparently there were agencies that sold the news items to the magazines and TV programs. They often got that news in an underhand way, using informers or freelance paparazzi. If there was any doubt how significant this phenomenon was, the newspaper published figures that spoke for themselves: celebrity magazines had an average of twelve million readers, and just seven magazines shared annual profits of twenty-five billion pesetas from their sales, plus another fourteen billion from advertising. The figures for television were equally incredible. It was a simple equation: where there is more money, there is more likely to be crime. I was beginning to understand we were dealing with a case that could have very important ramifications. To begin with, the hypothesis of a hired killer became more reasonable. In a context where the millions were more common than pigeons in city squares, it was easier to get rid of someone by employing a professional than to run the slightest possible personal risk. The easy answer—that it had been Valdés's ex-wife who had shot him in an act of jealous revenge, and then cut his jugular—began to seem increasingly remote. Why look for passion when there's serious money involved? Things like that only happen in pulp fiction, and even there they seem far-fetched. Besides, who wreaks vengeance on their ex-husband after so many years? No, we were taking our first steps on a newly discovered planet, so what we needed to do was to learn to walk on it.

The article went on to say that the most valuable scoops usually had to do with sex. In other words, pregnancies, births, baptisms, illegitimate children, adoptions. All of a sudden the coffee sat heavily on my stomach. I found it impossible to understand why anyone would be willing to spend even one peseta on finding out about this kind of thing in somebody else's life. Don't all babies look exactly the same? Was it such a big deal to see photos of them? There must have been a special attraction that I just couldn't get. When I went to the hairdresser's, it never even occurred to me to glance at these celebrity magazines. I had always preferred women's magazines to do with fashion, beauty tips, decoration, and other delightfully frivolous things. For example, it's enjoyable to read ads for beauty products: complicated names of chemical compounds that are guaranteed to tighten your skin, photos of stunningly beautiful adolescents next to pictures of potions that look as delicious as ice cream or cake. Who isn't fascinated by the possibility of becoming beautiful, so close at hand? Besides, I had recently realized that this kind of publication is also crammed with photographs of handsome young men. Male models with pouting lips doing their best to look really sexy for the cameras. Actors posing suggestively in tight trousers. I found all this breakdown of traditional taboos very encouraging. And it wasn't just the photos: whenever I read the magazine articles, I was constantly surprised at the freshness of the language and ideas. Things such as "Is your boyfriend shy in bed? Twenty ways to awaken his desire" showed that the young women of today were much more liberated than any woman of my generation could ever hope to be. That's life, I thought: nowadays what seems like a game is what we fought a revolution to obtain. Although, in order to enjoy the game, perhaps you have to pay the price of a revolution first. I wasn't really sure that was any consolation, but, at least, by analyzing things this way I didn't feel such a fool.

I left the papers piled on my bed and decided to get up and have a shower. That was enough of Ernesto Valdés: that little weasel had no right to infiltrate my private life the way he had always done to others! But it was going to be really hard to wriggle free of him. After my shower I went into the kitchen to make some eggs and toast. I turned on the TV, and in less than two minutes there was his dark angular face once more. The presenter said that his death could have been a crime of passion, and that the police had no firm leads. What dim-witted spokesperson had given out this version to the press? The names of several of my colleagues came to mind, but I decided against having it out with them. Fine, they could say what they liked, they could make it sound fascinating . . . journalists liked that kind of thing, and I wasn't going to put them straight. If it was passion they wanted, that was what they were going to get! Perhaps they weren't so wide of the mark anyway. In the end, all this fuss represented society's revenge: the man who made a living out of crawling in between other people's sheets now had his own shroud on show.

After I had wolfed down the eggs I felt a lot better. In fact, I felt so relaxed I wasn't even annoyed when Garzón called and suggested we get to work. All I said, as politely as I could, was:

"No, today I'm not being paid, so duty doesn't call."

"It's not exactly working, Inspector, it's more taking a look at some stuff I've recorded."

"Hard-core?"

"Pretty much. I've got several videos of Valdés's TV programs, and the last things he wrote for magazines. I thought it might be useful to see what he was up to, and seeing how we don't have much time during the working week . . . "

I grunted something incomprehensible.

"Did you say something?" he asked.

"No, I was only throwing up my breakfast at the thought of seeing Valdés's videos."

"It'll only be a couple of hours. Just long enough to have a drink and talk things over."

"I can't do it this morning, I'm going to a Chagall exhibition."

"And this afternoon?"

"Not then, either. I'm going to the movies. There's a film I've wanted to see for ages."

"It must be one of those Danish ones, with subtitles."

"You're right, it is Danish! How about Sunday evening?"

"Well, actually, that's when I'm . . . "

"There's not usually much going on."

"But there's an important football match on television."

"Don't be so pathetic, Fermín. Football is always the same!"

"What about Chagall's paintings? He's dead, so there's no way he's going to paint anything different!"

"You may be right, but it was your idea to work on the weekend, not mine."

He gave in. He had no choice if he really wanted to get the work done. Why was he like this? Did he really love his job so much that he couldn't cut himself off from it? I was afraid it was a question of age and habit, which meant that someday the same would happen to me.

When Sunday evening came around, I realized we had not agreed which of our two apartments we would meet in. I called Garzón. He took me by surprise, telling me he had prepared a snack for dinner. I was round at his place like a shot at nine.

Everything was prepared for a serious work session. There was a pile of celebrity magazines on the coffee table, and beside them a package of videos. Could I bear it? Garzón tried to encourage me. This was nothing more than a bit of muck: did I really prefer the sordid underworld crimes we often found ourselves caught up in?

"I'm not sure, Fermín. At least there you know you're dealing with the dregs of society, those who for one reason or another find themselves left out. But here it's vicious nonsense that eighty per cent of people appear to enjoy."

"So? Surely that's a good thing. If that weren't the case, that would mean that criminals are a race apart, and you know that's not true. Everybody goes crazy over gossip, other people's dirty linen, scandal . . . Nobody is perfect, Inspector."

"Yes, but whatever happened to beauty?"

I opened one of the magazines. A group of guests at a celebrity baptism were crowded together so that they could all appear in the photo. They could hardly have looked worse: the women wore tight, pastel-colored dresses well above their saggy knees, broad-brimmed hats drooping from their heads like rubbish in a tip, gold jewelry glinting in every nook and cranny. The men were dolled up in shiny alpaca suits, their throats choked by sky-blue ties and their feet squashed into patent leather tubes with long pointed toes. A troupe of trained monkeys would have looked much better.

"Who on earth are these men who look like stuffed animals?"

Garzón looked over my shoulder at the picture.

"Christ, Petra, if you think they look like stuffed animals! Look what it says in the headline: it's the baptism of the Marquis de Hoz and his wife's children. Everyone you can see is part of our aristocracy."

"I thought the aristocracy had hit rock bottom, but from this it looks as though they've still got a way to go."

"Wait till you see the third-rate singers, the Gypsy folklore entertainers, the TV presenters, the children of celebrities who've reached an age to . . . "

"Don't go on, there's still time for me to pull out of this."

"Don't get too depressed. As you'll see, Valdés's specialty was to lay into them. You'll end up liking him. Look for his column in the magazine."

Discouraged, I flicked through page after page of freaks and horrors. I finally reached a column where Garzón made me stop.

"That's it, read it," he said with delight.

I read, much less enthusiastically than he:

"'Young Alberto de las Heras, who has left untold debts and unpaid bills in Marbella, now informs us he is to open a restaurant in Madrid. The truth is, we have no idea which part of the establishment he intends to work in. Will he be the kitchen assistant, or on the till so that he can dip his hand in before paying the staff's wages? The most likely scenario is that he will take his turn with the customers, especially the ladies, whom he is bound to please as he has always done. As far as we can see, Alberto's only talent is living for, with, and off the ladies.'"

I was astounded. I turned towards the sergeant, who was waiting confidently to see how I would react.

"See? I knew it would surprise you."

"But he is insulting him openly! What I don't understand, Fermín, is why the guy he talks about here doesn't sue him immediately."

"Because young Alberto must be an out-and-out rogue, someone who is also probably proud to be talked about, even in those terms. Most of his kind live from publicity, and there's no such thing as bad publicity."

"But some things must harm him."

"Of course, but they have to put up with them, because all too often the insult is right on the money and they don't want to stir up trouble. The fact is, lots of people complain about Valdés all the time, and the people he attacks try to get their own back, but he's hardly ever had to face a court case."

Garzón had really done his homework. I thought he must have already decided we would end up investigating Valdés' professional life once we had got nowhere with the private sphere. Suddenly curious, I went on reading out loud:

"'Nacha, the youngest of the Domínguez family, seems finally to be getting hitched. Her bridegroom-to-be is the Latin American singer Chucho Alvarez. We've no idea how successful Chucho is in his own country, but here in Spain he's a nobody. That does not matter, because it is public knowledge that Nacha has inherited a load of money from her grandmother. What we

don't know is whether or not she spent it all on the plastic surgery she has had in the lead-up to the wedding. It may be that
she is no longer a rich young lady, but, to judge by the amount
of silicone that's been poured into her lips, at least she will
always be able to give her Latin lover a passionate kiss.'"

I stammered and stuttered before I finally managed to get
out:

"But Fermín, this is terrible! It's pure slander!"

Garzón burst out laughing.

"What did you expect, inspector?"

"How can anyone be so cheap, so underhand, and use such
a nasty style?"

"It came naturally to Valdés, he didn't have to force himself."

"Some guy he must have been!"

"That was Valdés. And that was the world he was involved
in—the world we're going to have to become involved with
too."

"I was afraid of as much. That's why I tried to put it off for
as long as possible, but I never thought humiliation could
reach such depths."

"Let's have a bite to eat, then we can watch the TV programs."

"I think I've lost my appetite."

"You'll get it back when you see the meat pie I've made
you."

However many ingredients my colleague may have put into
his concoction, it could never have contained the mixture of
bad taste, spite, and unpleasantness that Valdés served up. I
could see the change of style in celebrity journalism that the
article I had read the day before had mentioned. What I could
not get was why Valdés had been so successful. Who could
enjoy seeing so much mud being thrown around? Doubtless
the people on the receiving end of all this muckraking would

never appear on the list of Nobel Prize-winners. They were not great men or women, or benefactors of humanity. Nor could it be said that any of them were honest people above reproach, but how on earth could anybody get any pleasure from seeing them humiliated like that in public?

Garzón did not feel the same. He thought that most of mankind has more than enough to put up with in their daily lives. At work, at home, in their everyday relationships, ordinary people have to lower their heads and swallow their pride time and again.

"That's why they love to see that those who are apparently so much better off than they are treated in exactly the same way in the end!" he said, spitting out crumbs from his pie.

"That's a sad consolation."

"There's no such thing as a happy consolation, Inspector. And, besides, this one is cheap, you can talk about it with your friends, exaggerate it a bit, compare it to other famous cases, and . . . "

"At this rate, you're going to tell me that Valdés had found a cure for all society's ills!"

"In some sense he had, although I don't think that's the reason why the formula has been so successful. That's more to do with the money to be made."

"It's a dirty, cheap formula."

"Potatoes are dirty too, but look how many people eat them. And talking of eating, what did you think of my cooking?"

"Quite sublime. How did you manage?"

"With patience and love."

"Would you give me your recipe?"

"I don't think it's proper for two police officers to be swapping recipes. Let's move on to our dessert à la crap instead."

He put a video in his machine and turned down the lights.

"Ready, inspector. Let us bask beneath the shining exploits of our dead hero, our very own El Cid."

Noisy credits announced the start of a program called *Heartbeats*. A semicircle of chairs appeared on a garishly colored set. Various men and women were sitting in them. Facing them on a kind of platform was a single chair where the guest of honor was placed. Garzón told me in a stage whisper that the panel consisted of journalists, all of them associates of Valdés, who himself occupied a prominent position from which he directed the proceedings. The first victim was a lively looking young woman. "She's the wife of the actor Víctor Doménico. He's just left her for an Iberia stewardess," my colleague explained. What followed was a very odd spectacle. It was a kind of repulsive game in which the journalists encouraged their guest to make bitter, poisonous declarations about the man who was now her enemy. In a roundabout way, well aware of human psychology and also probably knowing the girl was not that bright, the journalists touched on the most delicate issues they knew were guaranteed to make her react with a furious diatribe. And just as she was confessing such secrets as that her husband had a violent temper and a drinking problem, or that he had hired a lawyer to make sure she was left with nothing, Valdés leapt in and transformed her from accuser to accused. I was left with eyes as big as saucers as I watched that little man with his penetrating gaze and hook nose round furiously on her with accusations, like "But isn't it true that you incited him to drink by flirting with his friends all the time?" or "But you've also hired a lawyer and told him to go for the throat, even if he has to pay false witnesses." The poor woman defended herself as best she could. More than once she showed that even imbeciles have got a gall bladder full of venom they are ready and willing to spit at any attacker. To tell the truth, I thought it was a disturbing spectacle, and it made me feel ashamed for them. I lamented the fact that wolves were becoming extinct just so that civilized man could have more room for himself.

When this farrago—all of it conducted at the tops of their voices—had finally come to an end, the sergeant wound back the tape and looked expectantly in my direction.

"What did you make of it?"

"It's an insult."

"I knew you would think it was ghastly."

"But it's not what I think that matters, Fermín. What matters is what it tells us. Any one of those people that Valdés humiliates like this could have wanted to kill him."

"Don't be so naïve, Petra. The people Valdés has on his show are paid to appear, and they know exactly what they are in for."

"I don't think you know all the secrets of the human heart, Fermín. They may be ready for anything when they become the tiger's prey, but what about later, when they are alone in their rooms and they start to go over and think about what happened to them? I'm convinced that more than one of them found the role they were forced to play unacceptable. Just put yourself in the shoes of someone trying to sleep after they've been dragged through the mud in public by that man. Wouldn't you get a mental picture of moments during the interview when Valdés's sly face is accusing you, and those rapacious eyes of his, the way he was drooling over your misfortune?"

Garzón thought this over. I could see him going through image after image of the melodramatic scene I had painted for him.

"Well, if that's how you see it . . . Does that mean you think that revenge was the motive?"

"Hold on, I never said that! Let's not jump to any conclusions. But it's obvious we're going to have to investigate the places where our victim worked."

"And all the while keeping an eye on his ex-wife."

"And his daughter. And the phantom lover."

"And everything and everyone else."

"That's right. Let's see, Fermín. Can you arrange visits to both the magazines he worked for, and the television station? Get a look at who works for the company: see who his bosses and his subordinates were. Find out about his work timetable and the resources he had to make his programs with."

"The magazines are in Barcelona, but we'll have to go to Madrid for the company. Valdés used to spend two days a week there. He'd record the program, then come back here."

"Fine. Get onto Coronas and tell him we'll need a contact in Madrid. And find out where Valdés stayed when he went to the capital."

"Don't worry, I'll see to all that."

"There's something else we're forgetting."

"What's that?"

"Is there anything new about the possible hit man?"

"No, but I arranged to meet Inspector Abascal at ten tomorrow. He and his team are the ones who have all the information about hired killers. They've been cross-checking our information."

"Good."

"But with all you've given me to do, I'm not sure I'll be able make it at ten."

"I'll talk to Abascal. Is there anything special I should know?"

"No. You just have to listen to what they say."

"At this stage in life, that's about the only thing I know how to do properly."

We had organized our work quickly and efficiently, even if it was meant to be our day off. We deserved a medal, but since I was sure nobody was about to give us one, I had to make do with a warm feeling of satisfaction. I got home ready for bed, although if I thought back to the scenes we had seen on the video I would probably not manage to get a moment's sleep all night. As I went through the living room, I saw that my answering-machine light was blinking. I was moderately surprised to hear my sister Amanda's voice saying: "Petra, call me at home tonight. It doesn't matter how late it is." I glanced down at my watch. Midnight. Normally I would never have called her at this time. My sister Amanda was an orderly, conventional woman who loved her routine. Married to a successful surgeon and with two teenage children, she had moved to Gerona after her marriage, and lived the peaceful, contented life of a housewife. Despite being two years younger than I, she had always been the more sensible and mature one. That was why her message and the fact that she had interrupted her Sunday night in this way puzzled me.

When she answered the phone, her voice sounded distant, drained of emotion.

"Is something wrong?" I asked anxiously.

"No, I simply want to spend a few days in Barcelona, at your apartment. Is that all right?"

"Of course it is! I'll have to work, though."

"I know you will. I promise I won't be in the way."

"I'll leave a key for you at the corner bar. When you get here, tell them you're my sister and there'll be no problem. Are you sure nothing's wrong?"

"We'll talk about it," she mused, giving fresh rein to my anxiety.

I hung up, wondering what could be behind this surprise visit. Every possibility that occurred to me seemed real and well founded: problems with one of her children, a medical check-up, her husband, Enrique, having an affair with someone else . . . Nothing frivolous or spur-of-the-moment, that's for sure. Amanda was not the sort of woman who decides late on a Sunday night to go shopping in Barcelona. And yet there was no point my speculating like this: it was no more than a professional tic. So I went to bed with a book that had nothing to do with crimes or celebrity magazines.

I arrived for the meeting with Abascal at a quarter to ten. I was surprised to bump into Moliner coming out of the office at the same moment. He had also been to consult Abascal. Apparently the society woman's murder could have been carried out by a professional hit man. But he didn't seem very pleased with the result of his interview.

"Not a single damned lead. They can't tell a thing from his modus operandi, apart from the fact that he's a guy with steady nerves who works alone. Which doesn't exactly narrow things down a lot. He's given me a couple of contacts we can follow up, and that's all."

"Did you think the killer would leave more clues?"

"Yes, the fact is, I did. The case is a real nightmare. Well, we'll see, something will have to give."

"It's not easy."

"You can say that again. Listen, have you got time for a coffee? Abascal won't be free for a while, they've just called him from Madrid."

We trudged over to the Jarra de Oro. Moliner was in a dreadful mood. He did not stop moaning—about difficult murder cases, about the lack of resources we had for tracking down professional killers. We had never had much direct contact, but I remembered him as usually being an optimistic, cheerful sort. Suddenly, as we sat with our cups of strong coffee, he stared at me intently and blurted out:

"Petra, you've been married twice, haven't you?"

Astonished by this abrupt change of topic, I tried to make light of it.

"For you, professional hit men tend to get you thinking about marriage, do they?"

His reply left me even more astounded.

"It's marriage that gets me thinking about bad things. My wife is going to leave me."

What do you do when somebody you hardly know makes such a personal confession? You can't exactly laugh it off, can you? So I turned serious, and muttered:

"Good heavens!"

"Good heavens and hell's bells! She's gone!"

I tried to relax. After all, it wasn't so extraordinary that someone should want to tell you their life story. People need to talk about these things with others they don't have close links with. I plucked up my courage, and asked:

"Why?"

"I've no idea, Petra, no idea. I understand less about what's happened than about the murder of the woman I'm investigating. Haven't a clue, in fact."

"Well, what does she say?"

"She says we've been married ten years and that I've never really paid her any attention. She says I don't like her, that she's never felt involved. What do you make of that? Involved! What does she want, for me to put on a show, complete with love scenes?"

"Well, you've always been very dedicated to your work. Sometimes we women need to feel we're the center of attention. Although my guess is she'll soon come out of her crisis."

"Yes, but when she does, someone else will be waiting for her."

"What do you mean?"

"That she's going off with a much younger guy. Her personal trainer, to be precise."

I didn't know what to say. *Touché.* It seemed as though we women were aiming higher and higher. What could I have said? That I was pleased, that deep down I thought his wife was freeing herself because she didn't feel happy with him? But Moliner was staring at me as though he was expecting my official reply on behalf of womankind. I cleared my throat. Horrified, I realized I didn't even know his Christian name.

"Do you have any children?" was all I could think to ask.

"No."

"That will make it easier, won't it?"

"Easier for who?"

"Look, Moliner, I don't know what to say. For a start, I don't know your wife . . . "

"But you think like a woman, and, besides, you've been divorced twice, so you must be able to tell me something."

I couldn't get over it. It was going to be very difficult to explain to my colleague that not all women think alike, that we're not all part of a single collective awareness, that women such as Marilyn Monroe and Madame Curie were very different. Basically, it was going to be hard trying to explain anything about the female sex to him, so I opted for making a common-sense observation. That usually works.

"Look, Moliner; first of all, keep your calm. Let her think it over for herself: don't put any pressure on her or do anything silly."

He could have sent me to the devil, but I had hit on something inside him that still responded, and he calmed down.

"Thank you, Petra. Of course I won't do anything stupid. I've seen too much in my job to make me even want to go near the edge."

I felt reassured too. I had no idea whether Moliner was a violent man or not, but when someone has a gun it's better to take things steadily.

I was still thinking about all this when I arrived at Abascal's office. The news he had for me did not exactly make me jump for joy. As an expert, it seemed to him that the crime could well have been committed by a professional. In that case, why had Valdés's throat been slit afterwards? According to the autopsy report, this had happened immediately after he had been shot. Did this mean that the presumed hit man had been instructed to commit this atrocity: in other words, that it was an act of revenge? A sort of tailor-made murder?

"Is that kind of thing common?"

"No," confessed the inspector. "As you can imagine, this kind of contract doesn't often go into such detail. In some cases—with the Mafia, for example—they do these things as a warning, but normally if you're just trying to get rid of somebody, shooting them is quickest and easiest."

"So then revenge is unlikely but not impossible?"

"That's a good way of putting it. The hit man killed him with a bullet, then added the butchery."

"Unless, of course, he wanted to make us think it was an act of revenge, just to throw us off the trail."

Abascal nodded, admitting this was a possibility.

"What can you tell me about who did it?"

"I'll give you the details of a couple of informers. They know people who use this kind of weapon, but I must warn you it'll be very difficult to get any information out of them."

"Why? Aren't they reliable?"

"A professional job like this is a serious matter, Petra. Asking questions about a hit man is like mentioning the devil. Everyone knows it's very dangerous terrain."

He handed me a sheet of paper with names and numbers on it. I sighed. I wasn't keen either on having to delve into the world of professional killers. I would have much preferred one of our usual simple amateur throat slittings. And the general information Abascal gave me about professional killers in Spain did not exactly cheer me up either. He said that a few years ago, nearly all of them had been foreigners: penniless people who got into the country illegally. It was cheap to hire them for anything from a beating to a murder, and it was relatively easy to catch them. Later, things became more sophisticated. The killers were still foreigners, but they were more professional. Catching them became more difficult, because once they had done the deed they had a plane ticket waiting for them, and it was impossible to get your hands on them without co-operation from Interpol. The price rose to half a million pesetas, and when they saw the business was so lucrative, Spanish criminals decided to get in on the act. Their asset was security, because they were only rarely willing to leave for another country. They moved around in the shadows, and almost nobody was willing to give them away without being paid a huge sum. Their price now was said to be around two million a pop. Some of them were involved in groups that made sure they got paid, and although these were closely investigated, so far there had not been enough evidence to put anyone away.

"You talk as though Spain were an ideal place for hired killers."

"It's our good weather that's to blame. Foreigners have started flocking here again, and lots of foreign criminals and Mafia men have come to our coasts to retire. You know what Marbella is like."

"Yes, and I suppose all this big game isn't exactly easy to hunt down."

"Quite right, Petra, so keep your eyes wide open even if you get a lot of dust in them."

Fine, I thought: dust in my eyes, and muck all over my shoes. Not exactly an enviable situation.

Back at the station, Garzón was waiting for me with a bulky file in his hands. I passed him Abascal's note with the names of his two informers. He glanced at it, wrinkling his kindly stag's eyes.

"Do they ring a bell?"

"No, they're no one I know. My informers are small fry, Inspector. They could never help us catch a hired killer."

"What is it about hired killers, are they some sort of élite?"

"The good ones are. The bad ones tend to be the worst kind of lumpen, and we usually catch them in two or three days. They're either part of marginal groups, people in the last stages of a terminal illness with nothing to lose, or habitual offenders who need the money. Amateurs."

"Our man doesn't seem to be an amateur. Abascal thinks he's a real professional."

"Then my informers won't be able to tell us anything. Don't worry, I'll make sure I talk to the two on your list."

"No, I'll do it."

"It could be dangerous. Every informer is capable of playing it both ways."

I sat smiling at him, staring him in the face until he became uncomfortable.

"What's the matter?" he asked eventually.

"What's the unspoken deal here, Fermín? You do all the dangerous stuff, and I get what's less dangerous?"

"No, no, I was just trying to be a gentleman."

"That's what I thought."

He looked daggers at me. He was right to be thinking as he did: he did not deserve a boss like me.

The truth is that discovering we were dealing with a professional killer worried me a great deal. I had no experience with them. I was completely in the dark. But to confess my fears to Garzón would inevitably have led to him wanting to protect me, and I could not allow that. I could not bear the thought of him going all paternal on me. I had to make sure I kept a careful balance, and not take on any responsibilities I could not handle. And, just in case I needed any further discouragement, the report on Valdés's diary shed no new light. The phone numbers were all perfectly normal professional contacts, or personal ones like his dentist. Apparently, Valdés was someone who had succeeded in leaving not the slightest trace behind.

The Barcelona magazine where Valdés worked was not really a celebrity magazine. Its publicity slogan was "news for the woman of today," and it was called *Modern Woman*. I read a copy through before I turned up at the office, but there was nothing in it that was really new. In fact, everything in it could well have been news in ancient Egypt. Fashion, make-up, hairstyles, decoration, recipes, and a bit of gossip about the worlds of show business, the aristocracy, the rich and famous. Valdés's column was in this last section. I read what was in front of me, not expecting to find anything extraordinary. I wasn't wrong. Valdés talked about TV presenters I had never even heard of, and singers and dancers about whom I was equally ignorant. There was something I did recognize: his venomous, cheap and nasty style. I did not really understand what someone like him was doing in this kind of magazine. Why would a lady who wanted to learn how to get rid of her cellulite, or what to wear when she went out to dinner, or how to cook a sea bream, suddenly want to plunge into such a spiteful article? All the things the magazine was proposing seemed pleasant enough; there was nothing aggressive about them. What could be the logical connection between seeing what curtains were right for your living room this year and learning about a split in a show-business couple's marriage? Suddenly, another equally random question made me look back at the magazine. I turned to the pages devoted to decoration. Quite a find! They were run by a woman, Pepita Lizarrán. There was no photograph of her alongside the editor's note. I tried to gauge whether the furniture shown in the magazine was at all like the new pieces Valdés had installed in his apartment. I didn't know enough about interior design to be able to identify any similarities. It all looked the same to me: curtains in muted pastels, nondescript paintings. The text accompanying the article did not give me any clues about the author's personality either. She could be young, middle-aged or old. About a bottle-green sofa, she wrote: "The warmth of the upholstery, combined with a shape designed for comfort, is bound to offer hours of reading and relaxation. Pleasure on four legs!" Good God, how could I expect anyone to give the slightest hint of their personality when they were talking about a settee! If I had been asked to write a few lines on a similar topic, I'm sure I would have fallen into the same clichés. I wondered how Pepita Lizarrán would manage in the next issue when she had to describe yet another sofa. But that was not the kind of question I should have been asking myself: I was allowing myself to be carried away by the frivolous side of our investigation. I went to look for Garzón.

"Sergeant, I want you to come with me to talk to *Modern Woman*."

"But I still haven't finished all the preparations for our Madrid trip."

"You can do that afterwards. I want you to come with me."

"With all due respect, Inspector, you don't want me to go with you when you talk to crooks, but you do when it's a women's magazine. Sometimes I don't get you."

"I want you to provide a counterpoint to my subjective view of it. Do you understand now?"

"Less than ever."

"Too bad. If we only ever did what we understood, we'd end up spending our lives sitting on a sofa, reading. Pleasure on four legs!"

"Whatever you say, Inspector. You're the boss!"

He treated me indulgently, as if I were a madwoman, although deep down I'm sure he thought things would be easier if he had Groucho Marx for a boss. But why on earth should I be any more logical than the society in which we lived, where people like Valdés rose to the top and then got shot, and where someone took the trouble to describe sofas one by one?

The *Modern Woman* editorial offices occupied a mezzanine floor on Diagonal. The editor was a woman of around forty, who seemed to age ten years when she heard that we were from the police. Her glamour was incapable of fending off such a deadly blow. She grew nervous and could not decide whether she ought to express her condolences for Valdés's death, as if we were family members, or stick to a more neutral and professional attitude. Unfortunately for us, she chose the former. She launched into an interminable eulogy. When it seemed as though it really could go on forever, I butted in rudely.

"Thank you. We are aware that Valdés' was a good journalist and an excellent colleague, and yet you can't deny that many people thought he was a downright son of a bitch, can you?"

She steered her fragile dialectical craft into these choppy waters.

"As you well know, inspector, in some professions, fulfilling our responsibilities means that others look on us suspiciously. You two, for example . . . "

"Are you trying to tell me that the police are also seen as bastards?"

Her cheeks blushed an intense red that contrasted sharply with the pretty white silk blouse she was wearing. She stammered:

"Inspector, I . . . "

Garzón was not in favor of me giving her the third degree like this, so he immediately started to translate for me:

"What Inspector Delicado means is that given the vehement tone of señor Valdés's articles, he might have made some enemies. Do you know whether he received any threats or complaints, by telephone or by letter?"

She shook her head vigorously.

"Did he have his own computer here?"

"Yes, he wrote his articles here, but he erased them afterwards. He was worried about keeping things private: you know what he was like by now. If you like, I can make a copy of his documents on a diskette, but I'm sure they'll be empty."

"There's something else you can do for us. Is the editor of the home-decoration pages here?"

She looked at me as if this were the strangest question she had ever heard.

"Of course, she's at her desk."

"Could we speak with her a minute?"

While she went off to find her, Garzón could not resist saying: "Are you thinking of redoing your living room as well?"

"You see, that's why I wanted you with me so that you could correct my subjective view of things if necessary."

"Well for a start, your subjective view was a bit off."

"What do you mean?"

"You were rather rude to the editor."

I lowered my voice.

"This magazine gets up my nose, Fermín."

"But there's hardly any gossip in it!"

"I know that, but . . . I'll tell you later."

The sound of footsteps behind the door signaled the arrival of the editor, closely followed by Pepita Lizarrán. She was petite, neither ugly nor beautiful, shy-looking. Could this be Valdés's lover, the woman who had unfrozen his icy heart, the one who was going to change his life just like she had changed his living room? At first glance I really had no idea. She did not look like the kind of woman for whom anything gets changed, not even the water in a jug. Then again, Valdés was no ordinary man, so he could have seen this wallflower as the ideal counterpoint to his high-risk lifestyle. She did not behave suspiciously in any way. Her face was non-committal, which was normal enough when one of your work colleagues has been murdered.

I realized that the editor seemed to want to remain in the room while I conducted the interview, so I thanked her for no reason. She got the point, and left.

"I'm sorry, we just wanted to ask you a few questions about your colleague, señor Valdés."

"Whatever you say."

She had a tremulous voice, and her round eyes seemed constantly frightened.

"Did you have any relationship with señor Valdés outside work?"

"Not at all! We didn't even get the chance to have a coffee together. Ernesto was never here for long. As soon as he finished his article, he was off. He went to Madrid every week to make a television program. He was always rushed off his feet."

I noted that she had been in too much of a hurry to answer, and that she had poured out her response. Bad signs for a lie detector.

"Given your expertise in the area, did you ever help him redecorate his home?"

"Me? No, he never asked me."

"Where were you on the twenty-third at nine at night?"

"At a decorators' conference held at the Majestic Hotel. I went to cover the event for the magazine."

"You can prove that, of course."

"Yes, I had press accreditation, and I have photos of me throughout the evening with various colleagues."

When we were back in our car, Garzón told me he thought Lizarrán's alibi was watertight. Besides that, he thought there was no reason for her to lie about her relationship with Valdés. She could quite easily have admitted she had given him a hand as a work colleague to help him redecorate his apartment.

"No, she couldn't! That would have meant that she had been at his place, that she might know who the murderer is . . . that makes it complicated for her."

"But why deny or confirm something we could perfectly well find out about by asking the other journalists who work there?"

"The way I see it, they must have kept their relationship a

secret. A guy like him must have had loads of people just waiting to get their teeth into his private life."

"Inspector, you brought me here to tell you if I thought you
were looking at things too subjectively. Well, I'm telling you
now."

"As objective proof, I've got the tassel."

Garzón looked across at me to see what dove I had magically pulled from my sleeve.

"What do you mean, tassel?"

I rustled the pages of *Modern Woman* beside his head.

"In the photos of the home-decoration section, everything
has got a cinnamon-colored tassel on it: curtains, upholstery,
tablecloths . . . and how about this for a coincidence: Valdés's
living room is full of tassels too!"

"Maybe they're in fashion!"

"Oh, come on, sergeant, you don't know a thing about fashion or home decoration!"

"It's true, I don't understand anything about anything.
Like, for example, why you've become so obsessed with this
magazine."

"I tried to explain it to you before. I find this sort of
women's magazine worse than the gossip ones. When it comes
down to it, the problems of the rich and famous is a general
topic, but these magazines are proposing something much
worse: real slavery for women."

I took advantage of us having stopped at a traffic light to
show him what I meant.

"Just look at this. Beauty section: care for your skin with the
proper creams. Look at the choice: one for deep cleansing, one
for the morning, another for nighttime, another for sun protection, another for after sunbathing, another for your eyes, for
your lips, another to get rid of dead skin, another for your
body, another for your bust. Health section: healthy slimming
diets, diets to make your hair shine, to give you strong finger-

nails. An everyday gymnastic routine. Ultraviolet sessions. Suggestions for cosmetic surgery: eyebrows, liposuction, increasing or decreasing the size of your breasts, how to plump up your lips. Cookery tips: how to offer your family a different menu each day. Home decoration: make sure your home is up-to-date. Discover how to change your own wallpaper."

We had left the traffic lights a long way behind by now.

"Shall I go on?"

The sergeant shook his head and lapsed into a deep silence. I guessed he was thinking it over, and decided to see if we agreed on the conclusion.

"Do you think any woman can worry about all that at the same time? Do you think there is any space left in her mind or her timetable for something truly interesting, even if it's only her private pleasures?"

He still did not say a word. I was about to continue with what had already become a dogmatic-sounding harangue when Garzón finally admitted:

"We men usually read sports magazines."

"So?"

"If you worry about team selection, if the manager has been changed, how many points your team has, what the players are saying, and all the other nonsense, you can seem just as stupid."

"Well, so we've finally found something we agree about tonight! Will you take me home, Fermín? I've had enough for one day."

"What about the tassels?"

"Beg your pardon?"

"What do you intend to do with Pepita Lizarrán?"

"We'll see if we can get Mallofré to identify her."

"What! And how the devil do you propose to do that?"

"I'll think of something. I haven't got the time to think now, I've got an important decision to make about what cream I've got to slap on before I get into my pajamas."

Even before I got to my apartment, I could see the kitchen light was on. Had I forgotten about Amanda? Not at all. I clearly remembered she was due to arrive, and intended to take her out to eat at a nearby restaurant. I called out to her as soon as I opened the front door. She came out to greet me, but when I saw her I realized I had forgotten exactly what she looked like since the last time we met. It was a very special feeling of real joy, and a recognition that I had deprived myself for far too long of someone I was close to.

Laughing, we hugged each other in the hallway, glad after all that we were sisters. Then, almost before I knew it, I saw that Amanda had gone from laughter to tears.

3

I made her tea. It's a way of comforting people that for some unknown reason seems to work with the English. We sat at the table to talk. She dried her tears and tried to calm down.

"It's Enrique," she began in classic style. "He's having an affair with a nurse. I think he's going to leave me for her."

"To go where?"

"It's just a way of putting it, Petra! What I mean is they're probably going to move in together. Enrique's abandoning me!"

"Has he told you that?"

"We've talked it over. He's crazy about her: those were his words. He's not sure about the future, but I'm sure he'll leave."

"I see."

"She's a lot younger than me."

"Do you know her?"

"I may have seen her at the hospital, but I don't know who she is."

"The married doctor who falls in love with his young nurse; it's a common enough story, isn't it?"

"I suppose these stories are always the same."

"You bet they are. What are you planning to do?"

"For now, I decided to come here to think it all over. I left him on his own with the kids. He can take care of them without me."

She stared me up and down, obviously expecting some

clearer sense of what I made of her predicament. She sighed deeply and said:

"Life is such a load of crap."

"Yes, it really is. Are you giving him time to think it over as well?"

"I don't know. I haven't even begun to think what it is I really want."

"I'd advise you to start looking for a job."

I could tell from her voice she was little short of scandalized.

"I appreciate your common sense, Petra, but first of all I need to understand."

"Understand what?"

"My husband's behavior."

"Amanda, love isn't something you can analyze. You either feel it or you don't, but it's very rare that there's any rational basis to it."

She slammed the teacup back onto the table.

"Rational basis! Good God, Petra! Do they teach you cold terms like that in the police?"

"But, Amanda, what I meant was . . . "

"Tell me whether there's a rational basis to the fact that we've spent all these years together, that we've got two children, that I abandoned my studies to marry him!"

"O.K., fine, so it was an unfortunate expression, but that doesn't alter the real question: Enrique is not going to be able to give you any proper reasons for why he's doing this because he doesn't have any."

"What is it men want, Petra? You should know, you've been married twice. How do those tiny minds of theirs work?"

My strength left me. I could feel how heavy and dull my muscles were. The same question yet again. Men and women. Impossible generalizations. The need to make your pain as impersonal as possible, to spread it out to cover an ancient, generic group. No surprise there; the only odd thing was that I should be considered such an expert when I considered myself such a failure. Doesn't a divorce mean a failed marriage? What did I know about the serried ranks of the children of Adam and Eve after they had been expelled from the Garden of Eden? Although probably no one was really expecting any answer from me: all they wanted was someone patient and friendly to talk to.

"Men are very selfish," I said, almost ashamed of being so crass.

"Enrique has been a perfect husband."

"Well, then . . . "

"Well, what?"

"Well, then, let him go and don't hold it against him."

At that, she burst into tears so bitterly I was scared. Her tears rolled down her cheeks and fell onto her jersey. If only we could avoid these heartaches, humankind would be omnipotent, I thought. But nothing would comfort her. She did not even know exactly what had brought on such despair: sorrow at her loss, fear of the future, social humiliation, regret, the sense of all that wasted time . . . In a few years' time, this mixture could be seen as experience and would count in her favor. Would it help her suffer less if I told her so? No; more likely she would throw the teapot at me if I dared say anything of the kind. Nor was I so sure whether knowledge and experience went hand in hand quite so neatly. Wasn't it better to study in books, to ponder on these things in the abstract, rather than to stumble along in real life? Didn't experience, in fact, make it harder for you to think these things through? I poured another cup of tea. My sister was crying her eyes out, and all I could do was philosophize. I wondered what exactly she expected of me in a situation like this. It was useless trying to pretend: we are what we are, so I asked her openly:

"Do you think that feelings are part of human knowledge?"

Amanda laughed once more, in the midst of her tears.

"My goodness, Petra! Is this how you solve your cases? Whenever you see a butchered body in the morgue, you start to ask yourself, 'To be or not to be?'"

I laughed, too.

"Yes, sometimes I do. Which really annoys my partner, Garzón."

"I'm with him."

Both of us had been brought up with a sense of humor, which is perhaps the most valuable legacy. I took advantage of the lightened mood to try to make sure things stayed that way, at least for the rest of the night.

"In fact, I'm dealing with a case which is all about how wonderful it is to be a woman."

"Oh, good, I can tell you all about that too!"

"I'll tell you everything about it that isn't a professional secret. But, first, here's my plan. I'll take tomorrow afternoon off, and we'll go and try all the things that in theory are so bad for us, but which perhaps in practice aren't so bad."

"Where are you thinking of taking me?"

"We'll go and have a nice relaxing, draining, and every other sort of massage. Then a skin-cleansing treatment. Later on, a good haircut. Makeup, manicure, pedicure, and sun lamp. After that, we'll try to force our way through the hordes of crazed admirers on the streets and find somewhere to have dinner."

"All that just to end up in a Chinese restaurant?"

"A Chinese restaurant? What are you talking about? My dear, I'm going to take you to a restaurant where they serve the unimaginable: aphrodisiacs, mead, and ambrosia just for starters."

"Do you think they could do me a grilled pork chop?"

"They can even slow roast Adam's rib for you, should you require."

"That might get stuck in my throat."

We both burst out laughing once more. Quickly, before her laughter could turn to tears again, we went to make up her bed and sort out her room.

Having to get up early the next morning was the last thing I needed, but, if I really wanted to have a free afternoon with my sister, there was nothing for it but to get up when the alarm went off. I reached the station at what seemed to me like daybreak. I asked for any messages, grabbed the addresses Abascal had given me, and set off at a trot before anyone could see me. I needed to have a clear mind. Nobody had told me how to deal with informers, so I was going to have to rely on a fair amount of improvisation and my hidden talents.

The first address Abascal had written down was a bar. The informer's name was Francisco Pazos. When I asked after him, the woman behind the bar said he usually dropped in for breakfast around ten. I could have had another couple of hours in bed, I thought, and sank down onto one of the stools rather like a whore coming in from a tiring night's work. The proprietor must have been thinking along the same lines, because she asked me straight out:

"Would you like a coffee? You can't stay here without ordering something."

"Yes, of course I want a coffee. And a croissant."

The woman sighed deeply and shook her head, doubtless feeling sorry for the wasted life I was leading. I looked at myself in the chipped mirror behind the bar. Did I really look so much like a prostitute then? In the unforgiving glass I looked more unkempt than anything else. My hair was all over the place, I had put on a black jersey that seemed like something I had inherited, and the raincoat that was meant to hide all the mess was clearly not in the first flush of youth either. Obviously if I carried on neglecting my appearance this way, I could soon expect to be spending the night in lockup accused of vagrancy. But no prostitute would have dared go out looking as bad as me. Deep down, I was amused that anyone could think I led such a hazardous existence. Perhaps I could be taken for a middle-aged junkie, too? When the woman brought my coffee, I put on a sad expression: I could not stop myself from hamming it up. I leant exhausted over my cup, and blew on it wearily. She stared at me and finally commented:

"Didn't have a good night, did you?"

"Dreadful," I said, as though trying to overcome it.

"It takes guts to spend the night out around here. I often think of you lot and the hard lives you must have. Is there really no other way you can earn a few cents?"

"I suppose there must be," I ventured.

"Yes, but that's too much like hard work, isn't it?"

I tutted, afraid I was letting the misunderstanding go too far. I dipped my croissant in my coffee, hoping against hope that the woman would just forget me. That was enough of a joke. But my hope was not fulfilled, because she went on to ask:

"Do you have children?"

"No."

"Well, that's something. The worst thing is if innocent creatures have to pay for our mistakes."

I thought of telling her to get lost and leave me in peace, but at this point her conversation veered off in an unexpected direction.

"The girl who helps in the kitchen left the other day. She says she found something better. I doubt it, but the thing is I've got no one to give me a hand now. I can manage in the mornings and the evenings, but a lot of people come in around midday. We have to leave the potatoes and the vegetables ready the previous evening, but I'm too exhausted . . . "

It took me some time to realize that she was offering to take me on then and there.

"If you'd like to stay . . . It's not a great wage, but it's enough to live on if you're not too fussy."

I stared at her in horror, and almost choked on my croissant. At that moment, a suspicious-looking character appeared: to me he was a knight on a white charger. The woman paused, then said, nodding towards him dismissively:

"That's the man you're after."

I turned towards the newcomer, who was none other than Francisco Pazos. I picked up my coffee cup and gestured for him to follow me to a table. It was all I needed for the proprietor to listen in to my conversation.

Logically enough, the man asked:

"Who the hell are you?"

To which, now that my coffee and I were safely out of the proprictor's earshot, replied:

"My name is Petra Delicado. I'm a police inspector."

When he heard this, Pazos's attitude changed from one of suspicion to outright anger. He leapt to his feet as nimbly as a circus acrobat and shouted:

"What? What the fuck is this? What are you doing here?"

From her position at the bar, the proprietor was equally vociferous:

"That's enough of that, Pazos! We don't want any violence in here. Be careful, or I'll call the police, I'm warning you!"

Pazos lowered his voice. He looked at me desperately.

"Why'd you come here?"

"Can you think of anywhere better?" I snapped back.

He sighed as though he were dealing with the dunce of the class. Then all of a sudden a look of terror flitted across his face.

"Did you bring a car?"

"It's in a car park on Calle Comerc."

"You go ahead, I'll follow."

I paid for my drink. I could feel the proprietor's eyes on me, and as I reached the door, she called out:

"Hey, don't forget what I was saying! At the very least, you wouldn't have to put up with guys like him! You might find it was a better life."

"I'll think about it," I said, to avoid any further discussion. And heard her say, in a weary stage whisper:

"No, you won't think about it."

I walked along the street, casting an occasional discreet glance behind me. Pazos was following me. No sooner had I got into my car than he opened the door on the other side and climbed in. He was furious.

"I don't know how many times I've told the inspector: if you're not careful I'll stop doing this. Why on earth did you come to the bar where I have breakfast every day?"

Obviously I had made a mistake, and such a bad one that all I could do was to try to turn it to my advantage. I deepened my voice so much that even to me it sounded completely fake.

"Listen, Pazos, don't try that with me. Coming to the bar was just a warning, to make sure you're thinking straight."

He did not allow himself to be cowed, but shot back:

"What? Who the fuck are you? The police never talk to me like that."

"Too bad, it's my way, and I have no intention of changing it just to avoid hurting your feelings."

He shook his head, still indignant.

"What do you want to know, for Christ's sake?"

"The journalist Ernesto Valdés was bumped off by a professional. We think you know who it was."

He let out a falsetto laugh that echoed round the car.

"Fantastic! Would you like me to give you his name here and now, or shall I send a fax to the station?"

"I don't think that's even remotely funny," I muttered.

"Listen, Inspector, I haven't the faintest idea who murdered Valdés. Have you any idea how hard it is to find out who did a job like that?"

"We'll pay more than we usually do."

"That's not the point; I really have no idea. In case you hadn't realized, this isn't like a teacher asking you a question in class."

I couldn't stand him making fun of me because he had guessed I had so little experience of dealing with informers. I whipped out my gun and stuck it between his legs. Astonished, he pressed his back up against the seat in terror.

"Listen, slimeball, I may not be a teacher, but there's one thing I'm going to teach you. If you don't tell me all you know right now, I'll shoot off that tiny soft thing you've got hiding in there."

"The police never . . . "

"Shut the fuck up! Right now, I'm the police. If you don't believe me, I can prove it. I'll follow you everywhere, Pazos, and in uniform. You've seen I don't mind who knows what I am. I'll follow you and wait at the entrance to your house. I'll point you out. And if within four days nobody has finished you off, I swear to God I'll castrate you."

The sweat had started to pour off him: he was convinced I was so crazy his position as informer would not be of any help to him.

"I'm sorry, Inspector, sorry. I didn't mean to offend you, I really didn't. But I don't have any idea who killed Valdés."

"Tell me what you've heard."

"The other day Higinio Fuentes said something, but I think he had just picked up some gossip."

"What did he say?"

"Nothing much, except that the cops would have a hard job solving this one. That's all. Talk to him."

I put my gun back in the holster. He sighed with relief. He did not dare complain, but I could tell from the way he was looking at me that he still thought I was off my head.

"I don't know what got into you, Inspector. There was no reason to treat me like that. I always collaborate when I can."

"And what do you do with yourself when you're not collab-
orating?"

"I have a few sidelines."

"You're a pimp, aren't you?"

"I've got a few girls; it's not a bad business."

"I don't know what disgusts me more, Pazos: the fact that
you're a procurer or an informer. But you do disgust me. Get
out of here. And don't forget: if I find out you know something
and are not telling me, I'll pay you a visit in uniform. I look
good in uniform."

He vanished quicker than a flash, convinced that there
must be something seriously off-kilter in the police force. I
knew I had gone too far, but I had got what I wanted. Seeing
the woman behind the bar take pity on me had stirred me up.
It was true, walking the streets cannot be much fun, especially
if you are protected by guys like Pazos.

I checked, and Higinio Fuentes was the other name on
Abascal's piece of paper. I was on the right track. I gave him a
call, and he agreed to meet me the next morning in a bar in the
Olympic Village. So uncovering hired killers was not that difficult. All you had to do was to get angry and charge like a bull.
Even so, I realized that the difficulties Pazos had talked about
were not simply pessimism or fantasy. I was bound to find the
going tough.

I met Garzón in the mid-morning. I told him how it had
gone with the informers, but said nothing that might have lowered his esteem of me. I have to admit, though, that the first
thing I did when I arrived at the station was to go to the washroom. I wanted to comb my hair and tidy myself up enough to
dispel the sad image I was giving. There was the question of
image once more: obviously a case creates its own atmosphere.

Garzón asked me what on earth I was going to do with
Pepita Lizarrán.

"Give her a call and ask her to come down to the station."

"But why?"

"Call Mallofré as well."

"Inspector, we'll be giving our game away. I thought you wanted to have her followed, in case she turned out to be who you thought she was. She might perhaps lead us to something."

"Come off it, Fermín. We can't waste any more time on that cupcake. We bring her in, put pressure on her, and sayonara. If she really was involved with Valdés and tries to hide it, she'll have to explain herself. If she doesn't, we'll have her charged, and put more pressure on her. She'll talk."

"You know best. I still don't get the tassel idea."

"That's because you're a man of little faith. Besides which, you like to get under my skin."

"You're particularly cutting today."

"Ever since I've had to deal with informers and hit men, I've changed my tune. Do you know I was offered a job washing up in a dump of a bar?"

"Fantastic! Are you going to take it?"

"I'll have a quick look at the chef, and if he's any less of a moaner than you . . . "

"Tell me if you get it. I'll come and try your cooking. I'll bet it's spicy."

Garzón loved a bit of verbal fencing before he got down to business: it made him feel happier in his work and sharpened his wits. As he was leaving, he turned to me and asked, with almost religious resignation:

"Who shall I call first, Lizarrán or Mallofré?"

"Call both of them. Don't let them see each other when they come in. I'll talk to her first, then show the decorator in."

"You do like a performance, don't you, inspector?"

"You know I'm crazy about vaudeville."

Somewhere between vaudeville and classical tragedy lies a

genre I had to practice every day: the police report. I switched on my computer and wrote a report of everything that had happened earlier that morning. This was the part of my job I most disliked: my greatest difficulty came from trying to translate facts into official jargon. I could never get used to the idea that, for the police, a "quick look" was a "visual inspection"; and I detested verbs such as "to present oneself," "to be domiciled," or "to proceed." At first I had tried to avoid using these stereotypes, but, once I realized that no one else was going to write my daily report for me, I gave up trying to make sense and simply tried to get it over with as quickly as possible. "The individual presented himself at the place where he was usually domiciled," and to hell with style.

An hour later, just as I was putting the finishing touches to my bureaucratic masterpiece, Garzón poked his head round the door and announced:

"Señorita Lizarrán is here, inspector."

As shy and unremarkable as when I had first seen her, Pepita Lizarrán came into my office. She did not even try to hide the fact that she was frightened. If, as they say, dogs go for people they know are scared of them, then any passing canine would have gobbled her up whole. She was wearing a pale beige dress, and her oblong glasses made her look frankly unattractive. I tried not to smile or seem friendly.

"Take a seat," I almost ordered her.

With a touch of irony that only a practiced ear such as mine could detect, Garzón asked:

"Would you like me to stay in the room, inspector?"

"No, you can go to your desk and await further orders."

This military-style command was more than the poor tassel expert's heart could take. She looked at me as if she could not wait for all this to be over.

"I'm sorry to have brought you in like this, but I wanted to confirm what you told us the other day in the magazine office."

"Yes . . . ?" she said querulously.

"Do you still maintain that there was no bond of friendship or any other kind of relation between you and the deceased, Ernesto Valdés?"

"I . . . " She took a deep breath, searching for words that would not compromise her. Before she could speak, I went on:

"You were neither his friend nor his lover, am I right?"

"That's right," she said with a sigh.

"And you didn't do any work for him, or give him professional advice?"

Contrary to my expectations, she replied firmly:

"No, I didn't do any work for him."

So there was life in her yet. Had I been completely wrong in judging her to be so weak? I picked up my phone.

"Sergeant, is everything ready?"

Garzón replied: "Everything set."

"I'll see you in my office then."

I did not look at her, but busied myself with some papers as if they required all my attention. The atmosphere was tense, but my visitor said nothing more. She did not cave in. Shortly afterwards, Garzón appeared, accompanied by Mallofré. I indicated for him to sit in the empty chair next to Lizarrán. At first, neither of them gave any indication of recognizing the other, and I began to think I had made a big mistake. Then, a second later, I saw a light shine in the decorator's eyes, and a thunderous look appear in hers. He greeted her, without the slightest idea of what was going on:

"Hello there, how are you?"

Pepita Lizarrán had no choice but to respond to his greeting with a slight nod of her head. Things were going to go smoothly after all. I took charge without waiting any further.

"Señor Mallofré, do you recognize this lady?"

He looked surprised, still not sure of what was expected of him.

"Yes, of course I do. I'm really sorry about what happened to señor Valdés," he said to her in all innocence.

"Would you like to tell me how you came to meet Pepita Lizarrán?"

At that moment he realized he had been brought in to identify her. He found it hard to speak with her sitting right next to him.

"We met in the decorator's studio I run. This lady came with the deceased señor Valdés to advise him on the choice of new furniture. Don't you remember?" he said, trying to make things easier for her.

Pepita Lizarrán did not deign to deny it or even to speak. All she did was briefly nod her head once more.

"You can go now, señor Mallofré. I'm sorry to have taken up your time like this."

The poor man was baffled, and yet he could not help being curious about the person he had helped identify. He glanced so insistently at Pepita Lizarrán out of the corner of his eye he was in danger of giving himself a permanent crick in the neck. I was sure he would ask the sergeant questions on the way out.

I was left on my own facing her. I looked her in the face until she dropped her eyes, unable to bear the tension any longer. I hated myself for behaving as though I were enjoying this. I got no pleasure out of it at all.

"Do you have anything you want to tell me?"

She burst into tears. Tears always bring some dignity to any situation, but after a while having to watch dignity in action makes me feel impatient.

"Calm down and talk, señorita Lizarrán. This is a police station, you know."

She did not seem to care whether it was a police station or not. She went on weeping buckets. I mentally cursed the fact that the whole world seemed to have ganged up to pour their unhappiness out on me. Eventually she produced a handkerchief, blew her nose, stared up at the ceiling, and finally launched into the story I had been waiting so long to hear. By the time she had got out three words I thought we were back in the world of women's magazines.

"I'm broken-hearted, inspector. Ernesto meant everything to me. We met two years ago and fell head over heels in love."

"Why did you try to hide it from me?"

"We decided to keep it a secret; you must know by now that Ernesto had many enemies. Not on a personal level—I mean those scoundrels he used to denounce on his programs. I can assure you that in his private life Ernesto was a wonderful man: tender and affectionate. Then there was his ex-wife."

"What about his ex-wife?"

"She's a cold, capricious woman, who made nothing but demands on him. It was as though between her and her daughter they were trying to ruin him financially. They were always asking him for more money, bothering him, hassling him. She could never accept the fact that he had left her."

"She didn't seem like that when I questioned her."

"You shouldn't trust appearances, inspector."

"I usually don't. Anyway, I don't see what all this has got to do with the fact that you decided not to tell the police anything."

"What else could I do? We managed to keep our secret: no one knew we were together. We had decided finally to make it public, and to get married next month. When he was murdered, I was very scared."

She started crying once more. I stopped her in her tracks.

"What could Valdés's enemies have done if they knew he was about to be married?"

She stared at me, unable to understand that I couldn't understand.

"They were out to get him, Inspector. They would have pounced on the story of his divorce, and other dark corners—which he had like anybody. They would have made my life impossible. They would have banded together to sink him."

"Isn't that exactly what he did to others?"

"Are we here to judge him?"

So the blancmange packed a punch. Worse still, she was right.

"No, we're here so that you can tell me all you know about his murder."

"Do you think if I had known something I would have stayed silent?"

"I think that it's me and not you who asks the questions. Tell me who Valdés was in touch with in the last days before he died."

"He never talked about his work with me."

"So you think his murder has to be work-related?"

"Ernesto had very few friends. I filled most of his personal life, apart from his ex-wife and his daughter, of course, but he did not see much of them."

"I know. But he might have told you something in passing."

"I haven't even thought about it."

"Well, try. I'll give you my cell number, and if you remember the slightest little thing, I want you to tell me immediately. Besides that, you will have to come back and make a statement to the judge about why you did not come forward in the first place. You can go now."

I could tell from the way she looked at me that she thought I was an unfeeling monster. And she was not far wrong: this case had anesthetized all the pity I might feel for humankind. Perhaps I was coming to realize that even our emotions are up for sale.

Garzón poked his ruddy face round the door again, anxious to know the result of my interrogation.

"The lover," I said, before he could even ask.

"Why didn't she say anything?"

"She was afraid of the scandal. Nobody knew they were together."

"Does she know anything?"

"She says not, but she's pointing the finger at the ex-wife."

"The rival," the sergeant said darkly.

We looked at each other. No need to say anything more. We had reached such a level of understanding that soon all we would need to do would be to grunt like animals.

"In that case, we can go and have lunch."

"Don't count on me today. I'll just have a sandwich. I've got an appointment in a beauty clinic."

"I don't believe it."

"I'll ignore that last remark."

"But I mean it!"

"In that case, you'll be pleased to know I'm taking the afternoon off. And do you know why? So I can have someone massage all my muscles until they feel like they're falling apart, then take a swim in perfumed waters, and then let myself be embalmed in moisturizing creams . . . In short, so that I come out like a rosebud."

"But you're that already!"

"Well done, Fermín. That was much better. Afterwards, I'm having dinner with my sister, who's staying with me at the moment. Why don't you join us?"

"Will I have to be embalmed too?"

"No, just make sure you change your shirt."

"Fine, give me a call and tell me where you are."

"All right. Ah, and this afternoon I expect you to do the work for both of us!"

He raised his eyebrows as quizzically as Socrates must have done in his day. Why had I invited him along? That would prevent any heart-to-heart talk between my sister and I. That must have been why. Anyway, she was worried about what made men tick, and here I was offering her a real man. She could ask him rather than me.

Amanda was waiting for me at the entrance to the beauty clinic. A pair of dark glasses hid eyes that were red from crying. Why is it that we women weep until we are dehydrated? Surely there must be some other way to show how unhappy we are.

"Have you been crying?" I asked somewhat unnecessarily.

"No!" she lied.

"Well, then, the Barcelona climate is no good for your eyes. Nothing that they can't sort out in here. Ready?"

She smiled, and we crossed the threshold into the clinic for the defense of vanity.

When we arrived at the massage tables a young woman built like an oak took me in hand. Lying naked and defenseless on her table, stripped of everything, I began to feel a bit like a corpse on a slab. I tensed up, and the walking wardrobe felt it at once. She asked me to cooperate a bit more:

"Why not try to relax?"

Why on earth should she think I could relax? I had abandoned a case to be here, I had a sister whose marriage was on the rocks, and, to top it all off, I had no experience of someone other than me having utter control over my body. Thinking all this led me to tighten my muscles still further. The masseuse stopped kneading my back and bent over my face.

"Excuse me, but how long has it been since anyone looked after you?"

"Well, if you mean looked after properly . . . " Her question had taken me by surprise.

"Why not think for a moment that you deserve to have someone look after you properly? Seriously, that's what you ought to be thinking, because it's true."

I smiled inanely. I felt like a real idiot.

"Would you look after me if you weren't being paid?"

"Of course I would, no doubt about it! But that's not the point. The point is you have to allow yourself some respite, to allow yourself some free time, have a massage, devote a whole day to yourself if you feel like it. We shouldn't always be struggling like beasts of burden and at the same time feeling guilty about it; that's something we women really need to learn."

This was probably a bit of cheap psychology she had been taught to say. Or not. Perhaps she was an out-of-work psychoanalyst. At any rate, she was right. How long had it been since anyone looked after me, myself included? The closest I had got to anyone worrying about me was when that big-hearted woman in the bar offered to take me on as a skivvy. Was that so bad? No, I didn't need anyone to take care of me. I could look after myself, or at least I could pay somebody to do it. Yes, the masseuse was right. I relaxed.

By the time she had finished with me I felt I was reborn. I thanked her from the bottom of my heart, and felt so liberated I walked over to the steam rooms wearing nothing but a tiny towel. Amanda was already there, wreathed in thick clouds of steam. Three or four other women, of all different ages, lay sprawled on the marble.

"How's it going?" I asked her.

"A lot better. Two more hours in here and I'll forget I was ever married."

I gestured to her not to talk so loudly, because the other women might hear. She shrugged as though this didn't matter in the slightest. I understood why when a woman well into her sixties replied, with her eyes tight shut:

"Lucky you! I've been married for thirty-five years, and can't forget it for a single moment."

This caused chuckles on all sides, and several naked bodies sat up.

"Your husband didn't leave you, did he?"

"Don't tell me yours did, love."

I couldn't believe my ears: my own sister was talking about her marital crisis in public to perfect strangers. And that was not the worst of it: the worst was that all these females, young or old, were immediately interested in what she had to say, and then not only told their own stories, completely naturally, but launched into a series of blistering comments about men in general, the unreasonable way they behaved, their interior fragility, their inability to cope with growing older . . . They gutted and slaughtered them with more expertise than a butcher in any abattoir. Thankfully, none of them minded that I said nothing: I would have been incapable of saying anything in that collective lynching. To top it all off, at a certain point one of the women sighed and said almost casually:

"But what can we do? That's the way men are."

All the others agreed, and what had only moments before been denunciations magically turned into words of acceptance, inevitability, and eventually jokes, which became more and more daring. These culminated in an uproarious exchange about the size and thickness of the other sex's commonest member. When I was on my own again with Amanda, I pounced on her:

"How could you, in front of everyone like that . . . ?"

"But, Petra, what do you think Roman matrons did when they went to their baths? It's all part of an ancient tradition."

"I really don't get it."

"I think you've been in a man's world too long. We women talk about our feelings. There's no shame in that, is there?"

"Shame, no . . . but a degree of intimacy . . . "

"Intimacy is a story invented so that we all suffer on our own."

I could not understand it. My sister may have been right, but I would have been unable to do it. Too much time spent among men? Too much on my own? What did one gain by keeping silent, what did one lose with such open talk? I wasn't sure, but I preferred to be sparing with details of what I felt.

Then it was the facial treatment. That almost completely finished me off: all the different creams they massaged into me and then rubbed off with gentle, sinuous movements left me on the verge of sleep. All that was left was the makeup session. I had less chance to relax then. I had to look down while they defined my eyebrows, and up while they put eyeliner on my lashes. I had to stretch my lips, pucker them, then smile to see the overall effect in the mirror. I looked good. I felt good. I somehow sensed this was not the real me, but I dismissed the thought. The only problem was the time. It was nine in the evening. We had spent five hours enjoying the pleasurable experience of being looked after. I looked at myself again in the mirror. All the hours of work were visible: the relaxation, the layers of different creams. I ought to go and show off the new me to my protectress in the bar.

Amanda looked wonderful too. Most important of all, the telltale signs of tears had disappeared from her eyes.

"What now?" she asked, wanting to know what else I had planned.

"Now, a champagne supper. Oh, by the way, I've invited my work partner. I hope you don't mind—I can still cancel him."

"Is he good-looking?"

"Sergeant Garzón? Well . . . he's big and strong."

"Strong enough for the two of us?"

"Yes, he can take it."

"Two from the same family?"

"Don't go too far: I'm his boss."

"Goodness gracious, Petra! Do you never lose your self-control?"

Self-control was what Amanda needed when she saw the sergeant arrive. The self-control of a Tibetan monk. Garzón was dressed to kill. He had on a pinstripe suit, with a black shirt and a lilac tie. I was used to his peculiar sense of taste, but even so, whenever I saw him dressed up like this it still took me aback. Impressed, my sister held out a limp hand, and he clicked his heels and kissed her hand in a demonstration of gallantry.

"Don't you think we look beautiful, Fermín?" I asked.

"Like two wild gazelles," he said without a moment's hesitation.

When Amanda heard that, she burst out laughing. She hardly stopped for the rest of the evening in the elegant restaurant we chose for our dinner. I have to admit that Garzón was in form, in one of those moments of grace when he could make fun of the most serious topic. He told us stories of his childhood, cases he had been involved in, everyday experiences as a widower on his own . . . and all of it was said in a mocking tone that was mostly directed at himself. I realized that the main aim of the dinner had been achieved: my sister was delighted. And she must surely have felt that the darkest clouds had lifted, even if the procession of martyred Christs and weeping Madonnas went on inside. Not that it took long for them to surface. Over coffee, when the euphoria died down and everybody stirred their sugar and meditated on the swirling liquid in the cup, Amanda suddenly asked:

"Could you fall in love with someone much younger, Fermín?"

Garzón did not realize her mood had changed. He joked:

"Can you see me seducing a teenager?"

"No, I'm being serious. Do you think that with the love of a girl in her twenties a man can rediscover his youth?"

At this, the sergeant realized something was wrong. He looked at me inquisitively, and I gave him a worried glance. He stammered out a few words:

"Well . . . I really don't know . . . perhaps in desperate circumstances . . . "

"What kind of circumstances?"

He ran his finger along his moustache.

"Well . . . like, on a desert island . . . "

"O.K., and on this desert island, if you fell in love with this young girl, would it make you feel younger and more alive?"

Garzón suddenly became serious too.

"You know, sometimes I see a young girl in the street and I stop and stare. I can't help myself—they have such lovely bodies, and such smooth skin . . . but I'm not sure I could fall in love just to feel younger . . . first of all, because I'm too lazy, and secondly, because not even God can give you your youth back."

"I know, but it's not just about looks, it's something more than that. Young people are clear-eyed, they have no experience, they have hardly had to suffer. It's as though they were brand new, as if the world had not ruined them yet. To live with them must be like discovering that all over again."

"I'm not a complicated person. I only discover what I feel in my own guts."

"Obviously my husband is not like you. He's fallen in love with a twenty-something and is planning to leave me to go and live with her. What do you make of that?"

Garzón made eye contact with me in a desperate plea for help, but I declined: I had no idea what to say either.

"It must be difficult for you."

"You can say that again. It would be easier if I really understood his position."

Garzón shrugged.

"I have only ever understood the half of what has happened to me in my life. Things happen: sometimes there's nothing to understand."

"That's just the way things are?"

We fell into a melancholy silence, the three of us staring into our empty coffee cups as though trying to tell our fortunes in the grinds. I summoned up my energy and called it a night. I paid, and we left the restaurant. After Garzón had said a friendly farewell, my sister spent most of the way home commenting on how wonderful he was.

When I looked at myself in the mirror, I was surprised at the professional makeover I had been given. I had forgotten all about it. Years, beauty, youth, love. The plans I had for my old age did not include love. I did not want to see anyone growing old alongside me, someone who at the same time would be a witness to my inevitable decline. I had decided to live in the countryside, to read, go for walks, and go into a nearby village every evening to share a drink with the local sailors or peasants (I still had not decided which). I would buy myself a shiny-coated cat, a friendly dog. I did not want to have anyone reminding me of the little horrors of everyday life: leaving the tube of toothpaste open, slurping their soup, or complaining about their aching muscles before they got into bed. There is a certain elegance in solitude, until death takes us from this world. And yet there was no denying I was upset at the thought of losing the beauty of youth. I did not think about it too much, but whenever I did . . . if only growing old meant changing to something else, but it didn't: it was nothing more than the slackening of your muscles, the degeneration not only of your brain-cells but of all your neurons, dying like flies. There was nothing to do to prevent it: you could spend hours stretched out on endless tables while efficient hands massaged you, daubed you, made you fragrant, or smeared on all kinds of marvelous creams. It made no difference: every minute, every second you had aged by another minute, another second.

What about experience, events, novelty, everything that was not physical that my sister had referred to . . . ? That was something else again: I had grown attached to my skepticism, and did not miss the sense of hope, the excess of vitality and lack of reflection that were so typical of youth. No, everything was fine, I would not have gone backwards even if I could. Period.

I washed off my eye make-up with a lotion. I put on my pajamas. Was there any way I could help my sister? No. Could I at least help soften the blow of the worst moments? Possibly, though, caught up in an increasingly complex case as I was, I would not have much time to find out.

4.

Inspector Sanguesa brought us the results of his investigation in person. I soon saw why. A hundred million pesetas! The louse had a Swiss bank account with a hundred million pesetas in it. The job of muckraking journalist obviously provided not only savings but also a considerable capital.

"Interesting, isn't it? Do you think he made the money interviewing the famous?"

"If you add together the three salaries he was paid, you'll see he didn't."

"Did he inherit then, or make money on the Stock Exchange?"

"Nope. Your man produced the money out of his sleeve like a conjurer."

"I'd love to know where he conjured it up from. Can you find out more?"

"I've searched everywhere. His name doesn't figure in any companies, and there is no trace that he was involved in business of any kind."

"When did the money start arriving in his account?"

"He made the first deposit two years ago. Ten million. After that he deposited an average of twenty million each time. There doesn't seem to be any pattern to the dates. He never took anything out."

"He was obviously thinking of retiring on the Riviera."

"Well, he doesn't seem to have been planning to go back to his native village and grow vegetables."

"You're right. I don't suppose he ever put in a check signed in his name."

"Of course not. He made the deposits personally, and always in cash. Nobody paid him checks."

"The old story: he took it in his suitcase."

"That's usually the safest way."

"It's also in keeping with his personality: he never trusted anyone. O.K., thanks for all your hard work, Sanguesa."

"I'll carry on digging, but I'm afraid I might not find much more."

"What you've already got is really useful. With that kind of cash up for grabs, we can forget about the idea of a crime of passion."

"How far have you got with the hit men?"

"Nothing so far."

It was no easy matter. Every new lead brought with it fresh motives for Valdés's death. By now we had more than enough reasons for someone to murder him.

"Are we also ruling out revenge by somebody he hurt professionally?" asked Garzón when I told him of Sanguesa's discovery.

"I couldn't be so certain, Fermín. Frankly, I have no idea."

"I've got two tickets for a flight to Madrid tomorrow. We ought to take a look at his TV program."

"Of course, we need to do that. But, first, I think we have to knock a few things on the head here first. Let's pay a visit to his ex and to his lover."

"Another turn of the screw?"

"Exactly. We'll take them proof: have Sanguesa's report photocopied and talk to our expert on hired killers. I want some photos."

"Photos of who?"

"I don't really care—people who have been savagely murdered by hit men. The more gruesome the better."

"What about you?"

"I have to see the other informer."

"And of course you want to go alone."

"Of course, out of pure stubbornness. And besides, we need to get a move on: time is pressing."

"Fine. With your permission . . . "

I nodded, but after he had taken two steps towards the door, he turned round and faced me without saying anything more.

"What have you forgotten?"

"Nothing. I just wanted to say . . . about your sister . . . well, it's very sad."

"Things like that happen every day. Don't worry on her account, she'll get over it. There are plenty more men, Fermín; too many, perhaps."

"That's what I get for opening my mouth."

He turned on his heel and stormed out, doubtless muttering to himself what a dragon I was. But I could not allow him to get involved in my family problems. And I really did not think you should pity somebody when they have lost the love of their husband or wife. Heartbreak was not one of life's great tragedies, it did not deserve to be given so much importance. My informer was waiting for me and I couldn't waste my time on these private speculations. Duty first, I told myself, and could not help smiling ironically at this phrase that is never heard anymore.

This time I knew exactly what I had to do. Even so, events took over and held a surprise in store for me. The sort of surprise I was always scornful of whenever it happened to me: the informer turned out to be a woman. She explained that her husband, Higinio Fuentes, who was the real police informer, had suddenly had to leave the city. When that happened, she said, she stepped in: they were always careful not to miss an appointment with the cops. I called to check she was telling the truth, and it was confirmed: the two of them worked together, and this was not the first time that the wife had taken the place of the husband. I examined her curiously. She could have been no more than thirty, and chewed gum as if her life depended on it. She was eyeing me with all the disdain she could muster. The pair of us were weighing each other up, and it seemed to me I came off worst. My mind was blank: I had no idea where to start. She was the one who tired first of this initial skirmish. She tossed her head and asked:

"Well, what can we do for you today?"

"You've heard of the murder of Ernesto Valdés?"

"I read something about it."

"We think it was done by a professional, and we want to know who."

She blew a bubble with her gum, then popped it expertly.

"Aha. So?"

"I've heard your husband might be able to help."

"He might, or he might not. These things need a lot of investigating. And besides, it's dangerous."

She fell silent and looked at me quizzically, but I did not react. She started to scratch her almost perfect nose impatiently:

"How much have they authorized you to pay?"

I hadn't even thought about that. I tried to bluff my way out of it.

"The usual."

"No, the usual, no! We're talking about professional killers here."

"Well, it will depend on the information you provide."

"However little that is, we need a hundred million. And if we unearth something valuable, make that three hundred."

"Shouldn't you check with your husband? He's our regular contact."

"There would be no point: I'm the one who always deals with money. Isn't it the same in your marriage?"

"Let's leave personal matters out of this. I'll have to talk to someone: the chief inspector."

"He'll say yes. Coronas is a very honest guy. As soon as my husband gets back, I'll give him your message. He'll know what to do."

"Fine, give me a call."

"Give me your cell number. We never call the station."

I gave it to her, wondering how on earth I should write all this up in my report. I still felt a complete novice when it came to dealing with informers. I found it hard, perhaps because deep down I considered it unworthy of a real professional.

Garzón was waiting for me, car at the ready. As usual, he had carried out my orders to the full. He was already in possession of the photocopy of Sanguesa's report and photos of victims. As we were driving up to the luxury estate where Valdés's ex-wife lived, I glanced at them. They made my stomach churn. The first showed a man whose entire body was covered in burns. He was emerging like a black ghost from a plastic bag. I swallowed hard. Garzón looked across at me:

"Good stuff, isn't it?"

"Charming."

"The trademark of South American hit men in the drug trade. Keep going, you haven't seen the worst."

The next one showed a body that had been chopped into pieces, all of them laid out on a sheet for the photograph. I could make out the limbs, the torso, and the horribly grinning head of a middle-aged man.

"That's a poor bastard who refused to pay a debt. It was the work of Poles."

"Disgusting!"

"Look at an Italian job. They're even more imaginative. Photo number ten."

I had trouble working out just what the bloody mess in the photo was, but I eventually deciphered it. A young man with his throat slit vertically, and with something pale and fleshy protruding from it. His own tongue.

"It's known as 'the necktie.' The throat is cut, then they open the mouth and fold the tongue down until it comes out at the front. Apparently they do it once the victim is dead. That one was a Mafia member who tried to run away."

"That's enough, Garzón. I think I'm going to be sick."

"Don't imagine that they're all foreigners, Mafiosi or some such thing. All the other photos are the work of Spanish killers, and I can assure you we're just as sophisticated."

I stuffed the photographs back into their envelope.

"They're ghastly. I just hope Pepita Lizarrán is as sensitive as I am."

"Are you going to spin her a line?"

"I'm going to play whatever few cards we have in our hand. We can't let the opportunity pass. She must know something, otherwise she would have gone to the police in the first place."

A maid in a pink apron opened the door for us. She did not let us in, but called out to Valdés's ex-wife, who then appeared. She looked as composed and stiff as ever, totally in charge of the situation. We were shown into the same small reception room as before. I skipped the polite chitchat, and fired my first broadside.

"We've discovered that your ex-husband had a Swiss bank account with a hundred million pesetas in it." She raised her eyebrows in a slight gesture of surprise. "Did you know anything about it?"

"Absolutely nothing. Am I by any chance going to inherit it?"

"I doubt it. The money will be frozen at once by the judicial authorities."

She smiled for the first time since we arrived.

"Inspector, you know what a separation is, don't you? People don't always declare their eternal love when they split up. Do you really think my ex-husband would have told me anything about his real financial situation or how he managed to accumulate vast sums of money?"

"I suppose not, but perhaps you were party to some of your husband's methods when you still lived together."

As she shook her head, her beautiful copper-colored hair swirled around her face.

"No, he never told me anything."

"And you didn't surmise anything from stray comments or from his travels?"

"I have my own job, Inspector Delicado. As a professional in an important position, I have to spend many hours each day sorting out problems. When my husband and I got home, neither of us talked about anything but personal matters. Besides which, when he became involved in the gossip business I lost all interest in what he did."

"I understand, but perhaps . . . "

She cut me short, but without raising her voice.

"If you suspect me of something, why don't you charge me? Otherwise . . . "

She fell into an expectant silence. I completed the sentence for her:

"Otherwise, you suggest we leave you in peace."

"I see you understand."

"Things aren't always easy in an investigation of this kind. Sometimes we have to ask questions even when we don't suspect the person of any crime. And if they do not cooperate, the normal thing is to go and get a warrant from the judge."

"Well, if that's the normal thing . . . "

"Fine. Thank you for seeing us."

As soon as we were out in the fresh air again, I said to Garzón:

"Make sure she's followed."

"Do you really suspect her?"

"Let's see, Fermín. This woman spends many years married

to a man involved in shady business. They separate, but remain on relatively good terms. He always pays his alimony, and sees his daughter from time to time. Do you really believe she knows nothing about anything, that she never heard him say anything about money or work, that she never even wondered about it?"

"I've known people like that, and they weren't necessarily hiding anything."

"Well, it won't do any harm to keep an eye on her. That way we can be sure she's innocent."

Our second visit that day was to Pepita Lizarrán. More than a visit, it was a deliberate attempt to intimidate her.

She greeted us as timidly as ever, and when we asked to speak to her somewhere more private than the magazine's reception area, she became nervous. She led us to a small, impersonal room with walls covered in magazine covers in colored frames.

"What can I do for you?" she asked, her body slumped lifelessly.

Taking advantage of her obvious emotional fragility, I decided to leap straight in. Without saying a word, I pulled out the envelope with the photographs. Equally silent, she picked it up and started to look at them one by one. While she was doing so, I said quietly:

"All the men you see there were victims of professional killers. As you can see, they don't always use humanitarian methods."

Her hands started to shake.

"These people are merciless. They carry out their revenge systematically, and always leave their mark. It may have been one of them who killed Ernesto Valdés."

She dropped the photos into her lap and began to sob, her face lowered on her chest.

"I know this is unpleasant, but I wanted you to have a clear idea of what we're dealing with. I know you have nothing to do with Ernesto Valdés's death, but I want you to realize what kind of people you are allowing to escape if you hide anything from us—or, rather, if you don't allow yourself to tell us even the smallest detail that could help us in our enquiries."

Her shoulders were still shaking with sobs. Garzón put his hand in his pocket and said:

"Would you like to see what they did to Valdés?"

At that she lifted her tear-stained face and begged him:

"No, please—have pity on me!"

I returned to the attack more gently this time.

"Pepita, just think. Don't think of us as a danger, not to your own safety; think if there is anything at all you should tell us. We've found out that Valdés had a substantial account in Switzerland."

She sniffed loudly, and seemed to try to calm down.

"My God! Isn't it enough to have lost the man you loved? Will I also have to live the nightmare of knowing how much he suffered?"

This sounded like something straight out of one of his magazines, but I still thought this was the moment to get her to talk. I was even gentler:

"Anything you say might help us catch those criminals. And we will catch them, Pepita, you'll see."

"He told me . . . " she stared at us, her mouth still trembling from her tears. Garzón and I were on the edge of our seats. "He told me he was earning lots of money, and that within a couple of years we would both be able to leave our jobs and go and live somewhere outside Spain. He said this was a country of gossips, but that nobody would know us in our new home, and we would be left in peace. He said he thought Canada was a good place to live."

"Did he ever mention a Swiss bank account?"

"No."

"Did he tell you how he had come by the money?"

"No, and I didn't ask, but it always seemed to me he wasn't talking about his job as a journalist, but something else. Sometimes he went to meet a person called Lesgano: he would always tell me it was safer to say nothing about those meetings, but he was sure that Lesgano was going to help us."

"Lesgano or Lizcano?"

"He always said Lesgano, quite clearly."

"Was he Italian, Latin American, Portuguese perhaps?"

"He never spoke about his nationality, or if he was young or old. I swear to God, that was all he ever said. He looked at me with those kind eyes of his and told me to trust him. I always begged him not to get mixed up in anything strange, that we already had enough between the two of us to live on, that I didn't want to leave Spain. But he had his mind made up; that's how he was."

"O.K., don't get upset. You have our phone number. Just remember that whatever comes to mind could be useful. Anything."

"Will you keep me informed of what you discover?"

"Don't worry, we'll stay in touch."

Garzón drove me home.

"Astounding, wasn't it?" he said.

"What do you mean?"

"That she could describe Valdés's eyes as 'kind.'"

"What I find even more astounding is that he could have the gall to say this is a country of gossips. Look who's talking!"

"And that tale about a little house on the prairies in Canada . . ."

"It's obvious he was involved in something so shady he would have to leave the country once it was over."

"Exactly. I'm becoming increasingly convinced we're mixed up in something big."

"Drugs?"

"He doesn't seem the type."

"Well, we'll see soon enough. Come and pick me up in two hours. Have you got your bags packed?"

"It's in the trunk."

"Mr. Speedy González. Good, you can use the time to find out how many Lesganos there are in the phone directory. Find out too if it's a Spanish surname."

"It could be an alias."

"In that case, get them to check in our police files."

My sister was not at home. She had left a brief note saying: "Going out to visit the city." I left her one in exchange, explaining I would be in Madrid for a couple of days. I was pleased she had found something to do. The fact that she had decided to go out was a step back towards normalcy. As she strolled round the streets of Barcelona she would have time to think about what was going on. Besides, in public she would not be so tempted to cry. Crying is disastrous: it may relieve tensions, but it robs you of the time to reflect, as well as lowering your self-esteem and turning your eyes to red puddles.

Exactly two hours later, Fermín Garzón rang my doorbell. I picked up the bag I had prepared with a pair of pajamas, my toilet bag, and a complete change of clothes. Later I noticed that the sergeant had packed even less. He traveled as light as a feather.

We did not have to wait for the flight, and the shuttle worked perfectly. By suppertime we were in Madrid.

Garzón knew the city better than I did from his days in Salamanca, so he offered to be my guide.

"I think we should try some tapas," he said.

I agreed. I was tired and hungry, and I liked the liveliness of the city, the bars full of people, the impression you had of being somewhere with many years of history behind it.

We went to a place near the Puerta del Sol, right in the centre of the city. It was a bar with tiled walls and a bull's head presiding over proceedings. There were no tables, just a crowd of people jostling round the bar counter.

"It's crowded, let's try somewhere else," I said.

"No chance; just wait a minute."

As soon as he saw us, one of the waiters called out gaily: "What will it be?"

From the other side of the wall of people, Garzón shouted: "Two glasses of wine and two portions of salt cod!"

"On its way!" shouted the barman, decked out in an immense apron.

At this, in exactly the same way that the Red Sea must have parted for Moses, the crush of people seemed to withdraw slightly, leaving us room to charge forward and claim our glasses and food. This movement has been rehearsed for centuries: all of a sudden there was room for at least another fifty customers.

"You know your way around Madrid bars," I commented to Garzón. Chewing on his cod, he agreed.

"It's a whole way of life, inspector. There's nothing like it in Barcelona."

We visited five or six more similar bars until we had completely lost our appetites and much of our sobriety. But as we made our way back to the hotel, Garzón was strangely quiet.

"Are you tired, Fermín?"

"Yes. I'm beginning to wonder whether I'm getting too old for all this nightlife."

"You don't look it."

"You're just being charitable."

"I hate charity."

His cell phone rang.

"Anyone who calls at this time of night doesn't know the meaning of charity."

I watched out of the corner of my eye as he nodded briefly

and asked quick questions whose meaning I could not grasp. Finally he said curtly: "Wait for orders," and rang off.

"Problems, Inspector. It's Marta Merchán, Valdés's ex-wife. She's been followed to a poor-looking street in la Meridiana, and she's gone into an equally poor-looking house. She's been in there a while now. They want to know what to do."

"La Meridiana doesn't seem like the kind of place for someone like her, does it? It must be an interesting visit."

"We can't catch her in flagrante. We don't even have an arrest warrant."

"No, tell them to note down the address and to keep their eye on her. I'm sorry, Sergeant, but you're going to have to go back there. It could be something important, and I've got an appointment first thing with the TV people. If you hurry, you can still make the last plane."

"All right," he said with a sigh.

"Depending on how it turns out, either I'll return to Barcelona, or you come back to Madrid."

"You see how I can never allow myself to feel tired?"

"You'll have plenty of time to rest when you really are old."

"I suppose that was a compliment."

"Not at all, you're like a young kid."

"A kid whose punishment is not to be allowed to go to bed. It used to be the opposite."

I was truly sorry he had to leave like that, but I had no intention of telling him so. As soon as he thought I felt sorry for him, there would be no end to the wailing and gnashing of teeth. Just like all males of the species.

The hotel offered me its impersonal welcome. Perhaps I should have stayed awake worrying about the case, but I didn't. I slept like a deaf log. The minute I awoke, I called Garzón.

"Nothing out of the ordinary, Inspector. The lady went to see her maid. Apparently she likes to do good deeds, and pays her a visit from time to time."

"That's very commendable. Has she spotted us?"

"Our men were very discreet, but in cases like these there is always the chance that a neighbor might find our interest puzzling and tell the maid. She would be bound to tell her mistress."

"No matter, we'll have to run that risk. Find out all you can about the maid. See if we have anything on her, or if she has a kid mixed up in drugs. And find out if she has a husband."

"She's a widow. An old woman who lives nearby told us so."

"That will save you work."

"Shall I get someone to do all the checking?"

"I'd prefer you to see to it personally. And when you've finished, come back to Madrid. Did you manage to get any sleep?"

"A little."

"Take advantage of the three-quarters of an hour in the plane."

"Thanks, inspector; you're like a mother to me."

The director-general of Teletotal was expecting me at eleven, so I breakfasted on some typical Madrid *churros* and took a taxi to the TV studios, which were on the outskirts of the city. Along the way I revelled in the big-city feel, which was strangely mixed with that of a Castilian village. The fascination that anyone who lives in Barcelona has for Madrid is matched only by the curiosity people from Madrid feel for the birthplace of the counts of Catalonia. Two different worlds, one hour's plane journey from each other.

Avelino Sáez was an attractive executive around fifty years old who had not the slightest intention of wasting any time with me. He greeted me with a formulaic mix of willingness to cooperate and politeness, a formula he had obviously learnt in other circumstances. It was, of course, perfectly natural I should investigate Valdés's death, but he warned me he did not think I would find out very much there. What could his employees know of the crime when Valdés only appeared once a week? Besides, the journalist had been killed in another city. I explained that this was not so important, and that we were following up any leads there might be in his professional environment. Sáez did not seem to feel that this concerned him either: he had nothing to do with the details of the programming, he took a broad overview and, of course, looked after any mega-events as well as the finances. He sent for the producer of *Heartbeats*, the program Valdés starred in. When she came into his office, he stressed she should give me all the help she could, and make sure that everyone cooperated as fully as possible. Convinced he had shown himself willing, he left.

The producer looked as if she were about the same age as me. Like everyone else in the media, she seemed to be continually on the verge of collapse from overwork and stress. When I saw she intended to pass me on to two interns to get rid of the problem, I stopped her short.

"Could you at least tell me your name?"

"Maribel," she replied hesitantly.

"Maribel, I ought to tell you that I'm going to be here all day doing my job, and that it if I find anything interesting it may take me longer still. So, please, let's take this steadily. To start with, you could offer me a coffee."

She felt she had let down her public-relations image, and smiled at me.

"I'm sorry if I seemed in such a hurry, but do you have any idea the rhythm of our work in a TV station?"

"And do you have any idea of the rhythm of work in a police station?"

"No," she admitted.

"Well, it's very slow. We have to consider things, reconsider them, go back to the beginning . . . sometimes you only notice something that was staring you in the face after you've been going over it time and again."

"I understand."

"In that case . . . "

"Would you like to come to my office and have a coffee?"

"I'd be delighted."

I felt really pleased with myself, as though I had rescued a poor soul from the overwhelming pressures of modern life. Maribel's attitude changed completely: she even switched off her mobile phone.

"So tell me, Maribel, how does the program work?"

"Well, let's see . . . " she said, taking her time. "There are four journalists . . . Have you ever seen the program?"

I nodded.

"In that case, you know there are several people who agree to come and be interviewed."

"And they're all paid?"

"That's right."

"Are they all paid the same?"

"Not a chance! It depends on how big a celebrity they are, their prominence in celebrity magazines . . . There are huge differences. Then, as you know, the four journalists ask the interviewee a series of questions. And in addition, each of the journalists prepares a story on one of any number of topics: they go in the second half of the program. My job is to find them their topics, to dig around in society circles, what events or gossip make someone hot at a particular time . . . Do you follow?"

"I think so. Do you choose the stories too?"

"No, I coordinate them once they are done. It's up to each journalist to decide what story they want to do and how to do it. Valdés was a real expert at that."

"And they do all the work on their stories?"

"No, I have staff to help them."

"Who are your staff, Maribel?"

"Each journalist has someone from the production team

working for them. They are the ones who really make the programs. They make all the contacts, take the cameras out of the studios to film . . . Sometimes they have to hang around doorways for hours, waiting for somebody to come in or out. They uncover lots of secrets . . . It's very hard work, so most of them are quite young."

"Who worked with Ernesto Valdés?"

"A girl called Maggy. In fact, it was Ernesto who brought her with him; that's not usually the case. Now we don't know whether she will continue working for us; probably not."

"Were there any rivals who wanted to replace Valdés?"

She peered at me through the black gunge of her eye make-up.

"If you're thinking someone might have wanted to get rid of him to make room for themselves, you can forget it. Nobody will be stepping into anyone else's shoes. The network boss will choose an outsider who's famous in some other field. It's not a question of climbing a career ladder. Besides, Ernesto never had any problems with his work colleagues."

"O.K., let's rule that idea out. What about the people Valdés interviewed or did reports on?"

"What would you like to know?"

"Was there anyone who had it in for him?"

She burst out laughing, flicking back her impeccably groomed hair.

"You are joking, aren't you? They all had it in for him! What our dear friend Ernesto did here was common knowledge. But it was less clear cut than it seemed. Basically, they all wanted to be on the program; it was the most popular on TV. Even if some of them regretted it afterwards."

"Can you explain that?"

"Absolutely. Occasionally minor celebrities would call me to try and get themselves interviewed on the program. They thought they had everything under control, that they could face up to Valdés, but then he would find out things they had not bargained for, and bring them up live on TV . . . My God, the shocks they got! Valdés always made them feel sorry they had volunteered. He was incredible."

"How did he get information like that?"

"You'd have to speak to Maggy about that, I have no idea!"

"Was Valdés's life ever threatened?"

"Of course! He received some fabulous threats: they were going to pluck his eyes out, slice him up, wear his privates as a necklace, explode his liver . . . there wasn't a single part of his anatomy that hadn't been threatened at some time or other. He was very proud of it; he saw it as some sort of popularity index."

"Strange sort of index. What kind of people threatened him?"

"Sometimes the celebrities themselves. Or viewers who called or wrote in to the program. Remember that some celebrities, however disgusting they may seem to us, have fan clubs."

I broke out into a cold sweat at the mere thought that the murderer could have been an anonymous, crazy viewer. That would make the case impossible. Then I thought of the professional killer. A viewer paying a hit man? Highly unlikely, I reassured myself. Maribel was looking at me, unperturbed. I returned to the charge.

"Tell me something, and I want you to think this over carefully, although it is in no way an accusation or an obligation. Do you have your own theory about who killed him?"

The producer thought it over, pulled down the sleeves of her elegant two-piece, and then shook her head.

"As you can imagine, Inspector, these last few days the TV station has been buzzing with rumors and theories, each one more colorful than the last. But I can tell you that everything I've heard has seemed to me like a bunch of stupid jokes. I firmly believe that he was killed by someone from his private life."

"Do you have any reason for thinking that?"

"No, apart from the sheer mediocrity of the people we have on our program: singers, matadors, the occasional dim aristocrat, a businessman who wants to be on television, second-rate actors, TV presenters . . . I really can't see any of them being cold-blooded or determined enough to kill anyone."

"That's an interesting theory."

"Is it?"

"Yes, and a very sincere one."

She burst out laughing again.

"Would you like me to tell you something, Inspector? I'd love you to go on questioning me for hours! You've made me feel relaxed!"

"Perhaps we police do have something in common with psychologists."

This time we laughed together. All of a sudden, Maribel raised her bejewelled hands to her head.

"So relaxed I haven't even given you the coffee I promised!"

"I'll manage."

"If you like, we could both have one. There's a café on the ground floor."

"I don't want to take up any more of your time. Besides, I'd like to talk to . . . "

"Maggy?"

"That's right. Why don't you tell her to meet me in that bar?"

"I'd be delighted to."

She picked up her phone and asked her secretary to find Maggy and show her to the cafeteria. I noticed that as soon as she went back to business, the stress lines reappeared round her mouth. She showed me out, changing gears instantly and turning once more frenetic and anxious.

The cafeteria was not full, but the noise from the conversations filled the air with a dome of sound. The people at the tables were of different ages and appearance, although they all had a sort of fashionable sheen to them. Loose-fitting clothes, carefully styled hairdos, unusual frames on their glasses. I ordered my long-delayed cup of coffee and waited for Valdés's factotum to appear. After some minutes, a very young-looking woman came and stood firmly in front of my table.

"Are you the cop?" she asked challengingly.

"Yes, I'm Inspector Petra Delicado."

"And I'm Maggy. You wanted to talk to me, apparently."

I would never have believed she was the woman I was after. She was skinny, with washed-out jeans and a faded top. One ear was full of piercings, and her cropped hair was bright yellow. She looked like something out of a Bronx gang movie.

"Yes, I need to ask you some questions about Ernesto Valdés."

"There's too much noise here, let's go to the meeting room. My boss says you're not to pay for the coffee."

She signalled to the waiter, and set off ahead of me. We walked down a long corridor without saying a word to each other. I gathered that Maggy was not bothered about conventional manners, and was glad of it. That should help us save time.

The meeting room contained the usual furniture and a huge TV screen. Maggy slouched in a chair and stared me in the face.

"What do you want to know?"

"What do you think?"

"Who killed Valdés . . . But I have no idea."

"No idea?"

"No. If I had, I would have gone to the cops already."

"I know, but sometimes we have an intuition."

"Not in my case."

"O.K. How did you get on with Valdés?"

"Valdés was a louse, but I'm no angel myself, so we got on fine."

"You were the one who dug around in the private lives of the people who appeared on his program."

"Among other things."

"Who was about to appear when Valdés was killed?"

"There was a story about Lali Sepúlveda. She's just had a baby. I was in charge of getting hold of a cousin of hers whose boyfriend she stole—he's her husband now. She was happy to dish the dirt for money."

"What dirt?"

"You know, the usual crap: she had behaved very badly, she never answered the phone, had never deigned to explain anything. That sort of stuff, just to get her own back."

"Nice job you have, isn't it?"

"It's a living. When I'm a millionaire I'll make wildlife programs for the BBC."

She spat out this sarcastic comment, and never once smiled. I took a shine to her.

"Well, anyway, it doesn't seem like something so threatening that Lali would have had Valdés killed, does it?"

"No, of course not! We've done far worse recently."

"Can you remember what exactly?"

"No, I'd have to look in the files."

"That's what I'll ask you to do later. But for now, tell me: did Valdés leave any notebooks, a cell phone, anything like that . . . ?"

"When he was killed they got a warrant and came and searched his office, but they didn't find anything."

"Yes, I know, I just thought that maybe . . . "

"Valdés was very careful, he never left any traces. That was the way he worked."

"Did you take his phone calls?"

"Yes. Whenever he was in Barcelona he would call me, and

I would relay him the urgent ones. I would jot down the ones that could wait."

"Do you have a list of those calls anywhere?"

"No. I always wrote them on bits of paper that then got thrown away."

"Were there any people who called regularly?"

"Yes, I suppose so. His ex-wife used to call, and so did the Barcelona magazines . . . the occasional crazy viewer. I can't really remember, I'd have to think about it."

"Did someone called Lesgano ever call him?"

She was about to shake her head, but then stopped herself.

"Yes, I think someone called Lesgano did phone."

"Did he leave any messages, or a number where he could be contacted?"

She was obviously thinking hard, but the bored expression did not leave her face for one moment. It must have been in her genes.

"No, I don't think so, although now you come to mention it, he did phone quite a lot in recent months, and often said it was urgent. He didn't leave any number, though."

"Did he have a foreign accent; Italian perhaps?"

She puffed out her cheeks.

"Look, I really don't remember. I don't think so, but I couldn't swear to it."

"I understand. When could we take a look at your files?"

"This afternoon, if you like. Until I get a new boss I don't have a lot to do. Unless they fire me, of course."

"How about if I come around five?"

The shrug she gave was the only sign that she agreed. We stood up without another word, and when we were outside the room she disappeared with a brief "bye."

I switched on my cell phone. I had two messages from Garzón. When I got through to him I could hear airport noises in the background.

"I'm just about to board, inspector."

"How did you get on?"

"The maid's kids seem clean. We have nothing on them, they have jobs and seem like ordinary enough people. One is a bricklayer, the other—would you believe it—is a priest!"

"It's a job."

"Yes, but I find it odd. I had no idea where priests come from, then all of a sudden you find they're just like me or you."

Fortunately, I was already well used to Garzón's unexpected comments. "How did you get on in Madrid?"

"I'll tell you when you get here. Let's have lunch together. Do you know the Callejón de la Ternera restaurant?"

"Of course."

"I'll see you there at two."

I remember I once read a thriller that was set in Madrid. In it, an American guy says to a Spaniard: "Take me to any restaurant where Hemingway did not eat," and the other man says: "That's going to be really difficult." Nobody knows where, in fact, the writer ate: every owner of a halfway old restaurant in Madrid boasts that he dined there. But the Callejón is somewhere he definitely did visit. Besides which, their meat is excellent, and the place is attractive. I ordered some wine and spent the time waiting for Garzón to arrive examining all the signed photographs on the wall.

Garzón arrived at a quarter past two. He looked more dead than alive, and collapsed into his seat.

"Tired, Fermín?"

"Me, tired? Not a bit of it. I can go a week without sleep— I've proved it often enough. After that, the hallucinations start, and I drop dead, but so far I've never reached that point: is that what you're trying to do?"

"Don't exaggerate: you look fresh as a daisy."

"I won't say a word."

I poured him a glass of Rioja and we ordered food, then

told him what I had discovered, and what we had to do that afternoon. When they brought the first course, my colleague flung himself on the marinaded partridge as though he was afraid it might fly off. Duly fortified, he gave a deep sigh and said he felt a bit better.

"How wonderful it would have been! All the pieces fitted," he said. "Marta Merchán learns one day that her ex-husband has acquired a huge fortune. She hires her maid's son, a known delinquent, to kill him, but then can't lay her hands on the money because it's all in Switzerland."

"You're trying to square the circle there, Fermín! First problem: where did Valdés get all that money? What do we know about money that can't be traced?"

"That there's some dirty business involved! I'm not new to this, Inspector! Besides, how would his ex-wife have found out about it? And how could she expect to find the money if she had no idea where it was? All I was saying was how wonderful if would have been if it had all been that simple."

"Truth is, that money is a real problem. And what about this afternoon? Just imagine if we uncover a couple of really juicy cases where Valdés obviously had it in for the people he interviewed on TV. And then one of them decided to get their revenge and had him bumped off. That doesn't get us any nearer to solving the question of the money."

"It seems like what you're suggesting is that we should try to trace where that money came from, and forget everything else."

I rolled my breadcrumbs into a ball, and snapped back at him:

"How on earth should I know what we're supposed to do!"

"Don't let it get you down, Inspector! You'll see, one of our enquiries will uncover where the money came from, and a lot more besides. The real problem is that it's so hard to trace money itself: it's got no identifying features, it doesn't have a heart . . . "

"Would you kill someone for a hundred million?"

"I'd have done in Valdés for a hundred thousand. Or for free, even."

I laughed out loud, then finished my delicious lamb chops. As we were having coffee, the sergeant said:

"Did you know Hemingway used to come here to eat?"

"Yes, and to get drunk."

"Those really were the days! Bullfighters, Ava Gardner, drinking all night, flashy cars . . ."

"Old-fashioned myths! Nowadays in Madrid all you find are multinational executives and ministry officials."

"You don't get it, do you, inspector? You never let your imagination loose! Hemingway was a fantastic guy."

"A well-read tourist."

He muttered under his breath:

"Yes, of course, and Ava Gardner was a pretty young thing. You're just saying all that to contradict me."

I studied him more closely. I'd never heard him talk like that before. It occurred to me that once upon a time Garzón might have liked to stroll down the Gran Vía with a film star on his arm, or go to a movie opening with famous actors, or be an important bullfighter and have his dressing room full of millionaire American women, tipsy on whisky and all crazy about him. Obviously, even if that fantasy had ever been true, it belonged to the past, and now here was my Garzón, dog-tired and reminiscing about a past he had never even known.

"I suggest you go back to the hotel and have a siesta. I'll call you when I finish at the TV studios, O.K.?"

"I came here to work."

"Fine, in that case it's not a suggestion but an order. I've no intention of spending the afternoon having to put up with your bad temper just because you haven't slept."

There was nothing he could do but accept. I went back to the Teletotal studios where sweet little Maggy was waiting for me.

As was only to be expected, her manner had not improved from morning to afternoon. She flapped a hand in greeting and led me to the room where the files were kept. It was small, with a desk and a computer. The walls were full of shelves with rows of diskettes on them. She sat at the computer and asked:

"What do you want to know?"

I lit a cigarette and looked daggers at her. I drew on the cigarette once, twice . . . but said nothing. For the first time, Maggy started to look nervous.

"Is something wrong?" she asked, slightly less offhandedly.

"Look, Maggy, I don't enjoy my life much either, and the pleasures of civilization leave me cold. So, seeing that I'm neither kind nor gentle, I'd be really pleased if you changed your attitude and decided to collaborate a bit. Otherwise, I'm going to be forced to think you're involved in Valdés's murder in some way, and that you're trying to obstruct my investigation."

"Me? But I . . . "

"Yes, I know, you couldn't give a damn about any of this, and you're quite willing to help me. But tell me: what on earth am I supposed to start looking for on the computer? You're the one who has to show me where to look, the one who needs to think and select the cases where there was violence involved, or some other kind of controversy. Am I making myself clear?"

"Yes," she said, more resolutely. She had finally understood I was willing to play it tough, and she seemed to like this show of strength.

"O.K., how about if we start three months ago?"

"Perfect. Three months is a good length of time for someone to plan a murder if they didn't like what was said about them in a program."

"Here we go, then."

She pulled a grubby piece of gum out of her frayed pocket, started to chew it vigorously, and began typing. It was then I saw for the first time that she had two tiny silver skulls pierced in her right ear lobe. From the other ear dangled a tibia and a fibula bone.

"Okay," she said. "Let's see which of these assholes had a serious run-in with the boss."

Her language somehow led me to think she was warming to her task. Calmer now, I lit another cigarette.

"Oh, so you're another one who's determined to ruin her lungs!"

"Don't worry about my health, just concentrate, Maggy."

"My real name is María Magdalena, but, as I'm sure you understand, I couldn't go around with a name like that, so everyone calls me Maggy."

"Good."

"I'm only saying it in case you want to use my real name. I know you cops are such reactionaries . . . "

I counted to three before I spoke:

"Maggy is fine."

She shrugged to show she couldn't care less. Probably the right to call her Magdalena was one of the greatest concessions she made to other human beings, but I was not that sure I wanted to feel close to her. I could hear her singing to herself as she ran through all the documents on screen. Eventually she stopped at one file and brought it up.

"Beatriz del Peral," she read. "Here she is. Do you know her?"

"Not in the slightest."

"A real drag. She dances Spanish folklore. And I don't mean one of those from a proper dance company. She was completely third-rate, dancing in nightclubs for tourists, castanets and the whole Andalusian thing—though I think she was originally from Galicia."

"So what happened to her?"

"She made her name because she got together with Herminio Castelló, the banker. I've no idea what he saw in her, but it seems he was willing to leave his wife for her. Then we got word that she'd been seen with some DJ or other in night-clubs. I started looking into it, but none of the photo agencies had any pictures. I got in touch with a pal of mine, and between the two of us we started tailing her. We followed her everywhere without her cottoning on, and after two months we finally got something. I took a photo of her with a young stud: he had his hand down her dress. Bull's-eye!"

"What happened then?"

"Nothing special. I took the photos to the boss and he did the story. It went out on the program. It made a big impact because she and her banker had been so lovey-dovey in all the media, saying how devoted they were to each other. Naturally the wedding was off, and the banker must have been furious, although he didn't say a word. He'd been made to look ridicu-lous in public. The bank threw him off its board. They must have had their eye on him ever since he had said he was going to tie the knot with that old slag, but our program was the coup de grace. Shall I print it?"

I nodded, thinking hard. Maggy pressed the print button.

"Did they threaten Valdés?"

"I think they must have sent the banker off to the Sahara Desert, because he disappeared completely from Madrid, and was never heard of again. She threw a fit, and one day waited for Valdés at the airport. She made a scene: she screamed at him, insulted him, tried to hit him. But the boss had been expecting something of the sort, and so had a photographer with him. He took pictures of the scandal, and made sure everyone saw them. He threatened to have her charged with assault, so she backed down. She's never been seen again either: she must be hard at it in some brothel or other. Interesting, isn't it?"

"Are all the details in this report?"

"Yes, I'll see what more I can dig out."

I read what she had already printed. The phone numbers and addresses of both of them were there. I put the sheet of paper away.

Maggy was enjoying herself: she was typing away at the computer in that common, slickly modern way that characterized all her gestures and speech.

"I've found another possibility, Inspector. Jacinto Ruiz Northwell. Does the name mean anything to you?"

"Nothing at all."

"You should watch our program occasionally."

"I have other things to do."

"Sometimes swimming in shit is a good way to find out what's really going on."

"Do you always have to be so foul-mouthed?"

"You don't like the way I speak? You see how reactionary cops are?"

"Let's get on with it, shall we?"

"I'll watch my language, I promise—although 'get on with it' isn't exactly polite, is it? I would have expected you to say something like 'concentrate on the essential.'"

I could hardly believe my ears. I took a deep breath and smiled wryly.

"Who's our next possibility?"

"Oh, yes! Jacinto Ruiz Northwell, known as the 'marquis.' In fact, he is a real marquis. He's a relative of the Queen of England or some fuc . . . someone like that. He doesn't have a cent, but he's always at smart parties and events, because his presence adds glamour. He's a Don Juan, good-looking and always turned out like a movie star. We've done several stories about him, and we even interviewed him once. No problems: we paid him, and that was that. But then a property developer in Marbella chose him to appear in an ad campaign for a luxury development. They ran ads everywhere. The Marquis was the face fronting the whole scheme. But then the boss got some inside information from London about the marquis's financial past. So Remigio and me—Remigio is the pal I mentioned earlier, he's also what you might call my partner—set off for England. We soon discovered that Valdés's tip-off was on the right track: by asking questions here and there, and with a few bribes, we got all the lowdown: the marquis had unpaid bills even in his local pub. He had been accused of a swindle in a London company he worked for, and had even been charged with the possession of drugs. Not a great amount, mind you, it was for his personal use, but he was fined and has a police record."

"So you two brought all this mine of information back to Madrid."

"We sure did. The sky fell in when we aired it on the program, with proof and everything. The property developers were livid: they even had to change the name of the development. Let's see . . . yes, they were going to call it Marquis Gardens, but they had to change it to the Sunflowers—bit of a comedown, wasn't it?"

"What happened to the marquis?"

"He lost the job, and the possibility of doing anything similar. Now he's just a gigolo. At first, he got on his high horse and swore to everyone he would haul us up in court for defamation . . . but, of course, in the end he had to shut his trap. Interested?"

"Yes. Print it out for me. Listen, there's something I'm curious about. Did Valdés give you a bonus for a story like this?"

"No, he reckoned a fortnight in London was bonus enough, even though I was working my butt off, and he paid Remigio his expenses as well . . . "

"But that's not fair!"

"You're telling me!"

For this first time since we had met, I saw her smiling openly. She looked at me more indulgently.

"Listen, I don't mean to say that all cops are the same; there must be a few decent ones, it's just that . . . "

I interrupted this double-edged compliment sharply:

"Is there anything else?"

"I was thinking of another case in particular: would you like me to find it?"

"Of course, that's why I'm here."

The look of cosmic indifference returned to her face. She passed me the second lot of papers, and while I was glancing through them, she went back to her typing and chewing. I saw there were phone numbers and addresses in this one too.

It took her longer this time, but I had plenty to keep me busy, thinking and trying to tie up loose ends.

"Here it is. This one's very short. Emiliana Cobos Vallés. On the jet-set list. She made her name in business, and was invited to increasingly select dinners and shindigs. Photos, outfits, poses, rumors of romance with people in high society . . . in 1997 she was awarded the title of most promising newcomer by the National Society of Businessmen."

"What line is she in?"

"That's where it gets interesting. She designs and manufactures children's clothes. At one point she had two shops in Madrid and another in Barcelona. Her ads on TV showed angelic little blond kids taking their first steps in matching pants and tops made by her. And whenever she was interviewed, it was always the same question: 'How many children do you want when you marry?' And she would always reply: 'Personally, I'd like a large family, but I'm so busy . . . but in any case the man I marry should be aware that motherhood is one of my priorities.' Then one fine day, wham! We find out she had a child as a single mother at sixteen. The boy has Down's syndrome and lives in a Swiss clinic, where she has never so much as set her foot, not even at Christmas."

"Did you make a story of that? It's horrible."

"Believe it or not, I didn't research it. A freelancer offered it to Valdés, and he paid a lot for it. He even brought him photos of the poor kid with slanty eyes smiling at the camera. It was such a strong story there wasn't even any gossip about it; people had pity on her. But her factory has just gone bust, Lady Emiliana has never appeared in the press again, and her shops, at least the two in Madrid, are up for sale. Apparently a chain of 'traditional' fast-food restaurants is going to buy them—you know the kind of thing, sausage and lentils or beef stew to take away. Maybe they'll be a big success, who knows?"

"Give me a copy of that too."

She saw the way my face had tensed, reflecting my inner distaste.

"You think all this is really disgusting, don't you, Inspector?"

"To be frank, I don't know what on earth a young woman like you is doing here."

"I have to make a living somehow. A lot of my friends have got no job. Valdés gave me a helping hand; let's see if I go on being lucky."

"Hand out leaflets, join an N.G.O., or join the Catholic Women's Group: anything but getting mixed up in all this sleaze!"

"What we do may be sleazy, but the people we're dealing with aren't exactly sisters of mercy. Isn't it disgusting that a woman who wants to marry someone just for his money is incapable of being faithful to him even at the start? And what about an idiot who goes round the world leaving debts all over the place and still expecting everybody to think he's the bee's knees. And don't talk to me about the little earth mother who wants all those children but sends her own handicapped child to rot on the highest mountain in Europe, well out of her way! Isn't that just as disgusting?"

"But you're as bad as they are!"

"We're doing our job! You cops aren't exactly angels either!"

I looked down and bit my tongue. If I had had any sense I would never have started such a useless argument.

"Anything else?"

She swivelled away from me and began furiously typing again on the computer.

"I don't know. Those made the biggest fuss in the past few months. There was also a bullfighter whom Valdés called a shyster in public, an actress whose two cosmetic operations we were the first to reveal . . . but I'm not sure if those are reasons to kill someone. Although I bet you would have done away with the lot of us for much less."

"I wouldn't have wanted to get my hands so dirty."

Maggy was hurt. She glared at me. I handed her my card.

"This hasn't been a pleasant interview, but I have to admit you helped me a lot. Call this number if anything else occurs to you. May I remind you, it's your duty as a citizen to do so."

"If I call it will be out of a sense of duty; don't imagine for a moment it will be because it's a pleasure to help you."

During the taxi ride back to the hotel, my heart was pounding. I tried to think things over. How could I have been so clumsy, so stupid, and so full of myself? How could I have allowed myself to be carried away like that, so foolish? Who was I to judge anyone, let alone to do so right in front of them? Could this really be Inspector Delicado, famous for her level head, her irony, her imperturbability? I almost called the taxi driver a faggot so that he would dish me out a well-deserved smack. From the stories she had selected, Maggy had shown she was extremely bright. They all fitted perfectly into the kind of investigation I was involved in. And she had been friendly enough in her own style—I liked the way she looked, with her pirate adornments and her paella-colored hair! Whereas all I had done was get carried away by a complete moral stereotype, and allow what was left of my religious education to influence my judgment. As if judging others were not merely a sign of personal cowardice. To top it all, acting as a mixture of nun and left-wing activist like I had could actually harm our chances in the case. Maggy would not be exactly keen enough to want to call me with any new information, would she? No, I had really put my foot in it this time, or, as Maggy herself might have put it, I had landed myself in the shit, with only myself to blame.

I called Garzón from the hotel bar, and ten minutes later he came down, freshly showered and in clean clothes. The rest had put him into an ostentatiously good mood. When he appeared I was well into my first whisky on the rocks.

"How did you get on at the TV studios, inspector?"

By way of response I handed him the files Maggy had given me.

"Aha, as bad as that, is it? For professional or strictly personal reasons?"

"Just read."

He set about it without taking offence in the slightest. He read everything very closely, and finished just as I had downed the last of my whisky.

"Wow, this is worth its weight in gold! Any of these creatures had more than enough motive to want to see Valdés dead. And there's plenty of money in the circles they move in. They could easily have paid someone to bump him off. And it makes sense for them to do it in Barcelona—that way it was less obvious, further away from them in Madrid."

"That's all very well, but how do you account for the millions in Switzerland?"

He waved to the waiter and ordered himself a whisky. I asked for another. Then in a calm, easy manner, he explained his theory.

"As well as having a sleep, I've been thinking about the case. As you know, I'm expert at multi-tasking."

I nodded, not in the mood for jokes. He did not seem to notice, but sniffed his whisky and then took a satisfied sip.

"It's so good to get up at eight in the evening and have whisky for breakfast! We should do it every day."

I turned towards him impatiently.

"Apart from priding yourself on your many achievements and wanting the soft life a man of your talents so undoubtedly deserves, what do you have to say about the case?"

My sarcasm failed to shake him out of his beatific mood.

"The case? Ah, yes. I was thinking perhaps we shouldn't link the Swiss bank account so closely with Valdés's murder. What if he made people pay so that he would not publish all the dirt he found out about them? If they didn't cough it up, then he went ahead and wrote about them, or put them in his program."

"A hundred million is a lot of money!"

"But it quickly builds up . . . or, who knows, perhaps he got his hooks into a big fish."

"Blackmail."

"Nothing more, nothing less. He was in the ideal position. Just imagine, as he was looking for something else, or wallowing about in the usual muck, he suddenly stumbles on to something really important, involving someone equally important. The victim gets suspicious: should he publish or not? If he does go ahead, what might happen? He decides not to use it professionally, it's too big even for the kind of thing he does on TV. Do you think a bird of prey like him would have let a poor rabbit get away without at least trying to grab a piece of his flesh? No, he decides to try a different tack. Blackmail."

"It stands up as a theory all right, but if it's true, we're in trouble."

"Why?"

"How can we bring something like that out into the open? And where on earth do we start?"

"Well, we've started looking for the killer."

"You can forget that. The blasted informer hasn't even called me."

"Calm down, Inspector, any informer worth his salt takes time to get proper news. Even if it's only to tell you he has no news, he will call you; they always want to stay in the police's good books. In fact, I'd say the fact that he hasn't called you yet is a good sign."

"If you say so."

"O.K., now it's your turn."

"My turn to what?"

"To tell me why you're in such a bad mood."

"Oh, that? It doesn't matter. I'm just regretting having been rough with a girl who was trying to help."

"One of your little fits?"

"You think having 'little fits' is part of my character?"

"I reckon so."

"Fancy, and I thought I was such a friendly, easygoing sort of woman!"

"You're that, too. I'd describe you as easygoing with a tendency to your little fits, followed by remorse and possible depression."

"Don't say any more, you've destroyed me enough as it is."

"In that case, let's go for dinner. There's time enough tomorrow to see to those three poor offended celebs."

"I'm going to bed, I'm exhausted."

"So I'll have to go one my own! A poor country bumpkin in the capital!"

"By the way, make sure you call Barcelona and tell them we're staying here at least another day. It could take time to talk to all three of those ninnies."

"I'll see to it, Inspector. Get some rest."

I stood up and left him to it. He was enjoying his whisky in the bar as if he were Hercule Poirot in the Pera Palace.

I went up to my room and got undressed for a shower. Wrapped in a towel, I phoned home. Amanda came on the line immediately.

"Amanda, how are you? I'm really sorry, but I'm not going to be able to get back until the day after tomorrow at the earliest. Things have become rather complicated . . . "

"Don't worry, dear, I'm having a great time. By the way, there's something I wanted to tell you too . . . I'm going out for dinner with one of your colleagues tonight."

"What's that?"

"Yes, with Inspector Moliner. He's really sweet! He came here yesterday to talk to you about a police matter. I offered him a coffee, we got talking, and the upshot was that we've arranged to meet for dinner later."

"Amanda, do you realize Moliner is in the process of separating from his wife?"

"Yes, isn't that an amazing coincidence?"

"Wonderful! Except that it's no coincidence."

"I don't get it."

"Amanda, you're grown up now, so you know what happens with men who are separating."

"Are you warning me he might be so desperate he'll fling himself at me?"

"Look Amanda, I don't know, but . . . "

"I can't believe this, Petra! You giving me advice? What are you scared of, that I'll fall madly in love with him, or that he'll rape me?"

"I was only trying to fill you in about his background."

"Of course! Guys who've been rejected will fling themselves at anything, and women are pretty much the same! Listen, Petra, do me a favor: just forget about me! Oh, and tonight when you go to bed, ask yourself if you really are as liberated and as progressive as you've always thought you were!"

"We're both talking nonsense, Amanda."

"Especially you. Excuse me, I have to go now—Don Juan is waiting to take me to dinner."

She hung up. I hung up too. I gazed at myself in the looking glass. An old-fashioned progressive wrapped in a towel, with a mission to promote morality wherever I went. That was what I saw staring back at me. After that I clambered into the shower, convinced I would be doing everybody a favor if I slipped on the soap and knocked my brains out.

5

Not all of Garzón's rather tacky pet myths about the 1950s surfaced during our investigation in Madrid, but with the list of suspects we had—marquises, folklore artistes and high-society girls—I thought he might find something to suit his musty, decadent tastes.

Our flamenco dancer was not at home. Her neighbour had no problem telling us where we could find her, and gave us what she said was her work address. I was sure this would turn out to be to some flamenco dive or other that would whisk the sergeant off to the world of *The Barefoot Contessa*. But the soul of the great Ava had long since deserted the Spanish capital. Instead of flounces and flashing dark eyes, all we found at the address we had been given were several sports-goods shops. And in the aerobics section, surrounded by swimsuits, trainers, and leotards, we came across the lovely Beatriz del Peral—whose real name, it turned out, was Josefina García. She was lovely though, so beautiful that I could easily imagine a financier falling for her. Slim, with dyed straw-blond hair, delicate features, and a well-defined bust—not even the drab uniform she was wearing could hide her charms. She was not exactly pleased to see us, but neither was she surprised: I guessed her friendly neighbour must have rung to warn her we were on our way.

She did not let us get a word out. Taking Garzón to be my superior because of his sex and age, she immediately spat at him:

"Not here. Or do you want me to lose this crappy job as well?"

The sergeant glanced at me as helpless as a little child. I nodded: I had no desire for any more fuss.

"I finish in an hour and a half. Wait for me in the bar opposite. I'm not going to run away."

For the sake of peaceful coexistence with a suspect, we did as she suggested. Besides, a couple of cold beers were not a bad idea. The spring weather in Madrid was so hot that Garzón was sweating like Louis Armstrong over his trumpet.

"What do you make of her?" he asked, his moustache covered in beer foam. "She doesn't look to me like someone who's been saving up to pay a hit man."

"Don't be too sure. She might have a lover who lent her money so she could get revenge."

"A lover who lets her work in a place like that?"

"Lovers ain't what they used to be, Fermín. I think the idea that you wouldn't let your loved one work went out the window long ago. The occasional dinner at the Ritz is quite enough. That you can charge to expenses . . . "

"Even I could try that, then."

"Can I ask you a personal question?"

"Go right ahead."

"How do you manage?"

"Manage what?"

"Sex and all the emotional stuff. You never say a word about it."

He stared at me as though he wished he could put a millstone round my neck and push me into the sea.

"Really, Inspector, I never thought I'd hear a question like that from you. It's unworthy of you."

"Are you shocked?"

"Yes."

"I don't know why."

"First of all because you're a woman: I hope you haven't forgotten that. Next, because you're my boss, and I'm sure you haven't forgotten that. So . . . "

"Yes, I'm sorry, it was rude of me. It's just that I'm a bit confused about emotional issues at the moment. Did you know my sister is apparently going out with Moliner?"

"Inspector Moliner?"

"Yes, they're both in the middle of splitting up with their partners. I don't know what might happen."

"I don't think it's that disastrous."

"My sister has always lived a sheltered life."

"In that case, maybe it'll do her good to have a bit of a fling."

"I'm not sure Moliner is the ideal person to be having a fling with."

"Do you know why you're saying that? Because the inspector is a cop too, and you've never had a high opinion of cops, have you, Petra?"

"We never have a high opinion of things we know too well."

"I trust you don't mind me saying so, but you're a very contrary sort of woman."

"No more than the rest of mankind."

"I don't agree. You're far worse than most. You call yourself a feminist, but you don't want your sister to have some fun. You're a cop, yet you think that we cops are not to be trusted. There are loads more examples I could give, believe me."

"Go right ahead, I'm sure they'd all be justified. But you're wrong about one thing: I'm not a feminist. If I were, I wouldn't be working as a cop, or be living in this country, and I wouldn't have been married twice. I wouldn't even go out into the street, I can tell you."

He was about to respond, but suddenly I saw him fall silent and start to look over my shoulder. I turned round and saw Josefina García coming toward us. She was not exactly dressed like a flamenco star, more like an ordinary housewife. The only traces left of Beatriz del Peral were her high-heeled red shoes and blazing hair.

She didn't thank us for not having questioned her in the store at all. She ordered a beer and sat down. I got straight down to business, and asked her where she had been on the day of the murder.

"At work, as usual, then I went home."

"Do you live alone?"

"No. I got married two months ago. My husband is an insurance salesman and earns good money. I've settled down, get it?"

Garzón showed no sympathy.

"Three months ago you had a different boyfriend. How'd you manage to find a husband and settle down so quickly?"

"He was a childhood sweetheart, and I almost lost him too. That bastard Valdés almost ruined my life for good. But I didn't kill him! I don't go around killing people who spoil things for me: if I did, it would be a long list. What I can say is that when I heard he had been bumped off I drank a whole bottle of champagne! And I wasn't the only one!"

"Has your husband ever had any problems with the law?"

A glint of hatred flashed in her eyes.

"Look, why don't you leave me alone? With all the nonsense that happened, my husband is jealous as hell, and it's going to take years for him to forgive me for what I did to him. All I need is for you to start poking around into his affairs. Don't bother honest people, and start looking where you should be looking."

"Where's that?"

"They say Valdés was mixed up in big money deals. Pretty shady deals, as I understand it."

"What deals?"

"Don't you think I would have blabbed about them already if I had the faintest idea? Unfortunately, I don't know a thing."

"So who told you about them?"

"Oh, there were rumours going about. They said Valdés made trips to Switzerland to deposit cash in an account . . . But nobody seemed to know where it came from. He was a sly bastard."

I tried to win her over by looking her in the eye and smiling.

"Josefina, you do know you have nothing to gain by Valdés's murderer getting away with it, don't you?"

"Of course I do. On the contrary, I want him caught, because I'm sure that louse Valdés was in league with him. But I swear to God I don't know anything more about it."

We were about to call it a day when Garzón had a sudden flash of inspiration.

"These deals you heard rumours about, were they in Madrid or Barcelona?"

Beatriz del Peral thought about if for a moment, then said firmly:

"In Madrid. They said he made the deals right here."

"O.K. Tell us your husband's name."

To avoid a further outburst, I explained Garzón's demand. "We'll check his record. That's it! He'll never know a thing. After that I promise we'll leave you in peace."

She glanced over at the entrance to the sports shop.

"Look, he's over there, across the road. Every day he comes to pick me up. He said we had to get married at once if I wanted him to take me back, but being married hasn't made him any less jealous. He wants to know what I'm doing twenty-four hours a day. I'll have to explain what I was doing in this bar. He might even have seen you."

"Tell him I'm a friend from your past life." I suddenly felt sorry for her. She shrugged in a weary, dismissive way.

"Oh, yeah? He'd never swallow that, and you know it. It's obvious that you and I could never have been friends. Anyone can see we're not from the same social class. I assure you this is one lesson I have learned, Inspector."

She smiled sourly.

"My husband's name is Lorenzo Alvarez Bailén. Have a good day."

She left the bar. We watched her cross the street and link arms with a young-looking man. They walked off, deep in conversation. I guessed he must be submitting her to a far more rigorous interrogation than the one we had given her. A wave of sadness hit me. I tried to deflect it by commenting angrily to Garzón:

"You see why I'm not a feminist, Fermín? If I were, I'd have gone out there and given that guy a good spanking. And her too, for thinking that getting married, whoever the husband might be, is the only answer. And I'd kill Valdés all over again for doing this to her. Then I'd give that financier a kick up the ass, for thinking he could buy her like a sheep. And to round off a good day's work, I'd put a bomb in the houses of all those who watch Valdés's program or buy those gossip rags."

The sergeant was too busy paying for our beers to pay me much attention.

"Have it your own way, Inspector. Join the Feminist Salvation Army, and when I'm lined up to be shot, remember we were friends once."

"You are the first I'd shoot."

He laughed as powerfully as an operatic bass, pleased he could pull my leg for a change. Then he suddenly remembered:

"Did you hear your cell phone when we were with her? Don't you want to see who called?"

I fished my phone out of my bag and listened to the message. The time for joking was over.

"Are you coming back to Barcelona with me or staying here?"

"What on earth has happened?"

"My informer wants to see me at five this afternoon at the Velodrome. He's got news for me."

"Good. I'll come with you and check out Lorenzo Alvarez on the way. Depending on what our informer's news is, maybe we won't have to come back here."

"Get a move on then. That lousy informer hasn't given me any other option. Who do they think they are, God almighty? Let's get back to the stinking air shuttle, Fermín, we won't even have time to pass by the hotel."

I arrived before five, and sat waiting in vain for over an hour and a half for God to show up. I called Abascal to ask him if he thought this was normal, or a tactic. He assured me it wasn't either. I asked for the informer's address, which was only to be used in emergencies. He gave it to me, but hastily added:

"Petra, this time I really don't think you should go alone. Send a patrol car first."

"Why?"

"They might stumble on something unexpected."

He was right. They found Higinio Fuentes on the reception-room floor, and his wife sprawled across their bed. Both of them had been shot in the forehead at point-blank range. A summary execution. The door had not been forced, and there were no signs of violence, which led us to believe that the murderer rang and Fuentes opened the door without hesitation. Either they knew each other or the killer had tricked him. At least we knew that the information Fuentes was going to give us must have been true, otherwise he would not have been killed. The place was a complete mess, and the sight of the woman's body filled me with sadness. I remembered her very clearly. She had died simply because she had been sleeping next to her man. I ordered a thorough search, even though I knew we would not find a thing.

"For the murderer to come here even when there was a risk we might be keeping watch on the place shows he's both audacious and desperate," Abascal concluded when all the specialists had done their work. "By the look of it, we might be up against a professional again. The fact he shot the woman too proves that. She was a possible witness, so he got rid of her. He must be a professional."

"A professional hired for a heap of money," Garzón argued. "Otherwise he wouldn't have taken the risk."

"What about the weapon?"

"The bullets have gone to ballistics to be checked."

I cracked my knuckles.

"Have you talked to the neighbours?"

"Without any luck. Nobody saw or heard anything."

"Shit, everything and everyone just vanish into thin air!"

"If the people involved are professional hit men and informers, that's the way it's bound to be. We're delving into a world of shadows."

"We must know something about the informer!"

"We know a lot, but I'm willing to bet none of it will be any use."

"He was shot so that he couldn't tell us anything. That almost makes us accomplices."

"I'm sorry to have to tell you this, Petra, but that's the way informers work. They know it's a risky business."

I went home drained and exhausted. Garzón called our hotel in Madrid and asked them to store our things. We calculated we would need to be back there in a couple of days.

As I came in, Amanda was getting ready to go out.

"I had to buy a couple of dresses," she said. "I didn't realize I was going to have such a busy social life."

She looked wonderful: elegant, sensual . . .

"Are you going out with Moliner?"

"Yes. He's just called. He said something has come up and he's going to be a bit late. He knows you're back in Barcelona and says he wants to talk to you about something."

"About work?"

"What else?"

"Perhaps he wants to ask for your hand."

"I doubt it; but I don't need your permission anyway, do I?"

"What do I say if your husband calls?"

"Tell him I'm out enjoying myself. He's already phoned today anyway."

"What did he say?"

"Bah! Who knows, he calls a couple of times every day. He tells me how sorry he is, that he's having such a hard time, and wants to know when I'm coming back. He must be in a hurry to leave with his lover."

"Amanda, I . . . I'm sorry if I seemed like a busybody. It's just that I'm not too happy about Moliner . . . "

"Because you feel it involves you?"

"We cops should never have families."

"If you prefer, I could move into a hotel."

"I don't think that's necessary."

"Look, Petra, I've no idea what the real reason is, but the fact is, I'd like to get involved with him. For once in my life I'm going to do what my body tells me to do, and I'm not going to let common sense, you, or Enrique change my mind for me . . . so don't even ask."

Well, what could I say? Did I have to admit it was nothing more than a personal obsession of mine? Why was I opposing my sister in this ridiculous way? I've never been over-protective or concerned about family. Could the real reason perhaps be my old, well-documented desire to be left in peace, to avoid complications, so that I did not have to think even for a moment about other people's problems? I really hoped that was it: I could not have stood the idea of becoming a moralist well into my forties.

We had a drink in the kitchen, then at a quarter to ten Moliner arrived. I was expecting to see him freshly washed and dressed, but it was obvious he had come straight from the police station.

"Petra, I need to talk to you."

My sister discreetly took her glass and left the room. Moliner began to speak, but I was not so much listening as observing him. He was not so bad after all: tall, good-looking, polite. Perhaps Amanda was not so misguided in her choice.

"I'm sorry, could you start again?" I begged him.

"I was saying, there may be nothing to it, but we've been sharing an informer again. Did you know?"

"No."

"Higinio Fuentes had asked to see me as well, a couple of hours after you."

"Too big a coincidence?"

"Perhaps. But what really got me suspicious was the way he behaved. He was worried I wouldn't keep my side of the bargain. He wanted me to pay him before he gave me the information he supposedly had."

"I don't see the connection."

"Have you thought that perhaps he was going to inform on the same person to both of us? The details he wanted to pass on may have been exactly the same, and in that case I could have refused to pay him. I find it odd he was so worried about payment: our informers know we always keep our word."

"I see. How is your investigation going?"

"His tip-off would have been a blessing."

"For me too. Do you know what I think, Moliner? I think the responsible thing to do would be to head back to the station and get to work. We need to compare our cases."

"What about Amanda?"

"It's our job, she'll understand."

"Do you mind if I tell her?"

The look my sister gave me as we left could have drilled a hole in the wall. Curiously enough, she was all sweetness and light towards Moliner. Too bad; work is work, I told myself crassly.

We met up in Moliner's office and made some coffee. He switched his computer on.

"What do you want to know?" he asked.

"Everything."

"The victim in my case is named Rosario Campos. She's a girl from a well-to-do family that organizes conventions. The only thing of any importance I've managed to find out is that the poor thing was the long-term lover of our Health Minister. She used to travel frequently to Madrid, where they met in a hotel."

"Good god! A real scandal!"

"Especially considering the minister is married, has seven kids, and is a member of Opus Dei."

My whistle was heartfelt.

"When did you find all this out?"

"Just a short time ago."

"What action have you taken since then?"

"I've kept quiet as the grave. I wanted to hear what the informer had to say before I made any moves. You know as well as I do that when you aim high you better be careful what you hit doesn't land on your head."

"And now?"

"Now there's no way I can keep the lid on it. I've talked to Coronas, and the magistrate wants to get a statement from the minister. Then there'll be all hell to pay."

"Do you think Valdés was involved in some way?"

"The bullets aren't the same as the ones used on her, and the way they were killed is different, but who knows?"

"I certainly don't. It might have been the same hit man who changed weapons or simply changed his method of killing. We'll see what ballistics has to say."

"It would be too easy, wouldn't it? For some reason—per-

haps because the minister had threatened to leave her—
Rosario Campos is determined to get her revenge, or simply to
put pressure on him. So she goes to see Valdés and offers to let
him publish her story. Then they both start blackmailing the
minister until he can't stand it anymore and decides enough is
enough. He hires a professional killer and gets rid of them."

"And how much time would it take for all that to happen?"

"I can't be certain—eight months, a year . . . ?"

"He'd been filling his Swiss bank account with cash for
much longer than that. The amounts are very similar, and
deposited at regular intervals."

"Blackmail payments. That could fit in."

"But not in your time frame."

"Could've been blackmailing other people."

"Shall I guess what you're thinking? Valdés is digging
around in the muck every day. Occassionally, he comes across
important stuff, out of the ordinary, and he uses it to blackmail
people."

"Exactly. But there's one thing that doesn't fit into that theory. We didn't find much money in Rosario Campos's accounts,
either in Switzerland or anywhere else."

"Perhaps she didn't have time even to start her vengeance.
At the first threat, the minister had her murdered. How did
you find out about their relationship?"

"The neighbours, one of her friends, her parents . . . we
heard snippets here and there. Eventually, one of his colleagues
from the ministerial team agreed to collaborate, in the strictest
confidence."

"In public life, there's always someone willing to stab you in
the back."

"In public life and anywhere else."

"Listen, your theory is a good one, except for the few loose
ends."

"The dates?"

"Not just that. To blackmail at that level, you need more people. Valdés wouldn't have been up to it alone."

"Are you looking into that?"

"At the moment, we haven't found any clues that fit. We're busy interrogating his most recent public enemies."

"Make sure you ask whether Valdés tried to do a deal with them for money."

"I will. And what are you going to do next?"

"As soon as Coronas authorizes it, I'm off to Madrid to flush out our ministerial game."

"I don't envy you! I suppose you'll be discreet about it."

"It's supposed to be my strong point. The magistrate will want everything kept under wraps, and for now we can keep it from the press, but his wife . . . "

This time I gave a wolf whistle.

"A wife in Opus Dei, a Health Minister with a young lover . . . Even *The Sun* couldn't ask for more! There might be a promotion in this for you."

"Or I could get thrown out of the force if they decide to bury the whole affair."

"There are too many bodies to hide, they couldn't do it."

"That's what I think, too. I don't want to boast, but I'm confident about my diplomatic skills."

"Shall we inform Coronas of our mutual suspicions?"

"Perhaps it would be better to wait. So far, everything is resting on pretty shaky foundations."

"No, I'm increasingly convinced that Higinio Fuentes was going to give you and me the same name. I'm almost certain of it. Informers talk even when they're dead."

I was hoping that Moliner could bring his diplomatic skills to bear on my sister. When she heard that he was on his way to Madrid as well, she would see intrigue everywhere, and would blame me for it. And, in a way, she was right: I should never have stuck my nose into her affairs.

By the time I got home, Amanda was asleep. I went quietly into the bathroom, and looked at myself in the mirror. Good God, that woman in the bar would have offered me a job again! All the glamour that the beauty parlour had lent me had long since disappeared. No two ways about it, a good image and hard work did not mix. As I smeared my face with night cream I read the description that came with it. I had noticed that reading the theoretical benefits of a product like this somehow made it work better. Free radicals, enzymes, newly discovered acids dedicated to making women beautiful. What nonsense! I thought, but I was wrong. Beauty is important. Because of beauty, a financier had fallen in love with a second-rate flamenco dancer, and a conservative, religious man had perhaps found himself driven to murder. Although neither of them had eloped with the girl like in a fairy tale. The first could not have withstood the public ridicule, and the second had not even considered changing his life. And neither of them stood by their newfound loves. That's the way things are: beauty in itself is not enough. I stuffed myself into my pajamas, feeling ugly as a toad. There is too much to take into account if you want to be happy. Fortunately, I had long since dismissed that hope as absurd, and so I set my radicals free and fell fast asleep.

Garzón was very skeptical about our theory when I told him about it on the plane shuttle back to Madrid. He saw the coincidence about the murders and hit men as leading strictly nowhere.

"The thing is, Inspector Moliner is trying to flirt with you. Perhaps he thinks it would be fun to go out with two sisters at the same time."

"I thought we weren't going to allow ourselves personal comments like that."

"I'm sorry, you're right."

We reclaimed our rooms in the hotel, and went to see the next suspect on our list: Emiliana Cobos Vallés.

Her eyes were a deep blue and her face looked innocent and childish. As soon as she started to speak, though, I realized life had not been kind to her.

"You suspect I might have murdered Ernesto Valdés?" She gave a sarcastic laugh. "My God, I'm no do-gooder!"

"You'll have to tell me where you were that day."

"Was he killed the day that the newspapers said he was?"

"The day before."

"I was in Ibiza. I spend many weeks there."

"Doing what?"

"Letting time go by. I made a lot of money, so I don't have to go back to work yet. As you'll know better than I, people will eventually forget that I have a retarded son in Switzerland or Sebastopol. In a year or two I'll be able to start up a new business. I'm a fighter, and I have lots of ideas. I'm not going to let anyone like Valdés get the better of me."

"Can we have your address in Ibiza?"

She scrawled the details on a bit of paper, as calm as could be. Then she glanced at me ironically.

"Are you thinking of interviewing everyone who was on Valdés's program? That's ridiculous—you'll have days and days of hard work before you."

"Did Valdés try to blackmail you in return for your silence?"

"No," she said in an offhand way. "Why would he? He was far more interested in destroying people than laying hands on their money. He had a grudge against society. Besides, if he had suggested it, I would have refused. I knew my son's situation would come to light sooner or later. I made a mistake opening that children's clothing business. If I had done something else, people wouldn't have been so obsessed with my story. I could have said my son was in the best place for him . . . but I'm not sure of any of that now. I don't even hate Valdés; in the end, it's all publicity."

Garzón stared at me to emphasize what she had just said. O.K., I got the message, and there was little more to add. I called Sanguesa and asked him to investigate Emiliana Cobos's bank accounts. To avoid any loose ends, Garzón phoned the station to get them to talk to Ibiza. That way we could find out if our suspect had any problems there.

We went for lunch, but the sergeant did not seem satisfied.

"What did you think of her?"

"Unless we find some evidence, I don't think there's anything we can charge her with."

"She's a cool customer."

"None of these people are exactly heavenly creatures."

"But that comment about her son . . . Sometimes I can understand Valdés."

"You think our dear deceased was doing it in the name of justice? Come off it, Fermín!"

"Of course he wasn't trying to do good, but a woman like her deserves being dropped in it!"

"You're reacting just like the readers and viewers of that vulture did! Sentimental claptrap. Oh, the poor mentally handicapped kid abandoned by her mother in Switzerland. Nobody should judge what happens in other people's lives."

"You do."

"I do?"

"You said you'd like to smack Beatriz del Peral and her husband, and lots of others too. You even wanted to put a bomb under them! If that's not judging, I don't know what is . . . The thing is, you only react when you think there's machismo involved."

I put the glass of beer I was holding slowly and deliberately down on the table. I sat in silence for a few moments, then looked over at my colleague.

"I'm tired, Garzón, bone-tired."

"Inspector, I didn't mean . . . "

"No, listen a minute. We're in the midst of a case which, instead of getting simpler, just seems to become more and more complicated. My sister's at my place annoyed with me because I won't leave her in peace. I realize I'm not young anymore, and I look a fright. And, as if all that were not enough to depress any normal person, the colleague who is supposed to be on my side never misses an opportunity to criticize my way of doing things, to point out all my contradictions, my prejudices, to call me a cheap, half-witted feminist."

"I didn't say any thing of the kind!"

"Do you know something, Sergeant? In the end, I couldn't give a damn. I've never been a saint, and if I had ever felt the need to help my fellow man, I'd be working in some N.G.O. or other combing some poor refugee's curls instead of finding myself up to my ears in this pile of . . . let's call it social rottenness. Am I making myself clear?"

"I was just trying to . . . "

"I'm really not interested."

"Fine."

Our soup arrived, piping hot. I knew what Garzón was like. I knew I had offended him and that he would spend the rest of lunch without saying a word. That is exactly what happened. We drank our soup, set to on the fish, and at no moment did his face relax from a disgruntled pout. Good, that way I could think things over.

I thought about how little either Emiliana Cobos Vallés or Beatriz del Peral looked like assassins. The little marquis we were going to interrogate that afternoon had probably not hired anyone to kill Valdés either. No, we were not on the right track. Just because someone has ruined your life does not mean you go out and employ a killer. Direct revenge is too up-front for a complex society such as ours. An unpremeditated crime of passion, maybe, but to kill someone in cold blood like that . . . you don't become a killer overnight. What about this Lesgano: who was he? Then there was the money question. Money, money, money, that was the key: what else drove all the characters in this piece of theatre? It was the money we had to concentrate on.

When we had finished our dessert in Franciscan silence, I gave Garzón instructions.

"Sergeant, I want you to call Inspector Sanguesa again. Tell him we need the bank details of all those involved in this case. All of them."

"By which you mean . . . ?"

"Not just Emiliana Cobos, but Beatriz del Peral, the marquis we're about to meet, Pepita Lizarrán, the owner of the magazine, of . . . have I forgotten anyone?"

"Marta Merchán, Valdés's ex-wife?"

"Her too. I want to know how much money all of them have got hidden around the world."

"The magistrate might not be willing to issue so many warrants."

"He will. If the link between Moliner's case and ours is proved, the magistrate will grant us more than we need. His case affects important people."

"All right, Inspector."

"Do you have the marquis's address?"

"Yes, Inspector."

"Fine. I'll see you there at five."

"Whatever you say, Inspector."

Perfect. Why do we always have to be close to people, to know what they're up to, to try to make friends with them? Much better this way: Garzón was my subordinate; I was his boss. We had a job to do. Let's get on with it, then. Unfortunately, our job did not involve a production line where we could get fined for talking. No, we waited together and travelled together; we had lunch and dinner as close associates. By now, Garzón knew me almost as well as I knew him. We were determined to act as each other's conscience, and out loud too! Something had to put a stop to that. Would it help if I asked Coronas to find me a new partner? That's what happens to monks. If one of them is feeling too settled in a community, the prior sends him somewhere else. I suppose for them it's to suffer greater mortification. In other words, for them to do their job better, as mortification is part of that. Perhaps I would be more efficient, too, without Fermín Garzón.

I was thinking all this over as I strolled around Madrid. I looked up at the cloudless sky, such a radiant deep blue because there was no sea nearby, as in Barcelona. I realized I was in some sort of crisis. Otherwise, how could I possibly explain being so upset whenever anyone else tried to become involved in my life? It was my own choice to be such a solitary person, and now it looked as though I was heading for an even lonelier phase. But it's not that easy: there are always people around, and people want to relate to each other, they give you things and expect things back, they smile, busy themselves around you, judge your actions, hate you and love you, speak to you, see you and want you to notice them.

When this case finished, if it ever did, I would ask Coronas for a whole month off. Then I would go to a convent. One of those places where they give you a bed and board. I would stroll in the countryside. I would fill a hole in my intellectual development by reading the complete works of Pushkin. I would marvel at the gregarious instincts of ants—unless it was in winter. I would ask the nun who dealt with visitors if I could be served my food in my cell. If I happened to meet anyone in the corridor, I would turn away from them so as not to have to greet them. And if, at the end of the month, I liked the idea, I would take my vows. However hard that might be. I was not a believer, would not be able to bear the vow of obedience, nor all the prayers, or getting up at five in the morning, or being part of a community. Not to mention the lack of books, music, cigarettes, whisky, and coffee.

I reached the conclusion that there ought to be convents for non-believers, bruised, exhausted people, in need of solitude, but who did not want to have to give up all the pleasures of life. What about sex and love? Would they all have to give that up, too, or risk the convent becoming a brothel within three days of being set up? What would the community live off? Where did monks and nuns get their money from, anyway? Did they still make sweet liqueurs and embroidery? How to finance the thing? That would be the greatest problem, as always. Money, money, money. I thought about the case again. How was Moliner getting on with the minister? We had arranged to meet at nine in the hotel, where he had also reserved a room. Perhaps he would tell me then . . . As I slid back into the real world, I looked around me. I hadn't the faintest idea where I was; I was completely lost.

I hailed a taxi and gave the driver the piece of paper with Jacinto Ruiz Northwell's address on it. It was nearly five already. The last thing I needed was to be late for my meeting with Garzón. The taxi driver tried to strike up a conversation.

"Do you think it's going to rain?"

"I don't speak Spanish," I replied.

I had to stop him talking at all costs, because then he would only move on from rain to the lack of it, from the lack of rain to life in general, and from life in general to how his poor heart was suffering, and end up asking: so what do you think? To hell with all human relationships! Fortunately it all went smoothly, and he did not even say goodbye.

Garzón was waiting for me in the reception area, still wearing the face of someone who had been deeply offended.

"The marquis is expecting us."

"Did he object in any way?"

"On the contrary, he said that if we hadn't come to talk to him, he would have called us. He wants to talk."

"What about?"

"I haven't the faintest idea."

"Interesting, don't you think?"

He shrugged. He must have thought there was no point giving me his opinion as we were on such bad terms. Deep down I sighed, and vowed to be patient. I could not bear it when Garzón sulked like this.

An elderly maid opened the door for us. We were shown into a small room stuffed with lace, religious paintings and bibelots.

"Tokens of ancient splendors!" I muttered.

Garzón was staring open-mouthed at a large painting that showed the archangel Michael treading on the head of the devil. The archangel was wearing a shiny breastplate over a short Roman-style tunic. His blond curls streamed out from his head to emphasize the drama of the action.

"That must be worth a load," said my colleague.

"As an antique, perhaps . . . because it has no artistic merit at all."

Garzón looked at me in surprise.

"It doesn't?"

We stood up and went over to the picture.

"No. Just look at the size of the devil's head—it's out of proportion, see? Besides, the colors have no sparkle to them. And what do you make of the archangel's hands? Can you see how badly they're drawn? It must have been painted by some local artist from a village in Castille."

"Aha."

"If you're ever worried about how good a painting is, first of all take a good look at the way the feet and hands have been painted. That's foolproof. Of course, that doesn't work if it's an abstract painting: they can slip any old rubbish into that."

"To me, they can slip any old rubbish into any style they like."

"Don't be so sure."

"The thing is, I'm not cultured, and I haven't studied the history of art."

He scowled at me. I felt a wave of contempt, and could have killed him on the spot. Fortunately, I did not have the time, because a voice came from behind our backs:

"So you like that painting, do you? It's been in my family for two hundred years, and it isn't the oldest we have. There are some very interesting ones in my country house."

Jacinto Ruiz Northwell was the spitting image of a perfect playboy: tan trousers, blazer, a silk cravat knotted beneath his prominent Adam's apple. He was young, fair-haired, athletic— I could see why he had been chosen for an advertising campaign. His way of speaking was so affected it was comical. I was sure he must be putting it on.

"Good afternoon, señor Ruiz, we would like to talk to you, if you don't mind."

"I know, Inspector, I know. What's your name?"

"Delicado."

"Good, Inspector Delicado: I want to talk to you as well. In fact, in a few days' time, I would have gone to the police station myself. I think things have gone way too far."

"Can you explain what you mean by that?"

"Yes. Let's see: you have come here because you consider me a suspect in the murder of that journalist Valdés, don't you?"

"Well, according to our information . . . "

"Yes, yes, I know that. I had motive enough to kill that pig Valdés, but, the fact is, I didn't. What's more, I could have done him a great deal of harm and got him into real trouble, but I was having none of it. That's the way things are. Let me explain. You probably know, that as a figure in the public eye, I had frequent contact with him as a journalist. I appeared on his TV program several times. I knew he was a rat, but these days it's the media who make us. Do you understand what I'm saying?"

"I suppose so."

"Well, on one of the occasion we met, I gave Valdés an invaluable bit of information. I told him the Health Minister had a lover in Barcelona."

My heart skipped a beat, but I restrained myself: I had to let him do the talking, and proceed with caution.

"You may be wondering why I did something like that. Well, I did it out of pity. I knew the girl, Rosario Campos: she was a truly promising young woman, beautiful, discreet, from a good family . . . but she was throwing all that away thanks to the minister. She spent the whole time depressed, in floods of tears, in the vain hope that the guy would leave his wife for her. I told her a thousand times not to get her hopes up in the slightest, but she never listened to me. Then one day while I was talking to Valdés—he was always trying to get gossip out of me—I told him about it. Purely to help the girl, you understand? Then someone must have done him in to keep the lid on it. As you can see, I could easily have threatened Valdés by telling everyone what I knew, or simply told everyone to show he was mixed up in the scandal, but I didn't. Much less murder him."

"Why didn't you pass on your information about Valdés to the police?" asked Garzón.

"Noblesse oblige, it's not my style. People may think I'm exactly the same as all of those who appear in the celebrity magazines, but I'm not. I have a family name to think of, and I didn't want to get involved in any dirty business."

"Did Valdés pay or promise to pay you for your information?"

I was expecting the sergeant's question to ruffle his feathers, but he did not react.

"Are you crazy? Valdés would never have paid anyone who appeared on his program. If he had started mixing them with informers, that would have been the end of him. Besides, as I said, I have my dignity. I know that doesn't mean much around here, but . . . in the end, perhaps, I'll decide to leave Spain, this country doesn't deserve me."

"You may be right, señor Ruiz, but, leaving aside personal considerations, there is something I don't really understand. Why would Ernesto Valdés be interested in a politician? The people he dealt with weren't part of that world. I would guess that the media outlets he worked for wouldn't have published that kind of story."

"I know, but he was always after information about influential people: politicians, financiers . . . I suppose he simply wanted more power."

"Can you remember anything in particular?"

"No, nothing in particular: he would even ask about the King, but if he ever got any information about him, I don't think he ever used it. He didn't even use what I told him about Rosario and the minister. He always preferred to publish tittle-tattle about the same old people; that was all he was good for."

"Can you remember how long ago it was that you mentioned the girl and the minister to him?"

"Well . . . five or six months perhaps? Something like that. Then about three months ago Valdés played the dirty trick on me that you know about, and I was left without the contract I had pinned my hopes on. And it was all lies, of course!"

"Señor Ruiz, I'm afraid you're going to have to make a statement to the magistrate and tell him everything you've told us. You may be charged with concealing evidence from the police."

"Because I didn't mention that thing about Valdés?"

"Exactly. You should have come forward at the moment Rosario Campos was murdered."

"That's ridiculous, Inspector. I didn't know the two deaths were related. Besides, I only found out days later."

"That will be for the magistrate to decide. Personally, I'd like you to speak to a colleague of mine, Inspector Moliner. He is the one investigating Rosario Campos's murder."

"I'd be delighted to talk to him."

"For the moment, I'd prefer it if you did not leave Madrid."

"I have no plans to do so anyway, until the ski season starts . . . "

Once we were out in the street, I did not have to wait long for Garzón's first explosion.

"What a creep! My family name, my country house, my dignity . . . He knows where he can stuff his dignity! If I were a petty crook, I'd refuse to be put in the same cell as him."

I allowed him to let off steam: at least his bad vibes were not directed at me for once.

"Do you think he's lying?"

"Of course he was, the whole time! His country house . . . When all he's got are those crusty old paintings of saints disembowelling lizards with faces!"

"I meant lying about essential matters. Do you think he's lying about Valdés?"

"Hmmm . . . I haven't really thought it through yet. What about you? Do you think he was lying?"

"I suppose I think he was lying around the edges but telling the truth about the main things."

"I'm not sure I understand."

"It's true he passed Valdés the information about the minister, but he didn't do it for any noble reasons."

"You think he was paid?"

"Not even that. I think he was all chummy with Valdés, that he did it to get Valdés on his side, so that he would be treated better on his programs. That's how he makes his living."

"Well, his plan backfired on him."

"We all know Rome does not reward traitors. He wasn't lying, either, when he said he was willing to talk to the police. Of course, what he didn't say was that he would do so only if the police were after him. Otherwise he would never have risked getting mixed up in something like this. Now he's terrified he might be implicated, so he's dying to talk to anyone who will listen. I think that's the sad truth about our distinguished nobleman."

"You're right! A cretin like him couldn't have murdered anybody, still less hired someone else to do it."

"I second that. At any rate, Moliner ought to question him. He's the one with all the information on Rosario Campos. At least we'll find out how he knew her, and it might give us more information about her and what she used to get up to. As you can see, Inspector Moliner's theory looks increasingly sound. I think we're sharing a case."

"Have you spoken to him?"

"I'll give him a call to fix up a meeting, he'll still be busy now."

I called him on my cell phone, and we agreed to meet for dinner in the café next to our hotel.

"Can I come along?" Garzón blurted out.

"What a question! It's work, isn't it? Of course you can come."

"Just checking that I won't be in the way."

I came to a halt and stared at him.

"Sergeant, you do realize that behaving like a spoilt brat could hamper our investigation, don't you?"

"Me, a spoilt brat? I've never in all my life been called that! I started work at fourteen!"

"What I mean is you seem to be always upset and in a bad mood."

"The thing is, Inspector, you may not realize it, but you say things . . . "

"I don't know what I can have said that offended you quite so much."

"You said I was meddling in your life!"

"Look, Sergeant, let's settle something. Let's come to an agreement. Neither of us makes any personal reference to the other, all right? Everything else can carry on as normal. We've always got on well, haven't we?"

"Yes, but lately . . . "

He grumbled a bit longer, but finally caved in.

"O.K., where do I have to sign?"

"Let's seal the pact with a ceremonial beer."

"Agreed."

"But first swear to me you'll stop looking so grumpy all the time."

"I'll do my best."

I suspected that as well as having to put up with me, he was annoyed that another inspector was involved in our case. The classic complaint of a cop.

We had a beer in a Basque tavern.

"That popinjay said a few interesting things, don't you think? Interesting that Valdés collected information about people who were really important."

"I don't know, Inspector. I was so incensed by him I could have throttled him. I didn't really take in what he was saying."

"I didn't realize how passionate a creature you were, Fermín!"

"There you go with your personal comments again."

"You're right, I take it back."

I was afraid the cure might be worse than the disease, and I was going to have to spend all day fighting with Garzón over what was personal and what wasn't. For now, though, that put an end to it, partly because my phone started ringing. It was Inspector Sanguesa.

"Petra? I've got a couple of little scraps for you."

"Only a couple?"

"Do you have the remotest idea what it takes to get this kind of information?"

"All right, all right. Just tell me what you've got."

"It's about Pepita Lizarrán and that flamenco dancer. Neither of them has a cent. The first has her journalist's wage, and nothing more. The second has even less, just her weekly wage."

"Nothing from Switzerland?"

"They might have watches from there, though I doubt it."

"O.K., so they're out of the picture. What about the others?"

"Good god, Petra, I could understand someone who wasn't a cop being in such a hurry, but you . . . "

"I'm sorry, Sanguesa, but you can't imagine how vital those reports are. I may even ask you to chase up some others. Will you be as quick as you can?"

"Well, since you put it like that . . . When push comes to shove, there's nothing like a woman's sweet ways."

"Really?"

"Yes. Any guy would have said: 'Get a fucking move on, you assholes, I haven't got all year.'"

I preferred not to go into details, so I replied:

"I know you're overworked, but please, please make my list a priority."

"Fine, Petra, I'll do my best."

"Sanguesa?"

"And while you're at it, get a fucking move on, why don't you?"

He was still cackling when I hung up. If you wanted to get special treatment from a colleague, you had to mix politeness and banter. It usually worked.

While I was busy on the phone Garzón had asked for some blood sausage. He could even have ordered seconds, because my phone rang again. This time all I had to do was agree and say goodbye.

"That was ballistics," I told him. "The bullets used to kill the informer and his wife were from the same gun that killed Valdés."

Garzón munched on his sausage and thought it over.

"What do you make of that?"

"I'm not sure, but I can tell you that tonight we're going to have one hell of a dinner."

6.

I did not know Moliner very well, but I could tell just from looking at him that he was a tired man. He was sunken-eyed, and his features were bleary. He was already seated, with a half-drunk glass of beer in his hand. He smiled the way we police always smile when we're exhausted, demonstrating the pride we feel in our devotion to duty. I was so eager to hear what he had to say I launched into it almost without saying hello:

"How are things going?"

He realized straight away that I was not asking after his health.

"Terrible," he replied, then added, feeling himself in the spotlight: "Too much tension."

We ordered dinner. I was so anxious that I did not even glance at what I chose. Garzón, though, was careful in his choice, and I felt another flash of pure hatred towards him. I could stand it no longer:

"For God's sake, Moliner, if you don't tell me right now what's happened with the minister, I'll slap you in front of everybody."

Moliner twisted his mouth as though to indicate he was much more of a professional than me, then began to tell his story with a theatrical flourish:

"Our minister was almost beside himself with nerves. I spent close to four hours with him. I advised him to contact his lawyer, but he declined. He denied any link with Rosario

Campos. I see that as a fatal error, but that is his problem. He contradicted himself several times, then corrected himself, changed his tune . . . I don't think there's any doubt he's mixed up in the affair. It was a real war of nerves, and I think he lost. There were times when I thought he was about to break down and confess, but he always rallied."

"How did you leave it?"

"The magistrate is calling him in tomorrow, so with any luck he'll think it over tonight and talk to his lawyer. I hope he realizes we have a sworn statement to the effect that he was Rosario Campos's lover. If he will only admit that, all will be smooth sailing. We'll also bring in the person who gave us the information, so I don't think he has much option but to confess."

"Do you think he killed her?"

"We can't be sure, but after the interrogation we can be more direct."

"I wouldn't like to be in his shoes," said Garzón, tucking into his vegetable quiche.

"Nor me: tonight he'll have to talk to his wife. I suppose it will be a disaster, although with women you never know: perhaps she already knew he had a lover and preferred to keep quiet about it."

I let the comment pass.

"Did he know Valdés?"

"You think he would have admitted it if he had? No, at the moment he's denying everything."

"One of the suspects in our case told us it was he who gave Valdés the information that Rosario Campos was the minister's lover."

"How did he find out?"

"It was the girl herself who told him. They knew each other. His name is Jacinto Ruiz Northwell and he's a . . . "

"I know who he is. My ex-wife used to buy celebrity magazines."

"Do you think it's plausible that they knew each other?"

"Yes, why not? Rosario Campos organized conventions. She was the daughter of a rich businessman from Barcelona. That was her world, and that must have been how she met the minister. How did you find Ruiz Northwell?"

"He was one of the people Valdés had harmed good and proper in the past few months on his TV program, but the fact that he also knew Rosario Campos looks like a complete coincidence."

"Nothing in the world we're investigating is pure coincidence, Petra. They all know each other, they meet at parties: always the same people, and not that many of them either."

"Seems like there are hordes of them to me."

"There are far more people who have to slog away every day like us."

"You're right there, Inspector," said Garzón, his sense of class solidarity aroused.

"Obviously, our two cases are closely linked. All we have to do is discover exactly how. Did Valdés try to blackmail the minister with the help of Rosario, and did he then get rid of both of them, and have the informer killed later on?"

"We need to tell Chief Inspector Coronas. Will you do it or shall I?"

"I'd prefer you did it, Moliner. I wonder what he'll decide. He may well take Garzón and me off the case."

"Why would he do that?"

"You're the one with prestige in the service. Besides, having a woman on such an important case . . . "

He looked at me in astonishment.

"You are joking, aren't you?"

"No, I'm being deadly serious."

"I don't know if you're aware of the rumors, but in the station everyone says you're Coronas's blue-eyed girl. Lately he's been giving you important cases, and, besides, you only have to listen to his comments: Petra Delicado is such a diplomat, you should see how she treats suspects, she's the sort of person you can trust . . . he's always setting you as an example."

"That must be to hide his real feelings."

"I think you're wrong, Petra."

"That may be so, but as soon as he heard that the Rosario Campos case involved important people, he passed it to you."

"Because I have experience in that area; I don't think gender came into it."

While this little tussle was going on, Garzón was busy with his dessert. He raised his head to give his opinion:

"Don't waste your breath, Inspector Moliner, you'll never convince her."

At that, he put on his martyred look, and the two men exchanged a look positively dripping with male bonding.

"Women . . . " Moliner began, but I cut him short.

"We women are not from another planet, or a social category, or a cursed race, Moliner. We have simply been put down throughout history. That may have created certain suspicions in us, but, in general, reality only serves to confirm them."

"You won't deny, though, that you have at least one characteristic in common."

"What's that?"

"You're completely unpredictable."

Garzón guffawed. He was delighted someone else was at last crossing swords with me. Moliner underlined the point he was trying to make:

"Petra, Petra, hard as stone."

"The philosopher's stone. Do you know what that was?"

"I have to admit, I don't."

Garzón gave another, unexpected guffaw.

"See, she's got you now, Inspector. Just when you're least expecting it, she throws in a bit of culture, and you're done for."

So now it seemed as if he was celebrating a supposed victory of mine in this absurd dialectical cut and thrust. I slapped Moliner on the back so he would not lose all sense of proportion.

"What do you say to us all going to bed and forgetting all this nonsense?"

Basically, Moliner was a decent guy; instead of getting really annoyed, he smiled and said:

"That's the only sensible thing that's been said all night."

The hotel was right next door, so we did not have far to walk.

As soon as we entered the lobby, I saw her. She was sitting on a sofa reading a magazine as calm as could be. Was it really her?

"Amanda!" I cried out, unable to stop myself.

Moliner was thunderstruck. He had obviously not been expecting to see her there either. He stammered some sort of greeting. The only one who had his wits about him was Garzón. He went over and shook her hand.

"Decided to join the group?" he said in a friendly way.

"My sister told me this was where you were staying, so I took a room here. I felt like spending a few days in Madrid."

"But . . . we're working," was all I could find to say by way of greeting.

"I know. I won't get in the way. I've got things to do as well."

Moliner stood next to me, like a dummy. Amanda, who had been staring at me in a challenging way, softened her look and turned to him:

"How are you: have you got time for a drink?"

My colleague had no idea whatsoever how to react. He looked at me like a little child, asking my permission. I decided to put an end to the confrontation. I took Garzón by the arm and announced:

"The sergeant and I are off to sleep, we've had a hard day. Call me in the morning, Amanda, and perhaps we can have lunch together."

"We'll see. Don't worry about me."

In the elevator, Garzón had a smug smile on his face, like a religious ascetic who has seen the light. I made the great mistake of not keeping my mouth shut.

"Why are you smiling like that?"

"I was just thinking that the inspector was right about how unpredictable women can be."

I flared up.

"Sergeant, I thought we had agreed we wouldn't make any personal comments!"

"Was that a personal comment?"

"Don't act dumb."

"See what I mean, inspector? It's always me who gets the blame. It's not fair."

"Good night," I said coldly. "I'll see you at eight o'clock sharp for breakfast."

I threw my bag onto my bed. I didn't know whether I was more annoyed with Garzón, with my sister turning up like that, or with myself for a series of stupid mistakes. What an idiot! I had created a situation between my sister and myself which was getting worse by the minute. I had got involved in a silly argument with Moliner by trying to be clever. And, to top it all, the sergeant was right when he said he was always the one to blame. The thing was, he was like the silly kid who annoys the teacher after she has been trying to stay calm the whole day, and it is he who receives the full force of her wrath, although all the others have deserved it too.

Bad, bad, very bad, I told myself. You wonder what impression you make on others, then make an effort to improve it. That's the first mistake; all the others flow from that. Nothing to be done. Doubtless it was all due to the tinselly world of the case I was on. Luckily, I had the feeling that it would not be long before we got to the bottom of it.

I went to the bathroom and while I was removing my make-up and brushing my teeth, managed not to look at myself once in the mirror. To hell with image! This was my rather childish attempt at passive resistance, but the same was said of Gandhi before he defeated the British with his inner strength.

I only managed to calm down by reading an essay on the development of Western civilization in bed. I fell asleep thinking that we were pretty much all still at the first stage.

The ringing of the phone woke me with a start. I looked at the clock: five in the morning. As I answered, my heart was pounding.

"Inspector Delicado? This is reception. I'm sorry to disturb you so early, but I don't know what to do. There's a call from a Madrid police station. They say they need to speak urgently to Inspector Moliner, but he doesn't answer his cell phone. He's not in his room either. I've called several times . . . Since you are in the same group, I thought you might know where to find him . . . "

"Yes, thank you. I do. Put me through to Amanda Delicado's room, please."

No more mistakes, no more mistakes, I told myself, pummeling my head.

"Amanda?"

"Petra! Do you know what the time is?"

"Yes, I'm sorry. Is Inspector Moliner there with you?"

"Petra, I'm warning you . . . "

"This is an urgent police matter, so put him on the line, would you?"

There was a silence, then I heard my colleague's guilty, sleepy-sounding voice.

"Moliner, get in touch at once with the station you're oper-

ating out of here in Madrid. They can't find you, and they say
it's urgent."

"I'll be right there."

I called reception again.

"Do you know Inspector Moliner by sight?"

"Yes, I saw him yesterday, remember?"

"Good. Well, when you see him in the lobby, tell him to
wait for me. I'll be down in a minute. If he ignores you, call me
in my room."

"Don't worry, I'll take care of it," the receptionist said in a
puzzled voice. Although I was still not convinced our two cases
were linked, I did not want to miss the first moments of this
crisis.

By the time we reached the minister's home, the whole gang
was there. People from the Tetuán station, a forensic expert,
the investigating magistrate . . . The minister, Jorge García
Pacheco, was lying in a heap on an armchair in his study. He
was wearing a pair of gray silk pajamas and a dressing gown of
the same color and material. As we were soon informed, he
had shot himself in the roof of his mouth with his hunting gun.
He had left two letters: one for his wife, the other for the magistrate.

"I should have seen it coming," said Moliner.

"You couldn't have done any more than you did."

"I made a mistake. I was having him watched in case he
made a run for it, but I should have taken him into protective
custody."

"Now we're even."

"What do you mean?"

"You've got two dead bodies, and so have I. Coronas is
going to be pleased."

"I can just imagine. The problem is, we'll have to wait for the
magistrate to open the letter; maybe there's nothing left to do."

"Where's the wife?"

"In the living room with the children."

"Has she been questioned?"

"They were waiting for me. Someone has to talk to her, although, without knowing exactly what happened, I've no idea what to tell her. Come with me, Petra, it'll be better if there are two of us."

We went into the spacious, austerely decorated living room. I was very struck by the sight that greeted me. In a corner formed by a settee and an armchair sat a group of people who looked as if they were posing for a family portrait. When they saw us they did not budge. The group was dominated by a fifty-year-old woman sitting in the centre. Arranged around her were six children of varying ages: boys and girls. They were not crying, or showing any emotion; they merely looked serious. The stiffness of the position they had adopted was what gave the impression that they wanted to be represented this way for posterity.

"Good morning to you all," my colleague said pleasantly. "We are Inspectors Delicado and Moliner, from Barcelona. First and foremost, I should like to express our condolences at your loss."

"Thank you," the woman answered, without the slightest flicker of emotion. She went on, in a clear, harsh voice: "These are all my children, apart from the eldest. He is married, and we have not been able to inform him yet. If you have no questions for them, I would prefer it if they left the room while we talk."

Moliner agreed. The children, who all had the family likeness, trooped out obediently. Not one of them gave way to the emotions they must surely be feeling at their father's death. Once we were alone, señora García asked curtly:

"Might I know what you are doing here if you belong to the Barcelona police?"

When Moliner glanced across at me, I took the lead:

"Well, it seems that this case may be related to one we are working on in Barcelona."

"I don't know what you mean by 'this case.'"

"Your husband . . . "

"My husband suffered a tragic accident while cleaning his gun."

"Apparently it was suicide," said Moliner.

She turned beetroot red.

"Don't you ever suggest that again in this house, or outside it either! We have always been a proper, God-fearing family, and that is what we will continue to be."

Seeing Moliner on the point of exploding, I cut in:

"You have made the matter very clear, señora: to anyone who wants to know, your husband did not commit suicide."

She resumed her expression of emotionless disdain.

"He left you a letter. Could we know what it said?"

"No."

"It might be necessary for you to show it us."

"Then get a court order."

"Señora . . . " said Moliner. "Did you know that your husband had a young lover in Barcelona who was murdered only a few days ago?"

"I won't answer a thing, especially if it is offensive."

A man around thirty-five years old, with the same washed-out look as the rest of the family, came into the room unannounced. He hurried over to the woman.

"Don't say a word, mother. The lawyer is on his way. The police have no right to interrogate you."

I looked at him with all the scorn of which I was capable, and let my voice drip with cynicism:

"You've no need to worry. Your mother is perfectly well aware of her rights. Besides, we already know exactly how things stand: your father did not commit suicide, and did not have a lover in Barcelona who has been murdered."

Moliner touched my sleeve, and we left without saying goodbye.

"All they're concerned about is keeping everything right and proper," he said as we emerged into the street.

"They're defending what they have left."

Garzón was waiting for us, wide-eyed. He already knew what had happened, but was waiting for a final confirmation that we found ourselves unable to offer him.

"So that ties everything up," he hazarded.

"Yes, I think it's likely his letter contains a confession in which he admits ordering the killings," Moliner agreed.

I was sorry, but I did not share his view at all. Would someone who had the cold blood to hire a killer to murder his lover decide to commit suicide? Wouldn't it be more logical for him to try to escape? I might not be very good at applied psychology, and hiring a killer might be a gentle way to kill someone— something you never really have to come to terms with, as if another person really had committed the crime. We would soon find out: the magistrate called the hearing for four o'clock that afternoon in courtroom ten.

Moliner went off to have lunch with my sister while Garzón and I had a bite in a bar. We exchanged only a few words, but this time it was not because we were offended or had hurt feelings, but because both of our minds were racing on their own.

As the three of us sat facing the magistrate, we looked like a family waiting expectantly to hear the patriarch's will. The magistrate was not particularly interested in what he was about to read, and somehow this gave the proceedings a bureaucratic air that did nothing to lessen the tension. After a few endless comments about the delights of the inhabitants of Barcelona, and after naming all the magistrates he was friendly with there (just in case we knew them), he finally opened the minister's letter. He cleared his throat, then began to read in a legalistic sing-song:

Your honor,

In full possession of my mental faculties and fully aware of what I am doing, I propose to put an end to my life today, the twentieth of this month, at three in the morning in the study of my home, using for that purpose the shotgun for which I have a proper license.

I wish to make it plain that nobody else is to blame for my death.

The reason for my taking so dreadful a decision is the suffering I am going through, and my inability to see any way out of it but death.

I have sinned. I have committed the unpardonable error of betraying the sacred bonds of matrimony, and falling in love with Rosario Campos, a young woman from Barcelona whom I believed to be pure and innocent. However, this woman, doubtless guided by others, tried to blackmail me by threatening to tell of our romance to the press. I was still reflecting on what to do, and had decided not to give way to her pressure, when somebody killed Rosario: one of her accomplices, I suppose, although I do not know for what reason.

Ever since that moment, I have lived in fear that someone else might emerge from the shadows and seek to threaten me. Nor can I bear the thought that I may have been the indirect cause of Rosario's death.

All this is too much for me. I do not have the strength to confess the truth to either my wife or the police. As a government minister, the scandal would be too great.

One further sin, that of taking the life that the Creator gave me, will be the last I commit. He will judge me and perhaps in his infinite mercy will forgive me. While awaiting his judgment, no shame should fall on my family, and I hope not to cause them any pain.

May God forgive me.

None of us spoke. The magistrate peered at us over the top of his glasses.

"That's all," he said. When we were still silent, he said: "What do you make of it?"

Garzón was the only one to answer.

"It's very well written," he said. "Like he'd been committing suicide all his life."

The magistrate gave a nervous laugh and stood up.

"I'll make sure you get a photocopy; I have to send the original to the magistrate who is dealing with the case in Barcelona."

We emerged into the street as if we had sat through a marathon eight-hour film session. Moliner found it impossible to react, but finally muttered, almost to himself:

"So Valdés got rid of the girl after some falling-out between them, and then . . . "

"Hold on a minute! Launching hypotheses into mid-air like that is pretty useless, don't you think?"

His cell phone started to ring. He answered in monosyllables. When the call had finished, he said briefly:

"I'll have to leave you, they want to talk to me in Moncloa Palace."

"Who does?"

"The prime minister."

Garzón took an occasional sip of beer and speculated out loud.

"Do you think someone about to commit suicide would lie, Inspector?"

"I suppose not."

"Not unless he was trying to protect someone. Who could the minister be trying to protect: his wife, some of his children, perhaps the mysterious Lesgano, the only man with that name in the whole of Spain?"

"I don't know, Garzón, as this moment I've really no idea. Not even of the next step we should take."

"The next step is to call Chief Inspector Coronas. He must be nervous as hell about the minister's suicide."

"Stop calling him the minister! He's not a minister or anything else anymore."

"My, what a mood you're in . . . !"

"What mood do you want me to be in? This case is getting so hellishly complicated I don't think we're going to solve it in a month of Sundays!"

"Let's try to focus, Inspector. From the information we have, what seems obvious is that his lover, Rosario Campos, was trying to blackmail him, and she wasn't acting alone. Was Valdés behind her? Let's assume he was. We have reasons for suspecting so. We've discovered that Valdés had enough money stashed in Switzerland to have come from blackmailing several influential people. We also have the snippet that our marquis friend gave us: Valdés was asking around about people who were way outside his normal gossip column interests."

"All right, all right, but where could he have published any of the information he had, if none of the editors of his publications would have dared do it?"

"Excuse me, inspector, but let's not be obtuse about this. He might not have been able to publish the stories, but he could have sold them on to someone in the gutter press. They thrive on political and other big-time scandals."

I made no reply. The sergeant was right. But even if his hypothesis was well founded, it still didn't explain the murders. When I pointed this out, he protested:

"It might not explain them completely, but at least it opens a possible line of enquiry. I know you don't like working on suppositions, but even you have to admit, we can't just throw away the clear leads we have."

"It's the links that are missing."

"We'll find them, Petra. This would be the first time we got completely stuck in an investigation."

"Everyone in the case seems to have a tendency to disappear."

"So much the better; we'll end up with the only one responsible."

"Don't you ever lose heart, Fermín?"

"I have my moments, but I get over them. I never allow myself to give in completely. Nor do you, if you think about it."

"Do you know something: you have a good head on those shoulders of yours."

"That's what my mother used to say, but I always thought she was just referring to its size. She was never one for praise."

I burst out laughing.

"I want to apologize, Sergeant. I suspect I haven't been very good company these past few days. I think this case has made me particularly nervous."

"Yes, me too."

"But you know how to hide it better."

"Only because I'm older than you."

"That's true, a lot older."

"And wiser."

"You sure know how to make up for your mother's lack of praise, don't you?"

At that, it was his turn to laugh.

When Moliner got back from Moncloa Palace we were waiting for him in the hotel bar. He still had the dignified air of someone who has been personally summoned to the prime minister's office.

"What did he say?" asked the sergeant.

"He recommended discretion and more discretion."

"Does that mean he can't speak?" said Garzón, already seeing himself a secret agent.

"No, he meant we should be discreet. Not a word to the press. They are going to put out an official communiqué saying that the minister died of a heart attack."

"I don't believe it!"

"That's how it is, Petra, my dear. As his wife quite clearly told us, he did not commit suicide."

"Suicide is only for prisoners, artists, and depressed supermarket cashiers, is that it? Important people, particularly if they are on the right, have to die a natural death. What a load of nonsense!"

"I have no opinion about that. The fact is, he did not commit suicide, got it? And if any journalist tries to make trouble, send them packing."

"Do you hear what you're saying? I'm sure we only get to know half of what's really going on in the world. But then there's Valdés, earning a living telling us all the details of some third-rate actress's latest cellulite operation or who is hiding a retarded child in the basement."

Moliner was frantic.

"Look, Petra, peace on Earth and all that to an exhausted man. You can go on complaining about it all night if you like, but just tell me you've understood what our instructions are."

"Of course I have."

"Well, you haven't heard the worst yet."

"Go on, nothing could surprise me."

"I spoke to Coronas on the phone. He says he wants to see the three of us right now, and he didn't sound in a good mood."

"What does he mean by right now?"

"It means we ought to be going upstairs to fetch our things. If we're lucky we can catch the next air shuttle."

"What good are phones and all these other sophisticated means of communication if people insist on meeting face to face to tell each other how angry they are?"

"Petra, do you deliberately protest at every order from your superiors?"

Convinced he was being funny, Garzón replied for me.

"Women detest authority . . . when they don't have it."

We shot out of Madrid like human cannonballs. Moliner was always very respectful where his superiors were concerned. I regretted not being in charge, not simply to be in authority, as Garzón said, but so that I could at least lay things out properly and give my opinion. Or did I really want to be in charge? Did I protest about orders because I wanted to be the one giving them? Perhaps the sergeant was right, and my most salient characteristic was always to want to contradict? But if I was constantly admitting that he was right, I would soon be saying that he never made a mistake, and that was far from being the truth. For example, when Coronas shouted at us, he took it like a little lamb, and so did Moliner. How could I fight alone against the ignorance of our bosses? Coronas was raging like the sea off the coast of Norway.

"You three really go too far, do you know that? Your highnesses are not entirely convinced that the two cases are linked, so naturally you don't bother to tell me a thing until you had proof. I was lucky not to learn about this from the newspaper. Although, considering the amount of progress you've made so far . . . "

Unable to stay silent any longer, I put up my hand.

"Sir, if we had called to tell you something we only suspected of being true, I'm sure you would have told us not to do it again until we were sure."

"Oh, so you're the spokeswoman, are you, Petra? Fine, and in addition to that it seems you're my psychiatrist as well! You know me so completely you can read my thoughts and my orders too. Wonderful—so what am I going to tell you to do next?"

"I don't know."

"Good, then I'll spell it out for you. When I put you on to these cases, there was one victim in each, remember? Now, a few days later, it's like a cemetery, or the aftermath at Waterloo. Shouldn't you be concentrating on what the murderer is going to do next, rather than trying to guess what orders I'm going to give?"

"That's not fair, Chief Inspector. If we had been working together from the start rather than going our separate ways . . . "

"Petra Delicado! Have you ever tried keeping your mouth shut?"

"I . . . "

"You have more bite than a piranha, and yet you expect me to allow you to always have your say. Well, no: you can shut up like everyone else and face the storm, because that's what you're meant to do! When you come to see me with some results, and not with another dead body slung over your shoulder like a brand-new bag you've bought, then I'll listen to you."

"That mention of a bag is going too far, sir."

Coronas covered his face in his hands in a theatrical gesture, as if he really did have to restrain himself from leaping on me and strangling the life out of me. All at once he dropped his hands and said in a grave, dull tone:

"I'll see you in the meeting room in an hour. Sort out all the material you have collected until now. We'll outline a strategy and a plan of where we go from here. Understood?"

We all three agreed as one. Coronas turned to me and added:

"What about you, Petra, have you understood?"

"Yes, sir."

"No objections?"

"No, sir."

"The Lord be praised! Now be off with all of you!"

As we walked silently down the corridor, I said to Moliner:

"See what I mean about Coronas not having any special regard for me?"

"On the contrary, Inspector. Do you have any idea what he would have done if I'd been as rude as you?"

Garzón couldn't wait to add his thoughts.

"He was tough today. Once, the inspector called him a machista and he only laughed."

"You men always idolize your leaders, but, if you show respect, you can always disagree."

"No, what happens is, it's not the same if a woman says it; you can get away with it."

Garzón approved with vigorous nods of his head. I came to a halt.

"Have it your own way, but, at the moment, none of us is carrying out Coronas's orders."

"What do you mean?"

"Have either of you thought about the material we need to bring him for our meeting?"

"The material we've got stinks."

"Well, then, the sooner we get rid of it the better. Let's go to my office, we can talk more easily there."

The session with Coronas was truly exhausting. We went carefully through the daily reports that both Moliner and I had been writing about our cases. Rodríguez, who usually worked with Moliner, came and joined us midway through. He also gave his opinion about what our next steps should be.

The chief inspector noticed that not all of the financial details had been filled in. When he complained, I responded:

"Inspector Sanguesa has not had time to complete that part, sir."

Grunting like a bear on the first day of spring, Coronas picked up the phone.

"What do you mean, you still have to get it into the computer? How often have I told you, a computer is a tool to speed work up, not slow it down! So tell me . . . Yes, dammit, the ones you have finished! O.K., wait, I'll take this down, the others here will know what it refers to. O.K., Sanguesa, I'll sort it out, but, for heaven's sake, get a move on: just because something is difficult doesn't mean it has to take forever. We need those figures, so get to work. And if you can't have lunch, too bad—eat a sandwich instead. That's what the Americans do, and look at what they've achieved."

I realized just how many skills I was lacking to be able to give orders like a real policeman. And in case I had forgotten, Coronas turned to me to complete the lesson.

"As for you, Petra, how come you didn't ask for the figures already?"

"I did, but I didn't want to put my colleagues under too much pressure."

Coronas laughed a hollow laugh.

"This isn't a golf club where the members take tea after a game. Here everybody takes responsibility for their own enquiry, and if they need information from another department to get ahead, they have to put pressure on them using exactly the same methods as you would with a suspect."

"Yes, sir."

"Good. Sanguesa has investigated the accounts of two more of our suspects, and found nothing. Two women by the name of Pepita Lizarrán and Emiliana Cobos. I can't remember who that last one is . . . "

"She's the one with the retarded son," said Garzón, as tastelessly as ever.

Coronas understood at once: they all seemed to consider the story of the retarded child worse than an armed hold-up.

"Something else important. The murder victim Rosario Campos did not have anything to hide, either. Her account matches her income."

"All that's missing are the marquis and Valdés's ex."

"We'll soon have their details. What about the minister?"

"They'll look into his financial affairs in Madrid, but I don't think it's going to be easy," said Moliner.

"You can count on that. I don't think there's any way of knowing whether he paid Valdés money."

"There were no recent deposits in Valdés's Swiss bank account. And it's obvious he didn't pay Rosario Campos a thing."

"So he didn't lie before he died."

"That was probably the only time he didn't," I said mischievously.

Strangely scandalized, Coronas looked at me and muttered:

"Let's leave the dead in peace, shall we?"

It was finally decided that Moliner and Rodríguez would dig deeper into Rosario Campos's circle of friends and family, and would stay in touch with the police investigating the minister's death in Madrid. Perhaps someone could tell them how good a blackmailer the girl was, or perhaps one of the minister's sidekicks would decide to talk. Garzón and I were to go back to Madrid and follow up the trail that Ruiz Northwell, alias the marquis, had put us onto. Was Valdés a professional blackmailer: was that where he got his millions from?

Theoretically, this was a good strategy, but I wondered how much more we could get out of someone who was going on hearsay, and who was still a suspect himself. Did we have to hang out in the bars of the Madrid jet set, stick our noses into the epicenter of the thousands of rumors that were always flying round the capital? The idea horrified me; there was nothing direct or effective enough to help get us out of the dreadful impasse our investigation was in.

Coronas's angry threats had ended with a peremptory order: we should not wait until the next day to get back to Madrid. He wanted us to be on the job by first thing in the morning. We had just enough time to leave our dirty clothes at home and pick up clean ones. Then it was back to the airport, where the last regular flight left at eleven. We would have two tickets specially reserved for us.

Garzón and I agreed to meet at the airport.

"We'll have time to grab some dinner there," was all he could think of to say as he jumped into a taxi.

By the time I got home, my nerves were still raw. All of this was filling my boiler with far too much steam: it was bound to explode at any moment. As I went past the hall mirror, I stole a glance at how I looked. A complete disgrace! My hair was a mess, and tiredness was etched on my face. Unfortunately, I didn't even have time for a shower. I went straight to my bedroom and began to take the dirty clothes from my case. At that moment Amanda appeared in the doorway.

"Hello."

I jumped, and turned to see who it was.

"You gave me a fright. I had no idea you were here."

"Are you leaving?"

"Back to Madrid. Things have gotten more complicated."

"I think I'll be leaving too."

"For Gerona?"

"No, I'm staying in Barcelona, but I'll move into a hotel."

"Why on earth do you want to do that?"

"I understand that my presence here upsets you."

"That's absurd, and, besides, I've already told you, I'm leaving. Moliner is staying in Barcelona for now."

"O.K., then I won't move into a hotel."

"That's better."

"I'm sorry for what's happened, but I really don't think you've helped. Why didn't you say something during all those years I wasted being married? That would have been the ideal moment."

"We always waste time, married or not. All of us have to die. But you're right, I shouldn't have poked my nose into your affairs. Now I've thought better of it: I couldn't care less whether you get off with a cop or fuck with an orangutan."

She stared at me with a look of hatred.

"Petra, you've turned into a hard, selfish, and insensitive woman. I'm not surprised you live alone; I think you'll be on your own all the rest of your life."

She left the room quietly. I could hear her moving around in the kitchen.

I finished packing, and said goodbye to her from the front door, as casually as if I were just stepping out the buy the paper. Amanda did not reply.

The sergeant was waiting for me at the airport. We had more than enough time: our plane was going to be two hours late. But eating was going to be a problem: the bar in the national-flights section was closed for the night.

"We could show our police credentials; I'm sure they'd let us wait in the international part. The café there is still open."

That is what we did. My colleague did not seem to want to miss a meal, and I was longing for a stiff drink. Being shouted at by your boss and then having a family row are two reasons that justify getting good and drunk.

There, surrounded by foreigners in transit, we gave our instincts free rein. Garzón chose a couple of rolls and brought me a tuna salad, which I washed down with lots of beer. Afterwards, we both moved on to whisky.

"That was a real dressing down from Coronas!" I commented.

"Huh, you should see what it's like in other police stations. Coronas had to pull rank a little, to make sure things were speeded up. The problem is, you're too sensitive."

"There is someone who thinks the opposite."

"That must be because they don't know you well enough."

"Do you think I've become hard and selfish?"

"That happens to all us cops; it's because we're always dirtying our hands in grim reality. And living alone makes it even worse."

"Can I ask you a question, Fermín?"

"So long as it's not personal . . . "

"It is."

"In that case, no. It was you who promised we wouldn't talk about anything personal."

"We could go ahead as long as we don't remember a thing the next day. Think you can manage that?"

"I don't know what right you have to ask, but I'll go along with it. Let's give it a try."

"O.K. So here's my question: does being on your own bother you?"

"I thought it was going to be something weightier, but I'll reply anyway. Of course it does, inspector, of course it bothers me. Most days I don't think about it, but sometimes when I go to bed I imagine I'm not going to wake up, that I'll die in my sleep. I think that no one would miss me, and that nobody else's life would be affected by my death. That is sad, it's disheartening. What do you think?"

"It's awful. What do you do when that happens?"

"Depends. Most often, I get up and have a bite to eat. You know, a snack, a piece of ham . . . after that I generally feel better. And then I think that if I did die in the night I wouldn't show up at the station the next morning, and Coronas would be beside himself and send someone looking for me. They would find my body, they would have to certify that the death was from natural causes, my colleagues would come, so would you, my son in New York would be told, there would be a funeral . . . a proper ceremony. So if what we want is for our death to be noticed, I wouldn't be doing so badly."

"That's not a bad way of seeing it."

"What about you, does solitude bother you?"

"Bother me? No—you know I'm on my own because that's how I like it. But there's one thing—it's so stupid I don't know if I can even bring myself to mention it."

"You can tell me: let's have another whisky to help you broach the subject."

"Well . . . there's one thing I've never learnt to do. In fact, I think I've always refused to do so. Do you know what, Fermín: I've never learnt how to put laces in a pair of new shoes."

He stared at me as though wondering whether it had been a good idea to order another whisky.

"You know what I mean, don't you? I can tie them normally all right, it's just that I don't know how to lace them properly through the holes."

"It's not that difficult."

"I know, but I always used to have someone to do it for me: my father, my husbands. I never wanted to learn; it must have been something to do with allowing myself to be loved, to let others fuss over me a bit. What do you think?"

"I think it's very you: very odd."

"I know it's stupid, but, even now, I try to find someone who will do it for me. I ask them to lace them for me in the shop when I buy them, or get my maid to do it. But, of course, it's not the same. I know that one fine day there's going to be no one to ask, but I still refuse to learn. I think it's something life owes me."

"I understand."

"And what does life owe you?"

"Life and I are at peace with each other. I don't ask anything of it for the future, but I don't want it messing me around or demanding things of me. No extra sacrifices or awkward moments. I've had enough of them!"

"You're right! That's the selfishness of those of us who live alone, but don't you think we've earned it?"

"Of course!"

We drank in silence, pleased with ourselves. The artificial light blurred the sharp edges of the plastic tables and chairs. All the passengers waiting with us shared an air of tiredness. Some of them glanced at the odd couple we made. I briefly wondered what we were doing in such a cold, impersonal, and transitory place. Garzón roused me from my melancholy musings with a curse. The alcohol had made light of our worries and the hours, as it was almost time to go. We went back to the national-flights area and boarded our plane.

The next morning I woke up in the hotel without knowing exactly where I was. The first thing I did was promise myself that, as soon as this wretched case was solved, I would tell Coronas I wanted to take all the leave I was owed. I was turning into a nervous wreck; what I needed was to pack my bags and head for somewhere where there were no gossip columns, no celebrity magazines. I thought about all the dead people strewn in our wake: Rosario Campos, Valdés, that poor wretch of an informer and his wife, whose murderer we were not even looking for, and, finally, the minister. We had struck a rich vein of death, and we were still floundering around in the dark. Coronas was right: we kept being overtaken by events, and there was no other word for our efforts than failure.

Garzón was busy tucking into his breakfast when I conveyed all my anxieties to him.

"What should we do?" he replied. "We could interview our little marquis all over again if you like."

"To hell with the marquis! He's already done his bit by telling us about the possible relation between Valdés and the world of serious blackmail. We won't get another drop out of him."

"Coronas told us to interrogate and pressure him as hard as we could."

"That's easy for him to say, but the marquis gave us a lead, you followed it up, now it's a possibility. What does Coronas want us to do? To forget it and follow his instructions like a pack of his private bloodhounds."

"I don't think we should risk him blowing his top like that again."

"Who is fundamentally in charge of this case: him or us?"

"Now, Inspector, there's no need to be like that!"

"No, you listen to me, Garzón: it's time we took up where we left off. We were talking about blackmail, weren't we? I'm convinced that poor minister did not have anyone killed. There must be somebody else. Do you remember that fellow Lesgano? We need to go back and trace him."

"How are we going to do that?"

"We need to return to the world of the media. Do you remember that girl Maggy, the one I was so friendly and subtle with? I think she is more important to us than the marquis."

"Good god, you're just asking for trouble!"

"Relax, Coronas isn't here in Madrid."

So we went back to Teletotal, where Maggy once again received us without the slightest flicker of interest or wish to collaborate. She had underlined her punk credentials by adding a couple of tiny studs to the right nostril of her small, snub nose. She said sarcastically:

"I didn't think we'd ever see you here again, as you're so horrified by our complete lack of moral scruples . . . "

Determined not to make the same mistake twice, I smiled and said:

"I underestimated you, Maggy. Out of all the people we've spoken to, you're the only intelligent one we've found."

"Wow, what an honor!"

"I'm serious, and I should also say that at this moment you can give us more help than anyone else in clearing up Valdés's death."

"I see, this is a summons, like 'your country needs you,' is it?"

"Call it what you like, but, the truth is, we do need you."

She brushed some tiny specks from her woolly ecological jumper.

"Well, what can I do for you?"

"It's simple. We know Valdés got hold of some information that was much more dangerous than a starlet's latest plastic surgery. Do you have any idea who he might have been selling it to?"

She scoffed and threw her head back, making the long spikes of her fringe wobble like a coxcomb.

"How would I know? The boss refused to keep notes so there'd be no chance of people reading them. Do you think he'd tell me something that precious?"

Garzón took over.

"We don't expect miracles, but you were the one who worked closest to him, you knew his contacts, whom he talked to."

"Forget it! All he did was get information out of me; he never shared anything he heard from other sources with me. I was never anything more than an office assistant round here, and soon I won't even be that."

"What do you think of the woman running this channel?"

She burst out laughing.

"Shit, as far as I'm concerned you can rough her up whenever you want, but I really doubt that this TV company is involved in anything like that!"

"Who would have been capable of publishing a scandal involving a public figure—a government minister, for example?"

"Are you joking? Everyone, Inspector, every single journalist in this country would! This is the modern world of journalism, or did you think that only those ghastly gossip magazines brought out that kind of shit?"

She was right. Sarcastically and totally right. Everyone. Any newspaper would publish the story. They would crucify the prime minister himself if they had a juicy story. They would club him to death. And if the political line of the newspaper was different from his, they'd be even more keen to do so. Any of the big-circulation papers in the country would fight to put that kind of dirty linen on its front page, whatever it involved: public or private, economic or sexual.

The fact that I thought there was some limit to the appetite of the press showed how many out-of-date preconceptions I still had. Nowadays we were all in the same gutter, covered in the same muck. And it took this young girl, with her big round eyes and bright yellow hair, to make me see it. I felt ashamed of myself.

"I suppose that's how it is, Maggy, you must be right. Do you remember if Valdés ever had an interview with the editor of a particular newspaper? Did he receive a call or an official invitation from government circles? Could Lesgano be a politician, perhaps?"

She shook her head several times, realizing I was becoming increasingly desperate. I showed how really lost I was.

"So what do we have to do, visit every newspaper in Madrid and Barcelona asking their editors if they paid Valdés for confidential information? Do we have to question every government department?"

"All I can do to help is go with you to our newspaper library. We can look up recent issues and see if they published any scandals about important people. That would represent an unsuccessful blackmail attempt. I can also ask my contacts about politicians or journalists. What do you think?"

"My God! That sounds very laborious, and very unfocussed, but perhaps it's the only way. And here was I thinking that in this world of celebrities we'd be doing nothing but going to parties! I hate working in newspaper libraries."

Maggy laughed out loud. I could see that deep down she was friendly enough, but I wasn't in the mood.

"O.K., Maggy. If we decide to take you up on your offer,

we'll give you a call tomorrow. In the meantime, please try to think of something that may have slipped your memory. Do you still have my phone number?"

She nodded several times, and when she saw how disheartened I was, she added:

"You see how our country can't really count on me? I'm sorry."

"I'm sorry, too, that I was so aggressive last time. I promise to try harder."

"Today you weren't bad at all."

She smiled her stray-cat-in-search-of-an-owner smile. She was a good girl underneath.

We walked slowly along the street in silence, creating a little cloud around us from our bad temper and sense of frustration. As there were no stones to kick, Garzón took aim at a cigarette butt.

"Do you think, with the number of dead bodies we have hanging round our necks, now is the time to go searching in old newspapers?"

"No, I suppose we should have done that earlier; it would be absurd now, and, besides, we'd lose a lot of time. How about if we set light to the journalistic forest? That might force out some of the creatures hiding in the undergrowth. And what about the politicians?"

"Just remember, Inspector, that the danger with newspapers is that they tend to publish things. If we start openly visiting editors and spreading suspicions, it will soon get out. And that will be the end of any discreet approach."

"You're right, it might damage us in the end, but at least it would stir things up."

"Or not. If Valdés was part of a network of blackmailers in the world of journalists, I don't think they're exactly naïve. They would think hard before they came out into the open. And I'm sorry to have to say this, but if we're going after big game, we need to make sure we have some proof. You can forget about intuition or psychological profiling."

"If that's the case, I think I'm ready to resign."

"Don't even consider it. If you did that, they'd transfer the case to Moliner and Rodríguez, just when we're onto something big."

"You might see it like that, but I'm not so sure . . . Besides, even if it were so important, it's such a sensitive affair it could all stay hushed up. What are you hoping for if we solve it: that they give us the keys to the city?"

"I just want to do my duty."

"Give me a break, Garzón!"

"O.K., maybe that's going a bit too far. Let's just say, my professional curiosity. Anyway, Inspector, this isn't getting us anywhere, we're just wasting time."

"We have more than enough time. What we don't have is leads."

"Let's go and talk to the marquis."

"All right, let's go and see him, but I'll bet you ten to one he'll swear he doesn't know anything more."

"If he does, I'll pressure him a bit. Do you remember that painting he has with that blessed angel stomping on the devil? That's what I'll do to him."

"Don't forget your flaming sword."

"What's that?"

"A sword with flames coming out the end: I think it runs on gas."

"There's no need for inventions; a good roughing up will do anytime."

Ruiz Rothwell's ancient retainer informed us he was not at home, so we had to wait for him in a nearby bar, from where we could see the entrance to his building. We decided to eat something.

"I'm going to call Sanguesa," I said. "It would be good to know something about the marquis's financial state before we talk to him."

"Do you think Sanguesa will have something by now?"

"According to Coronas, you just have to insult him to produce results."

As expected, Sanguesa had not finished his report on the marquis. And yet, without any need for insults, he did tell me that all his investigations so far led him to believe the marquis did not have any accounts in Switzerland. However, he did have a rather strange one in a Madrid bank. I began to see some daylight. The transactions in this account were very odd. There were several hefty deposits, which did not seem to follow any particular pattern.

"Could you be a bit more specific?"

"Well, I was going to put all the details in my report, but, as far as I remember, he put in five, six, or even ten million at a time. Bit by bit, that gets used up, until there's almost nothing left. Then there's another big deposit—but there's nothing regular about it."

"I get it, Sanguesa: you're an angel. I'm sorry the boss shouted at you the other day. If it's any consolation, I suffered, too."

"Bah, what kind of boss would Coronas be if he didn't get mad now and again? And what kind of subordinates would we be if we ever took it seriously?"

"That's a very good philosophy! But I stand by what I said: you're an angel. I don't know what we would have done without your help . . . in fact, I don't know what we're going to do with it!"

"Don't pay me any compliments until I've been through the whole list. That Marta Merchán is proving difficult."

"Valdés's ex?"

"Yes. I'm not saying there's anything strange. There probably isn't, but there's one element I can't put my finger on, investments, maybe . . . I don't know. I'll tell you later."

I turned towards Garzón.

"See? We've got more information already. And without having to rough anyone up or shout at them like Coronas!"

"A colleague isn't the same as a subordinate," he complained.

I blew my top.

"Why don't you stop talking nonsense and finish those squid you're eating? You ought to be going through the marquis's details before we go in and knock his teeth out!"

His jaw dropped. I smiled.

"Do you prefer that kind of style with a subordinate?"

He got the joke, and smiled back at me.

"Just because you don't shout doesn't mean you can't give orders. You do, and often, but you women have other ways of getting things done."

"A lot more delicate ones."

"A lot more complicated, I'd say."

"Worse, in other words."

He shrugged and changed topics.

"What did Sanguesa tell you?"

I gave him all the details. I felt much more energetic; in fact, I felt better altogether. The fact that Ruiz Northwell had such a fluctuating account, with no visible means of support, looked promising. We were back to our hypotheses. Could the marquis be some sort of intermediary between high society and Valdés? It might well have been that because he was "penniless" he did not rub shoulders with the real élite, but he could at least hear rumors that Valdés could sniff out with his professional talents.

We stayed speculating for another hour until we saw Ruiz bounding athletically up the steps to his apartment block. We waited a few more minutes then walked over.

The elderly maid opened the door for us, and we followed

her teetering shadow into the same reception room where we had been the last time. Garzón immediately sat down facing the archangel Michael painting, as though fascinated by it, although perhaps he was only looking for inspiration as to how to mangle the marquis as he had promised. A few moments later, Ruiz Northwell came into the room, beaming as though this were a social visit.

"Hello! So here you are again! How nice to see you!"

Before I could quite realize what was happening, Garzón had leapt up and backed him up against the wall.

"That's enough of that crap!" he growled. "Either you tell us all you know or I'll knock your coronet off!"

I was astounded: seeing Garzón in action like this made me want to burst out laughing. The marquis looked pleadingly towards me, as if praying for me to get my dog off him. I moved slowly alongside the new Saint Michael.

"I admit my colleague is rather impulsive, but, the fact is, señor Ruiz, that we're both running out of patience."

"But . . . why do you say that?"

"Because, in a case where so many people have died, it's not a good idea to hide the truth, still less to lie."

Garzón turned on him again.

"You know more than you're saying, asshole!"

"What are you talking about? I know my rights!"

"This may not be strictly legal, but neither is having such healthy bank accounts when you don't do a stroke of work. Where do you get all the money you keep paying into your account?"

Ruiz Northwell looked anxiously at us.

"Tell him to put me down, please."

Garzón saved me the trouble of having to treat him like a trained animal by letting go of him on his own account.

"Everything I have is above board, I swear. I pay almost all my taxes."

"That's not what we're interested in. Where do you get the money in the first place?"

"You've no right to . . . "

I suddenly felt immensely tired. Tired of going through the same old routine. I collapsed onto one of the uncomfortable rococo chairs.

"Listen to me, will you? We could make this last minutes, days, weeks, months. We could follow you everywhere and make your life impossible. It would be difficult, violent, exhausting for all concerned. It wouldn't be worth it, believe me. So just tell us where the money comes from, and we'll have done with it."

He nodded.

"All right, inspector, I'll tell you. I have nothing to hide. Come with me, I want to show you the rest of the house."

Without really understanding what he was doing, we followed him. As we went through the reception room, we saw the elderly maid dozing in a corner: she did not seem to have much to do.

Ruiz Northwell showed us the rooms one by one. They were almost completely empty. To judge by their desolate aspect, just about the only one in the entire apartment that had any furniture was where we met.

"Do you see? Do you think it has always been like this? There used to be Elizabethan furniture, valuable mirrors, paintings, silver cutlery, antique porcelain coffee sets. I've been selling it all off to survive. Things haven't been going well for me recently: this inheritance was all I had, and you can see what's happened to it."

"Have you been selling it to antique dealers?"

"Yes, and for most of the sales I have invoices. Others I've sold under the counter. I don't care if you want to report me for that. I thought things would change with the new contract I had, but that bastard Valdés ruined everything."

"Did you kill him?" Garzón asked.

"No. Can't you tell? I don't have the courage to kill a soul. I wouldn't kill anyone if I didn't get something concrete out of it. Revenge is a thing of the past. I have other problems to worry about."

"You told us Valdés was always asking for information about important people. Tell us more about that. Do you know someone called Lesgano?"

"I swear, I know nothing. If I had, I would have tried to get something out of Valdés, and been happy to do so. But I'm sure he was mixed up in something big. I'm not stupid, and managed to get something out of Rosario Campos, but not enough to be able to do anything with it."

"Did Rosario Campos say she was trying to blackmail him?"

"No, she never said anything specifically, but one day she was boasting about how she knew Valdés, on another she let slip she was going to live abroad. It was all very strange! But I couldn't get anything more out of her."

I could see a certain logic to what he was saying. He must have been trying to find something he could use against Valdés to pay him back in kind. Ruiz carried on, growing increasingly excited.

"He must have killed her himself, inspector! He had no scruples whatsoever! He was always using women. He must have had something on his ex-wife too!"

"What makes you say that?"

"One night I saw them in a restaurant together. Not one of the usual places you see people from our world in. What were the two of them doing having dinner together in Madrid when they could see each other whenever they wanted to in Barcelona?"

"Listen, Ruiz, I don't think . . . "

"Yes, but when he recognized me he almost jumped out of his skin. He tried to hide his face, but I saw him. Of course I did! And I knew who she was too. I'm sure he was trying to blackmail her. He was a pig, a real louse."

"O.K., O.K., we get the point. Make sure you don't leave Madrid, we might need to have another . . . conversation with you."

"I've got nothing to hide."

"Are you sure? Perhaps the tax authorities would be interested to hear about your sale of valuable antiques."

"You wouldn't get far by reporting me, inspector. I'm small fry. And I don't think you're the type to enjoy kicking someone when they're down. Just think of someone who comes from a noble background like mine being reduced to living like this; I'm sure you feel for me."

"You know where you can stick your noble background," snarled Garzón. "So don't count on us keeping quiet, right?"

It was obvious the sergeant regretted not having been able to play his avenging angel role to the full. I could understand why: Ruiz Northwell's final attempt to move us to compassion had been frankly pathetic. Out in the street, Garzón didn't let the passersby stop him from continuing his diatribe.

"Feeling sorry for that social parasite! I'd have him breaking rocks on a chain gang, on bread and water, that's what I'd do!"

"He's a nonentity, that's all."

"I hope you don't fall for that sob story about him being reduced to living like that."

"All I'm saying is that he's a poor bastard. He hasn't killed anyone, and I'll bet he doesn't know much more about Valdés either."

"What about the story of seeing Valdés and his wife having dinner together? Do you think it's any more than a smokescreen to hide something?"

"I thought it was more like a desperate attempt to show us he would tell us anything he knew."

"Was it true, then?"

"Yes, probably, although I'm not sure it was significant."

"Was Valdés on good enough terms with his ex-wife to have dinner with her in Madrid?"

"They must have had something to discuss. I bet it was pure business. Don't get me confused, Garzón; it's just taking us away from the essential. Let me make a call."

I called Maggy. I was sure she had taken our visit seriously, and had spent the time searching for something on Valdés. I wasn't wrong. The reedy voice of this sniper in the world of celebrity journalism gave me some reason to hope:

"I was about to call you, Inspector. There's something that might . . . I remembered my boss used a taxi service. He used them whenever he was in Madrid. It was always the same company: Taxi-Rapid. The TV company paid. It's not much, but it is something."

"Do they keep the invoices?"

"I think so, those from the last year at least. They must have them in administration. Would you like me to get them for you?"

"That would save time. We could be there in an hour."

"I don't think it'll take me long to find them."

At last we had found some trace of Ernesto Valdés's passage through this world. We couldn't get our hopes up, but it might somehow allow us to reconstruct his steps through Madrid. And since we were groping about in complete darkness, that seemed like a heck of a lot to me.

7

The addresses, almost all of them repeated, that Valdés had taken a taxi to in the previous year didn't mean much to us; we didn't know Madrid well. I had to ask the director of the TV company to allow Maggy to spend some time with us. Since Maggy had nothing to do since the death of her boss and benefactor, she could hardly refuse, although she was intrigued to imagine what such a small cog in her great wheel could offer.

Maggy explained what the addresses she recognized meant. She was able to solve the riddle of two of them at once. The first was the hotel where Valdés stayed whenever he was in Madrid. The second was a men's shop where he often bought clothes.

"He always told me he preferred to buy the clothes he most needed in Madrid."

"He had ghastly taste," I could not help commenting.

"Yeah, although he wasn't afraid of colors, he didn't go round dressed like an undertaker the way the rest of them here do."

I only had to glance at what she was wearing, a cross between neo-hippie and genuine rags, to understand what she was getting at.

Apparently put out by what he saw as a typically female diversion, Garzón tried to hurry us up:

"What about these other two addresses?"

Delighted to be doing detective work, Maggy looked at them more closely.

"No idea. One of them is only there twice; but the other is repeated sixteen times!"

"We'll have to go there."

Garzón looked at me anxiously:

"Do you think it will be necessary for the young lady to come along?"

Maggy awaited my decision with complete indifference; in other words, chewing her gum more furiously than ever.

"She might be useful. She can tell us if her boss ever mentioned the place."

Her little bovine eyes gleamed. She scratched an ear loaded down with studs and said slyly:

"Don't get it into your heads that I enjoy working with the fuzz. If you were in uniform I wouldn't go as far as the corner with you. I've got lots of friends who would never forgive me."

"We're convinced of that," I replied.

The general manager of Taxi-Rapid knew Valdés very well; he was one of their most distinguished clients. He was not looked after by one driver in particular; whoever was free took the booking. By chance, someone in the office remembered having driven him in the last month. He had nothing to add, though: he said the journalist was not someone who appreciated conversation. I decided we would not get much more there, so instead we headed off for the address that appeared sixteen times on the list.

It turned out to a perfectly normal-looking café, La Gloria. Locals and passersby dropped in to have breakfast, a snack, or a cup of coffee. It was neither luxurious nor shabby, and contained a bar and a few tables, nothing more. The owner remembered Valdés, of course; everyone remembered him from his TV appearances. Coming here sixteen times in a year did not make him a regular, but it was often enough for the man to be able to supply us with a few details. Valdés always met another gentleman, usually in mid-morning. He was able to give a brief description of the other man: about fifty years old, tall, well dressed, rimless glasses, and elegant-looking. They used to sit at an out-of-the-way table near a window, and spend at least an hour in conversation. He never heard what they were discussing. He had the impression that occasionally they were looking through papers. He even thought that he once saw them exchange colored files. He had always thought Valdés's companion must be someone important in the magazine or television world. One day, the other man came in with his wife, a very pretty woman about the same age as him. It seemed that Valdés must know her, because they were not introduced. The three of them sat and talked. He could not really describe the woman, apart from that she was tall and slim. He could not remember what color her hair was, or what she had been wearing.

When we were out in the street again, I felt a surge of excitement, but I did not want make any comments to the sergeant in front of Maggy. I decided to give her something to do elsewhere, without offending her.

"Maggy, you know the city and the important people here. If you'd like to carry on helping us, there's something of vital importance you could do."

A flicker of interest ran through her tiny monkey-like features. She immediately disguised it, and said, as though sparing my life:

"What do you want me to do? It'll mean me missing work, but they're going to throw me out anyway . . . "

"You won't have to leave the TV studios. Go back and look closely at a map of this neighborhood. Find out if there is any important bank near here, any newspaper, the office of any political party, the home of any prominent member of the jet-set. Do you follow?"

She shrugged. She was probably waiting for some further explanation of why this was so important, but I didn't oblige.

"O.K.," she said, unconvinced. "And what should I do when I've finished?"

"Give me a call."

She nodded briefly several times, then left us without so much as a goodbye. We watched her gawky figure disappear down the street.

"Thank God for that!" Garzón puffed. "That kid makes me nervous!"

"What's wrong with her?"

"That couldn't-care-less attitude, her way of talking and chewing gum . . . and, besides, I hate amateur detectives."

"That's very ungrateful of you. She's put us on to a valuable lead. What do you make of Valdés's meetings with this mysterious man?"

"I suppose he must be Lesgano, the man who bought information from him."

"And was perhaps his murderer, or the person who hired him."

"Possibly Rosario Campos's murderer too."

"It looks as though between us and Moliner we've managed to gather a lot of bits and pieces."

"Now we simply have to put them together. You know how hard it is to use mere sightings, like those the bar owner was talking about. You heard him, a tall man, a woman . . . who were they exactly? Nobody knows. A lot of cases have ended up a blind alley because of evidence like that. The people who could really have helped us are dead."

"Not all of them. There's still the murderer."

"Or murderers. To make matters worse, we don't even know how many we're looking for."

"Don't worry; we've got enough bodies for a whole troupe of them. Off we go again?"

The second address the taxi company had given us was of a restaurant, Mesón de Sancho Panza, in the Chamberí neighborhood. It was all very authentic Castilian, although we did not know much more than that about it. The waiters—more than four of them—could not remember having served Valdés. The youngest did not even know who Valdés was, which gave me a certain amount of hope in the young generation. All of a sudden, a thought surfaced from among the thousands lying scattered around in my mind. I called the marquis. When he heard my voice, he could not disguise his annoyance. Yet he managed to hide his instinctive reaction when he spoke.

"You again, Inspector? Of course I can answer a question: for you, I'm always available!"

Although a celebrity education might not help anyone to be honest, hard-working or pay their taxes, it is perfect for hiding true feelings.

"Sancho Panza, the Mesón Sancho Panza . . . I'm not sure. There must be five hundred restaurants in Madrid called Sancho, and another thousand called Quijote."

"The one I'm talking about is in Chamberí. Could it have been there you saw Valdés having dinner with his ex-wife?"

"Ah, well, that's another story. You may be right: A friend of mine lives in the neighborhood, and I'd gone to visit him, but he wasn't back yet. So I went into the restaurant to have a coffee, and it was while I was waiting that I saw them. I think that's how it was."

I managed to escape quickly from his endless prattle. I hung up and turned to the sergeant, who had rolled his eyes as soon as he realized who I had been talking to.

"Underneath he's quite sweet," I said, to ruffle his feathers. "I can understand why some women go crazy over him."

"If you want me out of your hair for a few hours, just tell me."

"Don't bother, I'm sure I can resist his sex appeal. Anyway, I think he's just being nice to me so I won't denounce him to the tax people."

"In that case, he should be trying to seduce me as well."

"Why, are you thinking of passing on his details?"

"You bet I am! As soon as all this is over and that popinjay can't be of use to us anymore, I'm going straight to the tax inspectors so they can do their worst. I've had it up to here with all these parasites! Let them pay for once in their lives!"

"You may be right. At any rate, he says the restaurant was in Chamberí. It's obvious that Valdés and his ex-wife were a civilized couple after all, and they used to get together for dinner occasionally—perhaps every time she came to Madrid."

"In such a down-at-heel place? And why in Madrid rather than in Barcelona? I still think it's odd."

"It may be more people knew her in Barcelona, and they wanted to go unnoticed. I don't see it as so strange. You just think it is because they agreed to meet. I'm sure you'd never forgive an ex-wife."

"Luckily, I've never been in that situation, but you're right, I couldn't bear the idea that I'm paying for a woman who's got nothing to do with me anymore, and on top of that I'm supposed to smile at her . . . ?"

"That's what I thought."

"What shall we do now? I'm so hungry, I . . . "

"O.K., just so you realize what a kind boss I am, we'll have a bite to eat. But, first, let me call Moliner. I want to know how things are with him."

Things were not good. The initial financial information he had about the minister all seemed completely within the bounds of normality. He had not withdrawn any large sums of money, so it did not look as though he had been blackmailed. But was that really so important? No. The attempt to blackmail him could have been made anyway. Nothing in the minister's private papers made any mention of his extra-marital relationship, with the possible exception of regular payments to a florist's in Calle Muntaner. Every Wednesday, a bouquet of red roses was sent to the home of Rosario Campos. The name of the sender was always Frédéric Chopin.

"How kitsch can you get!" I could not help exclaiming.

"What do you expect? Anyway, things weren't all that different at Rosario's end. She dropped a few hints to her friends, telling them she had met the man of her life, that she had at last found true love . . . that's pretty kitsch, too."

"I suppose it was disenchantment that turned her against Frédéric Chopin. At some point, she must have realized that he was never going to leave his wife. That was when her plans changed; and Valdés was on hand to help her. Have her parents said anything?"

"They're suffering in silence. If they do know something, they're hiding it behind the excuse that their daughter lived her own life and told them nothing."

"That's understandable."

"It may well be, but, let me tell you, I've had it up to here with this world where nobody says anything. It's so different from crimes committed on the street. There you always find a witness, or family members who talk and talk until they say something that you can use."

"Yes, the poor are more defenseless against their enemies— there's a long tradition of it."

"Describe it how you like, but the fact is I'm fed up with it. Apart from anything else, I'm feeling too tired."

"Part of that must be from going to bed so late."

There was a long pause, but then Moliner came on the line again, and said calmly:

"If by that you're referring to Amanda, you're mistaken. We're not seeing each other anymore."

It was my turn to fall silent. Moliner went on:

"She's going out with Guillermo Franquesa, from the Drugs Squad."

"What?"

"We met him in a restaurant and I introduced them. They must have clicked at first sight, because Amanda dropped me and started going out with him. I already told you I find women incomprehensible; this just confirms it."

I was as surprised as he was, and told Garzón about it as we had a quick lunch in a bar. He came over all sympathetic.

"It must be a real blow to have your husband leave you. You probably think you were faithful with him for far too long."

"That's fine, and we've all been through that first completely lost phase, but why doesn't she go somewhere else to have fun? What's she trying to do, go out with the entire Barcelona police force?"

Garzón went on in philosophical mode.

"You can deny it, but you're worried about what others might say. However modern you may think you are, the social stigma still hurts."

"All right, Fermín, I've had enough of your agony-aunt act. What you say is true, and I admit it. I admit it, and I admit, I just wish my sister would go home and face up to her predicament. All she's doing at the moment is running away from it. At some point she'll have to go back and sort it out."

"All these things like divorce and relationships with ex-husbands are very complicated."

"Everybody has to find a way through it."

"You, for example don't want anything more to do with Hugo, and yet you have a friendly relationship with Pepe."

"There's no way of knowing which will be better; there are no models to follow. That's what makes it so intriguing."

"Do you think you'll ever marry again, Petra?"

"How on earth should I know?"

"It's not just an idle question."

"Why ask then?"

"To know if you're thinking of eloping with the marquis."

I laughed aloud. I looked at my colleague. As with all men,

there was a childish side to him that made him attractive. I was still smiling when I said:

"I don't know if I'll ever remarry, Fermín. If I do, it won't be to prove some theory or other. I've reached the conclusion that, like almost everything else in life, love is a jungle, a chaotic mess, an utter defeat. That's why I think it's absurd to make plans, but no more absurd than not planning anything . . . I don't know, it's scary trying to impose order where there isn't any. You end up realizing there's no damn reason you're here on Earth anyway, that you're nothing more than a poor little animal, a spore, nothing more than a link in the chain of life."

Garzón was listening to me as seriously as a religious devotee. He screwed up his eyes in his effort to follow my homespun philosophy, but said nothing.

"What about you? Do you think you'll marry again?"

"I . . . "

My cell phone rang again, interrupting him.

"I think it's our amateur detective again."

"Shit! Tell her to join the police academy, then she can get paid when she graduates!"

Garzón continued to look daggers and sip his coffee while I took the call. When I had finished, I turned to him again.

"Got it."

"Got what?"

"There are no party political offices or official buildings near the bar that Valdés used to frequent, but *El Universal* is based close by. What's most interesting is that they've reported several political scandals recently. As soon as you finish your coffee we'll go and see the editor. We'll see if he knows anything about the sale of sensitive information or possible blackmail attempts. Now, carry on."

"Carry on?"

"Yes, you were about to tell me whether you were thinking of ever getting married again."

"You're incredible, Inspector! We're in the midst of a tough case, and all you want to know is whether an old bachelor like me intends to marry again! How on earth should I know? Perhaps, if I find the right woman."

"A sweet little wifey who has your slippers ready when you come home from work?"

"Yes! And who blows on my coffee when it's too hot! Come on, Inspector, get off my case. I know you well enough by now—we've been working together far too long."

"Not so long I can't still surprise you occasionally."

"You can say that again! Let's just say you've more than enough surprises in you for an old man like me."

I enjoyed it when Garzón talked like that. It somehow kept my tiny personal myth alive, however much it was suffering from the wear and tear of daily life.

All we needed to gain access to *El Universal* were our police badges. It was rather more difficult to get the editor to see us. His name was Andrés Nogales, and apparently he was in a meeting, so we had to wait half an hour for him. We were in no hurry; all we wanted to do was talk to him and ask if any of the journalists on the paper looked remotely like the man Valdés used to have breakfast with in La Gloria. When he did finally appear, we had to change tack quickly. To our complete astonishment, he himself fitted the description that waiter had given us: tall, elegant, rimless glasses, around fifty years old. Garzón shot me a quick glance, and I narrowed my eyes slightly to confirm I thought the same. I had to react swiftly. Were we at last faced with Valdés's killer? I knew I had to be careful, and not jump to any conclusions. The editor of a daily newspaper is not some villain you can threaten without hard evidence. I had no idea how to begin, but I realized that to improvise would be the biggest mistake I could make. Garzón was still quiet as the grave as we sat in the two little armchairs opposite the big editorial desk. Nogales smiled, spreading his arms wide in a well-rehearsed gesture.

"What can I do for our beloved police?"

Either he was playing the ironic man of the world, or he was nervous. In either case, it was to my advantage. I smiled back at him.

"Just a quick chat."

"About anything in particular?"

"About the practice of journalism."

"I know the boundaries are somewhat blurred, but I never thought that being a journalist was in itself a crime."

"It isn't. All we are asking is that you clarify some journalistic practices."

"Such as what, for example?"

"How does one carry out investigative journalism, for example?"

He laughed out loud.

"Please, inspector, you're not talking to a child here."

"What do you mean?"

"I realize that's the only thing the police could be interested in. Besides, there is nothing else in a newspaper: all the rest is work done by agencies, and you know what that is like."

"Fine. What I'd like to know, then, is if it is your own journalists who carry out the investigations, or do you bring in people from outside?"

He shut a desk drawer firmly, without being rude but showing his impatience. His face had lost its smile.

"Look, I like playing games as much as anyone, but can we be sensible about this? I am the editor of a national newspaper, and I am privy to lots of things, and get to hear about a lot more. You are really not going to get me to believe that you came here out of an abstract interest in our working methods. Nor am I going to talk openly about matters when I have the professional right to stay silent. You are investigating a particular case: might I know which one?"

"The murder of Ernesto Valdés."

"Good, now we're getting somewhere. Let me see . . . Ernesto Valdés, Ernesto Valdés . . . yes, got it, the celebrity journalist. His death happened in Barcelona, didn't it? You're rather far from the crime scene."

"Someone saw Ernesto Valdés come into these offices shortly before he died. We wanted to know what he was doing here. We're checking all his last movements."

"Valdés here? I don't know: I'd be surprised at that, but I don't keep a close watch on all the sections. Perhaps he was being interviewed, or he gave us some information on celebrity magazines. Wait a minute, I'll check."

He picked up the phone. He put his hand over the mouthpiece and explained:

"I'm ringing the documentation center. They know what we've published recently. We'll see if they . . . "

He gave them the details, insisted, but naturally enough got only negative responses. Five minutes later, he hung up.

"Well, it seems as though you were misinformed. Valdés has not been in *El Universal* recently; in fact, they say he has never set foot in here in his life. We're all journalists, but we work in very different areas, if you understand me."

"I think so. Too bad then."

"Was that all?"

"I'm afraid it was."

"Inspector, I'm going to make a suggestion, which I hope you won't take the wrong way. When you have some police business to do, there's no need to ask to see me. My secretary or one of the editors would do just as well. Don't think I don't wish to collaborate: I have very good relations with the police. I also have a good friendship with the Interior Minister—he's in charge of you, isn't he? But I'm always so busy that . . . "

"I understand perfectly."

"Who gave you that information?"

"I'm sorry, señor Nogales, but I also have the right to keep silent about professional matters. Does that make sense?"

"Of course it does. I'll show you out."

"Do you mind if we go via the editorial office? The fact is I've always been really curious to know what a newspaper is like."

For the first time, I saw a hint of doubt creep across his face. But he quickly suppressed it.

"Of course! I'll ask my secretary to be your guide."

"Fantastic! That's really kind of you."

While we were waiting for his secretary, Garzón whispered in my ear:

"What a creep! Like he's sparing our lives or something."

"Calm down, Fermín," I urged him. "Let's keep everything very calm and polite. And keep your eyes peeled in case you see anyone else who fits the description. We have to be careful."

Not that careful, because nobody in the editorial office looked as much like the description the waiter had given us as Nogales did. He was our man: I would have staked my virtue on it, if only I still had it. I was so convinced of this that leaving the newspaper building felt like giving our prime suspect the chance to escape. But we still had no concrete evidence against him, so we could not rush things; we did not even have a clear idea of what crime he had committed.

We went to the Madrid police station that Moliner had been working out of. I asked them to intercept his phone, to follow his movements by satellite, and to put a man outside *El Universal* to take photos. After that, we returned to our hotel. If my suspicions turned out to be ill-founded, making all these demands would be as welcome as a cup of hot vomit, but we had to make the effort.

As I was going to bed, the phone rang. It was Sanguesa. I was surprised that someone like him would call so late.

"Sorry to ring at this time, Petra, but, the truth, is I've been getting nowhere with your damned report. This Martha Merchán is proving really difficult. I still can't find out much about her."

"What's the problem?"

"Have you any idea how closely guarded matters concerning government bonds are? You often have to give up, even if you're the police or a magistrate; those guys just won't talk."

"I know."

"But perhaps you also know I'm the best financial sleuth in the country."

"Of course I do!"

"Well, thanks to my high-level contacts, I've managed to discover that a fortnight ago Martha Merchán invested a considerable sum of money."

"How much?"

"Twenty million pesetas."

I whistled, though I was not quite sure whether I was meant to be impressed or not. Sanguesa went on:

"Strange, isn't it? Where did she get all that? It doesn't show in any of her accounts, and she doesn't earn money like that. Did she have it stuffed in a sock? Did she suddenly earn it? Anyway, that's as far as I could get; I don't have the authority to discover the details."

"I understand."

I sat trying to fit this new piece of information into all the rest. Sanguesa's voice brought me back to reality.

"Don't you have anything to say?"

"I'll have to think about it."

"Not even about the work I've done?"

Finally I realized what he was after.

"Sanguesa, I'm struck dumb. I can hardly believe my ears.

I knew you were good at you job, but to get to the bottom of this kind of investment! But it's not just that, it's the way you've worked on all the reports I've asked you for. I truly don't think there's anyone else in the service who could have done what you have."

A little snicker of satisfaction told me I had probably praised him enough and could stop.

"Well, Petra, I'm afraid I have to go. Take care, I wouldn't want anything to happen to the best inspector we have."

"Sanguesa, I adore you. Bye."

Men's vanity: so huge, and so easy to satisfy. You can over-exaggerate, praise them in an infantile, over-the-top way bordering on the unbelievable. They swallow it hook, line, and sinker, it never seems far-fetched. They are delighted with you, even if they know they do not really deserve it, because they see it as a mother's love.

I stared at the four corners of my room. Then I studied the eclectic pieces of furniture so typical of a hotel bedroom. Shit! There wasn't enough free space in my mind for any new information, least of all something that did not fit with the rest, which even went so far as to destroy the order I had managed to establish from my deductions and suspicions. What on earth did Valdés's ex-wife have to do with all that? How was she mixed up in the sale of confidential information? Was the sale of that information really the trigger for all the deaths? How far had we got with our investigation: were we simply back at the beginning again? I could feel my head start to spin, as though I were falling into a deep well with nowhere to cling to. Be careful, Petra, I told myself. Now was not the moment to start feeling insecure. No rushing ahead, but no going back either. Take it slowly: I was where I was, and something must have got me there. No point going over all the evidence yet again, recapitulating, casting doubt on everything. I could trust my policewoman's instinct, couldn't I?

I got up off my bed. Stay calm, it was only one more piece of information. Does a computer go into panic mode when it receives a new bit of data? What does it do? It archives it, that's what it does. But where? That was the problem. What if Sanguesa's nugget had nothing to do with our main enquiry? We were operating in a world of swindlers. Everyone in that rarefied part of society had something to hide, usually money. They were born thieves, with more opportunities than anyone else to make transactions that were difficult to trace. To them, the tax authorities were the devil. Possibly Marta Merchán had made an earlier investment that had never shown up, or had received a secret inheritance from Valdés which she kept with her lawyer so as not to have to declare it. Yes, that was a distinct possibility: after all, weren't they on good terms despite their separation?

What to do? What was my next step? To go back to Barcelona? That was impossible, with Nogales firmly in my sights and with the final shot ready to be fired. Send Garzón to interrogate the ex? She was not the kind of suspect that Garzón was at his best with. I took what I thought was the least bad option. I called Moliner. He was already at home. I asked him if he could go and interview Marta Merchán. Not only did he know all the details of the case, but we still were not sure that his and mine were not the same anyway, so it was good for him to take a look and see what he thought. Depending on what he said, we could make our move.

He agreed, of course. That was my problem solved, for the moment at least. I could breathe more easily, but fate was not going to let me off the hook that easily and allow me to sleep. Just as I was about to hang up, Moliner stopped me.

"Petra, do you know what was happening when you called?"

I commended my soul to any protecting saints who might be listening. I did not really know why, but I sensed a cataclysm was about to break. I told him I had no idea. The cataclysm broke.

"My wife has just left me for good."

"Listen, I'm sorry, I didn't even ask . . . I'm sorry, I won't keep you any longer."

He did not hang up. In fact, I doubt if he even heard me.

"In fact, she left a few days ago. She took all her things with her; she has a new apartment. But we had agreed to meet today for dinner, in a last attempt to keep it friendly . . . I don't know why, but I had some sort of stupid hope that perhaps in the end . . . but she's gone, Petra. I was roaming round the apartment when you called, thinking that I would never see her here again."

"Look, perhaps if you did manage a friendly goodbye, you'll see her again, you can talk, and as time goes by, you . . . "

"We didn't."

"Didn't what?"

"I blew my top. I couldn't help myself, I don't know what came over me."

I took a cigarette from the bedside table. Any attempt to interrupt him would have been like showing a lack of solidarity with mankind. I drew the smoke deep into my lungs and listened. That was all that was required of me, yet again.

"I told her everything I should never have said, everything I don't really feel. What was the point? It was a disaster, Petra. I'm such a fool, my wife must have lots of good reasons to go off with someone else."

"Don't give in to the temptation of thinking you're the only guilty one. That is usually almost as bad as blaming the other for everything."

"So what does work?"

"Letting time go by, and, if you really are interested in working out what went wrong, start thinking about it once all the pain, resentment and anger has faded."

"And when does that happen?"

"I don't know."

"Let time go by. That's easy to say."

"Well, if you really need something to put the blame on now, blame your profession—that's usually a good move. Do you have any idea how many policemen and women are on their own or are divorced?"

"I've never given it a thought."

"There are lots. It's quite normal, Moliner: not many partners can put up with the hours we work, the tension we generate, the sheer amount of time we put into a complex case, the phone calls we get at all hours of the day and night . . . "

"Do you think it's any consolation to be reminded that, while I was working so hard, she was screwing some other guy?"

"That's just being vulgar. If it's only your pride that's hurt, it's not such a problem."

I heard him give a sad laugh.

"Petra Delicado, always such original ideas!"

"Yes, they should give me a column in a gossip magazine."

"Listen, about your sister . . . "

"Am I my sister's keeper? As that celebrity Cain once said. Forget it, make sure you concentrate on something more interesting."

"You're right again, Petra. I'll make sure I go and question Marta Merchán. I'll make sure I'm as passionate about it as you would be."

"Even more, I should think: you've always been a better cop than I."

It's strange, but sooner or later there's always a bond of sympathy and solidarity between those of us who are divorced. I've always thought that one day we could make a powerful lobby. Politicians would mention us in their speeches so we would vote for them, we'd have our own special shops and clubs. Who knows, perhaps in the future we will be one of the pillars of civilization, replacing that shrivelled concept of a single marriage that is always such a stereotype, so predictable, so lacking in real emotions. By the time that glorious day arrived, though, I would be long since gone, so I had better not give in to fantasies and settle for what I most needed at that moment: sleep.

The police station we were attached to in Madrid was a model of efficiency. Early the next morning we already had the information we had asked for. They had followed Nogales all the time. Nothing suspicious in his movements the previous evening or night. He stayed at the newspaper office until very late. He left with the deputy editor, Juan Montes, and the two of them had a meal in one of those restaurants that stay open until the early hours. Then he went home. Nothing out of the ordinary in the phone calls he made either; all of them were apparently work-related. We were surprised at how well our third request—the photos of Nogales—had come out. They had caught him in silhouette as he left the newspaper, and almost face-on going into the restaurant. It was him without a doubt.

"Would you like some breakfast?" I asked Garzón.

"Only if it's at La Gloria."

Adolfo, the waiter, admitted he instinctively recognized Nogales as soon as we showed him the photos. He agreed straightaway, but then apparently thought better of it, and started to express doubts. This was a normal enough reaction: it's not the same thing saying you've seen an unknown person in a specific place as identifying him in a photo you are shown by the cops. To accuse a real, named person is a step not many are willing to take.

"Actually, I'm not sure, it could be him, but we see so many people in here . . . it may just have been my impression."

This was not the moment to tell him he would have to make

a sworn statement to the magistrate. To do that, we would have to catch him off guard again. I tried to get him to commit himself as far as possible.

"Can we say at least that he bears a greater than usual likeness to the man you saw here many times with Valdés?"

"Yes, he looks quite like him."

He was struggling with a feeling that he had put his foot in it by telling us what he knew, and a desire to tell the truth. I decided it was better to leave it like that, but as we were leaving, Garzón criticized me.

"You should have insisted more. He's not a witness we can trust. He could vanish at any moment, and then what will we do: tell Nogales we have a witness who thinks he saw him with Valdés, or perhaps someone who looked a bit like him? He'd laugh in our faces."

"It may be that the witness thinks it over and concludes that making a proper statement wouldn't compromise anyone."

"The conclusion most witnesses come to is that it's better for them not to get into trouble."

"O.K., so what should I have done?"

"Instill a bit of fear in him."

"Threatening him with my truncheon? No way, Sergeant, that would only give grounds to his lawyer to say he had been intimidated!"

"You could be right, but I don't agree with how you handled it."

"I'm not happy about it either. Let's cross our fingers and play the cards we have well."

"How are we going to do that? Are you going to tell Nogales the owner of the bar recognized him?"

That was the sixty-four-thousand-dollar question, the heart of the matter. If we said that to Nogales, he could react in a number of different ways: confess, because he felt he could not get out of it; do nothing, confident that it was a trap; continue to deny everything until he had been identified in a lineup; or, in the most extreme case, try to buy off the witness, or hire someone to intimidate him or even, if the worst came to the worst, get rid of him. If he really was behind the other two killings, why should he hesitate to commit another if it meant getting rid of the few clues that pointed to him?

"We could always have La Gloria put under surveillance. That way we could haul Nogales in if anybody tried to intimidate the witness."

"Do you think he'd do it in such a way we could trace it back to him? There's a hundred ways of intimidating the guy without even going anywhere near the bar!"

"Then we'll have the witness followed, and take photos of all the customers who go into his bar! We'll tap his telephone!"

"The chief inspector here will tell us to go to hell."

"We'll tell him that in Barcelona we do things like that all the time; that'll bring out his professional rivalry."

"O.K., give it a try, talk to him. Even so, we would not be covering all the possibilities. It might work if he sent a killer who had a record, but what if he didn't? He could have his own special man, someone who looks just like any other customer."

"Nothing ever covers the risks one hundred per cent, inspector, as you know perfectly well. You have to believe your adversary will make a mistake: even the most outstanding brains slip up sometimes."

"It's true: even me, when I chose you for a partner!"

He laughed out loud.

"Just to show you what a saint I am, and that I don't hold your typically unkind remark against you, I'll go to the chief inspector and make all those demands myself. That way if he bawls anyone out, it'll be me."

"O.K., I'll wait for you at the hotel. As soon as everything is in place, we can pay another little visit to *El Universal*."

A short while later I went up to my room for a few minutes of calm in order to prepare my strategy for the interview with Nogales. I took a whisky from the mini-bar and played back my messages. I had two, one from Maggy that I was keen to hear, and another from my sister's husband. He asked me to get in touch with him as soon as I could. Against my better judgment, I called him: something told me I wasn't going to find any calm or peace by talking to him.

"Petra, I've tried to keep you out of this, but things can't go on this way. What's happening with Amanda?"

"You might not believe me, but I don't know. She's staying with me, but for the past few days I've been on a case in Madrid. There's not much I can tell you."

"I know she's at your place, but now she's refusing to even come to the phone. On the few occasions I've managed to get through, she hangs up as soon as she realizes who it is."

"How do you think I could help?"

"Call her and talk to her. She can't just take off like that. We haven't had a proper conversation about the future, we haven't made any plans. I've no idea how long she intends to stay in Barcelona. Both the children and I are completely bewildered. It's not normal for someone to go off like that without any explanation. We need to see what we're going to do, how we're going to organize things. She has to face up to the reality of the situation."

"Are you in such a hurry to leave?"

He fell silent. I could hear him give a deep sigh.

"Petra, please! Do I have to justify myself to you? Do we have to split into family loyalties, or some friends who are on the husband's side, and others on the wife's? Can't I even avoid all that with you?"

"I suppose so. Anyway, Amanda won't talk to me either."

"Why?"

I hesitated a moment before replying.

"Well, I suppose it's because I was preaching to her, playing the experienced sister who only wants what's good for her."

"When are you going back to Barcelona?"

"I haven't the remotest idea. For the immediate future, I'm staying in Madrid."

"It's a really desperate situation, Petra."

"Give it time. This kind of fake truce can't last forever."

"All right, but promise me you'll try to convince her to come back, at least so I can know if she wants custody over the kids."

"I'll try," I said faintly.

Was I really such a model of the neutral woman? Would everyone in Spain who was splitting up come to me for advice? Had I chosen the wrong profession? Should I have dedicated myself to being a marriage guidance counselor? Even before I could hang up properly, the phone rang again. I almost jumped out of my skin. It was Garzón.

"Inspector? Everything's in place."

"Already?"

"It was all very easy. They're going to cover La Gloria properly, and they didn't even shout at me. Do you know what I think? I think it's harder to get things done back in Barcelona. Coronas is a hard nut to crack. Shall I stop by to pick you up?"

"No, wait for me at *El Universal*, I'll be there straightaway."

I looked at the finger of whisky sitting like burnished gold in the bottom of the glass. I went into the bathroom to pour it down the drain. I needed to be wide awake. In the end, I had no strategy for my interview with Nogales. I was just going to have to rely on my powers of improvisation, and of my knowledge of people like him. I changed my mind: I would drink the sacred brew. Facing up to the wolf without any fear would probably have been Little Red Riding Hood's best strategy. I drank the whisky down in one gulp. I was bound to win: Red Riding Hood didn't have a Garzón by her side.

We were made to wait again before we could see Nogales. He was in a meeting. Important people live in meetings, apparently. It's like a spiritualist session. An hour and a quarter after we had arrived at the newspaper, Nogales finally saw us. He was considerably less charming than the day before.

"What's this? Do the police really need journalists so much?"

Our verbal fencing had begun. I had to be careful he did not wriggle out of my reach. I plunged straight in.

"Señor Nogales, yesterday you stated that you did not know Ernesto Valdés personally. Do you stand by what you said?"

"Oh, so that was a statement, was it? I had no idea. If things are that serious, I should call my lawyer so that he can be present. That's my legal right, isn't it, inspector?"

He smiled with a measured cynicism. This intelligent, worldly man would take full advantage of any slipup I made, and I had committed the first one almost before I had started.

"You can do as you like. In fact, we don't want much from you today. Rather, we want to tell you something."

"Good! Is it publishable? I always admire good reporting, and I suppose as police you do the same."

"I don't know if it's publishable or not, but perhaps your readers would be interested to know we have a witness who swears he saw you with Valdés."

Beyond giving a smug snort, he did not react.

"As I already told you, Inspector, the media world is small and absurd. Anybody could have seen me near Valdés at a busy party, an opening night, some political do. I may even have exchanged a few words with him, although I don't remember having done so. That would not change what you call my statement: I did not have dealings with that gentleman. Is that better?"

As we had agreed, it was Garzón's turn to step in, while I watched for any sign of a reaction on Nogales's face.

"We're not talking about 'dealings.' You used to have breakfast with Valdés in a bar called La Gloria. You used to talk and exchange papers there. You met him at least a dozen times: sufficiently frequently for the waiter to recognize you."

I could have sworn Nogales's eyes narrowed slightly, but that was all I saw.

"Well, that is news! Where or how does this gentleman know me from? Did he take my photo while I was having breakfast with Valdés? Good God, I must have looked frightful, having to share a table with someone like him! Well, if this person is sure of what he says, I suppose he will be willing to identify me in front of a magistrate. In that case, fix a date, and I'll be there. I won't be too pleased to lose a morning, but if there's no other way! A newspaper editor gets involved in lots of strange things during his career, and I guess this will just be another one."

"Very well, señor Nogales, that is all for now. If you find you suddenly remember something, please call this station and ask for me."

"Just a minute, Inspector. Can I know what your theory is? What am I supposed to have done while I was having breakfast with Valdés? Were we gossiping about people in high society; did I kill him because he knew secrets about me I did not want revealed?"

"I'd prefer to keep my theory to myself. When I put it into practice, you'll be the first to know."

We slid out of the office as though we had left a time bomb that might explode at any minute. In fact, the opposite was true: Nogales had discovered our Achilles heel almost at once. Was our witness willing to identify him in front of a magistrate? And, even if he did, would that be sufficient to bring a possible case of the sale of compromising information to light? It was all held together with safety pins, and Nogales knew this as well as we did. We were not likely to be able to charge him for any economic misdemeanor: he was bound to have all that covered. It was frustrating, like having a wonderful cake within your reach, and not even being able to smell it. All our evidence was circumstantial, we needed facts, and those facts were stubbornly refusing to appear.

"Let's see if we can catch him in the operation we've set up round the bar," said Garzón.

"I wouldn't hold out much hope of that," I said.

"We should wait at least a day before we force the witness to testify."

"All right, but not a minute longer."

And with that, we went off to have lunch. Perhaps eating would calm my nerves. It certainly did wonders for the sergeant, who tucked into a plate of tripe as though eating it were the only wish of his immortal soul. The restaurant was as lively as they all are in Madrid. There was a general hubbub, voices in animated discussion, and the shouts of the waiters to add a final touch of hysteria. They called out the orders so forcefully they sounded like revolutionary slogans, urging the crowd on to claim justice and slices of ham. The background noise was so loud I barely heard my cell phone ring, though it was going at full volume in my bag.

"Yes?" I asked, trying to cup my hands to protect my ears.

"Petra, this is Moliner. I want you to listen to me carefully."

"I can listen, Moliner, but I won't hear much. Can you call back in half an hour when we've finished lunch?"

"I'm sorry, but I can't. Get out of there: go to the washroom."

I stood up like a robot, gestured to Garzón, and went out to the front of the restaurant. I felt a mixture of things: alarm, curiosity . . . what could it be about? My sister, Coronas . . . ?

"Petra, I've discovered Marta Merchán's dead body."

I found it impossible to reply. All the food I had eaten was struggling to come up again. I took several deep breaths. Moliner was already growing impatient.

"Petra, can you hear me or not?"

"I can hear you, Moliner. Are you sure it's her?"

"Are you drunk or something? Of course it's her! I found her. I had been trying to telephone her, but there was no one at home. So I decided to go out there without warning, and . . . Petra, you need to get here immediately. I'll tell you the rest in person."

I caught the next shuttle. Garzón stayed on in Madrid. We could not just abandon all we had set up there: if the sergeant's plan worked, Nogales could try something at any moment.

The flight seemed endless. The hypotheses flitted around in my brain like the changing images in a kaleidoscope. I thought I was going crazy. It had been yet another mistake to discount the financial information I had about Marta Merchán. She was obviously mixed up in all this: but in what, exactly, and how? I tried to drive the case from my mind with all the mental concentration of a yogi, but it was no use: as soon as I stopped focusing on attempts to explain everything, Coronas's face popped up on my little mental computer screen, and I heard him saying: "Another dead body, Petra. When are you going to solve the case—after the last suspect has been killed?" If he said anything like that, he would not be far wrong. It was like the black death, or a tropical hurricane. If things went on like this, we would discover who the murderer was because he would be the last one left standing. And the last one standing was Nogales.

I took a pen out of my bag and started scribbling on the paper napkin the stewardess had given me with my fruit juice. Nogales. Nogales. Nogales. I stared at it, hypnotized. Nogales. Nogales. Nogales. All at once, I saw it: No-ga-les. Les-ga-no. A simple switch of syllables. I had discovered the mysterious Lesgano. What more proof did we need? Nogales must have hired another killer: but why did he want to get rid of Marta Merchán?

As soon as I got to Barcelona airport I called Moliner. I

took a taxi to Merchán's house, where he was waiting for me. The police circus they had put on looked as if it had calmed down somewhat: they had already taken photos, checked fingerprints, searched for clues . . . all the routine stuff. The magistrate had allowed the body to be moved, and an emergency autopsy had been ordered at the police forensic institute. Coronas was on his way, and Moliner was prowling round the crime scene like a zombie. He was even more affected than usual, and I soon found out why. He had been the one who found her. However many dead bodies a cop comes across, they have usually been discovered by somebody else. But Moliner had turned up without the slightest notion that he would find a corpse, and such a find is always a shock.

"The kitchen door was open. It was lucky I even noticed. I rang and rang, and in the end I went in. She was in the living room, stretched out on the floor. There was blood everywhere. You could see the wounds a mile away: in her chest, her neck . . . her face was covered with blood too."

"What did the forensic expert say?"

"That they're stab wounds. He thinks she's been dead since eleven o'clock this morning; at least three or four hours."

"This wasn't a very professional job."

"No, it looks like a typical bloody crime of passion; it's not the work of a hit man. The doctor says he thinks she fought back. The autopsy should tell us for sure."

"Had anything been disturbed?"

"Only what you can see, and the study. There's a desk in there; all the drawers had been opened. Whoever it was, he was looking for something and went straight there. Nothing else has been touched. Either the murderer found what he was looking for, or he didn't want to risk spending any more time in the house and left empty-handed."

"Have you spoken to the neighbors?"

"The lady next door says she saw the daughter early this

morning. According to her, she was on her way to school as usual. It's the maid's day off."

"Any signs of a forced entry?"

"No."

"That means the person who killed her knew her, her house, and her daily routine."

"That's how it seems."

Coronas arrived, serious as a monk. Moliner told him what he had told me. I wondered what excuse he would find to shout at us today. Luckily, I had filed all the latest reports from my computer, and he had obviously read them before coming. There was no sign of anger.

"What hopes are there that Nogales will confess?"

"I'm not sure, sir."

"Well, at least you're honest."

"How could Nogales be involved in this murder?"

"I've no idea. The owner of La Gloria said Nogales and Valdés had a woman with them on one of their visits."

"O.K., Petra, leave all this to us and get back to Madrid. Have a photo taken of the dead woman and show it to that cretin of a witness in the bar. Make sure he's well aware how serious this is. Threaten that we'll charge him with being an accomplice if he won't confirm Nogales's identity to a magistrate. Tell him whatever you like, but I want us to be able to interrogate Nogales with some concrete proof in our hands. We've got to put our cards on the table, right?"

"What if that man really isn't sure that . . . ?"

"When you showed him the photos, do you think he recognized Nogales?"

"Yes, but to be fair . . . "

"You can take your idea of being fair with that guy and use it for toilet paper."

"But if I go back to Madrid I won't be able to interrogate the maid or Marta Merchán's daughter."

"Moliner can do that. Didn't you say your two cases were the same? Now's your chance to prove it."

"Garzón's already in Madrid."

I could see his dark eyes trying not to lose their patience.

"If just once in my life I could give you an order you didn't object to, I'd be a happy man. Don't you want to make your boss happy?"

"More than anything else in the world."

"All right then . . . get out of here! We need to act swiftly. One of the commonest and stupidest mistakes we police make is to have the prey in our sights and then let him escape. We'll keep you informed of the autopsy results and the interrogations of the maid and Valdés's daughter. And, for now, let's keep this death a secret."

I turned to Moliner, who was looking on as helplessly as I was. Coronas did not budge, waiting to see me leave.

"Moliner," I said. "Just have another little look round the house, will you?"

"Don't worry," he said in a low voice. Coronas turned on me again.

"Petra Delicado, do you have any idea how many years Moliner has been an inspector? May I remind you that things were running along quite smoothly even before you joined the force? Do you really think you are so irreplaceable?"

"I didn't mean to . . . "

"Get out of here, will you!"

I left with my tail between my legs, and that same feeling of having forgotten something that you get when you've packed your bags too quickly. But orders were orders, and, just as in the army, it was impossible not to follow them.

I got back onto the shuttle, which was turning into something like a bridge of sighs for me. I feel asleep in mid-flight, unaware of the stewardesses offering me coffee. I had not even had the chance to talk to my sister so she could bawl me out again. We cops fail not only in our marriages: we should not have families, either. We should be a race apart, and reproduce through spores, springing up like clumps of wild bushes and depending entirely on external factors like the climate and rainfall. That, at least, would save us our uneasy consciences and all the stress.

8

When I met up with him, Garzón was rather disappointed. Our man had made no move that made our complex police operation necessary. No compromising phone calls, still less any visit to La Gloria to try to intimidate the witness. The only appointment he had made was to see his lawyer, whom he had gone to visit at his practice. According to my colleague we were at a dead end, although he still thought the wait was worthwhile. I told him my word play discovery: No-ga-les and Les-ga-no. He was fascinated, but did not see how it could help us.

"You never know, Fermín. Tonight as he's shutting up, we'll pay a courtesy visit to the waiter. We have to get him to formally identify Nogales. Orders from the boss."

"It's always the same! A dead body turns up, and everybody goes hysterical. It's as if they don't realize that when they're dead, they can't possibly cause any more problems."

"You're talking as though the appearance of Marta Merchán stabbed to death didn't change anything at all."

"And does it? How?"

"I'm going to have to tell you what I told Coronas: I'm not sure. Though, God knows, I hate having to admit it. There's nothing worse than groping about in the dark, Garzón, hoping against hope that something you're doing will lead to the next step."

"So, you'd like to have your hypothesis perfectly worked out from the beginning, just like Sherlock Holmes, would you?"

"You can laugh, but, yes, I would."

"You've been an inspector long enough to know that isn't how things happen. You have to crawl around among the facts like a worm. It's not painting by numbers."

"How can you say that when we've cornered Nogales thanks to one of your own hypotheses? What you should be doing is trying again."

"Trying what again?"

"Trying to find a hypothesis that fits the murder of Valdés's ex."

"I'd have to use my imagination."

"Go right ahead!"

"Well, the simplest thing is to imagine that Marta Merchán only found out recently that Nogales had killed her ex-husband. Obviously, she wasn't pleased, and so she threatened to tell the police. So our friend had her done away with too, so that she couldn't talk."

"Your hypothesis is full of holes. First and foremost: how would Merchán have found out something like that? Did she know Nogales? Was she aware of what Nogales and Valdés were up to?"

"She benefited from it! Valdés paid her part of what he got!"

"Why would he do that? I admit, they had dinner together occasionally, they had a good relationship after their marriage break-up, but can you really see it being so good he would share his illicit gains with her? I don't believe it. I don't have that much faith in friendships after a divorce."

"You wouldn't share any of your winnings with your ex-husbands?"

"You bet I wouldn't, especially if they were illicit."

"Well, that's my best shot at a hypothesis. Besides, it's getting late, Inspector. We have to be going to La Gloria. It would be just our luck if they shut early today for some reason or another."

"I had no idea what time it was. All this shuttling between Barcelona and Madrid has completely confused me. I'm beginning to understand the stress that executives feel spending the whole week on a plane."

"See? You've found an even worse profession than being a policewoman—though, of course, they get paid a lot more."

"They can keep their money, I don't think it makes up for it."

"That's what I like most about you, Petra: you have class. I love the face you put on when anyone mentions the word money. It's as though you suddenly were reacting to something you'd eaten, or someone had put a disgusting bug on the table."

"Yes, all it takes is a bit of practice, I'll show you."

We asked for a patrol car from the station, and parked almost on the corner where La Gloria stood. After ten very few new customers went in. It was definitely not a late-night place.

At eleven we saw someone who must have been the cook leave. There did not seem to be any customers left inside, so we walked quickly over and went in.

When he saw us, the barman's face was a lesson in facial expressions. I caught surprise, fear, and a wish to vanish into thin air.

"Hello there. You scared me: I was just about to close."

We said nothing. In my worst tough-guy manner, I threw the photos of the murdered Marta Merchán onto the bar.

"Adolfo, take a look at these."

That man was as transparent as glass. His features immediately conveyed the emotions he was feeling: panic, horror, pity.

"My God!" he muttered.

Garzón started up his bulldozer. He brought his fist down on the bar with such a thump that two glasses that had not yet been cleared away shook.

"Never mind God or the Holy Spirit! Tell me straight out, just this once! Is this the woman you saw having breakfast with Valdés and the other man in here?"

The barman shrank into himself, as if the punch had land-ed on him rather than the bar. The sergeant returned to the charge, putting on his deep, threatening voice.

"Talk, dammit! That woman got herself killed because you didn't have the balls to swear that you recognized the man in the photo. What's wrong? Has someone threatened you, or offered you money? In case you didn't know, it's a crime!"

The barman stammered:

"No, nobody has said or offered me a thing, I simply said I couldn't be sure . . . "

"I couldn't give a fuck whether you're sure or not. The first time we came, you were sure of the guy's appearance. Then you began to have your doubts. Listen, either you tell us the truth or you're going to be in such hot water you'll have to sell the bar to pay the lawyer's fees!"

We were just within the bounds of being legal, or perhaps we had completely overstepped the mark. We would never have talked like that to Nogales. We were simply taking advan-tage of this poor man's defenselessness. That's life.

He was so scared he could not think straight.

"I've never done anything or been mixed up in anything in my entire life. I only work, have a family; I even pay my park-ing fines. If there's a need to collaborate with the police, I do so. I think you've got the wrong impression about me, based on a misunderstanding."

"Would you give a sworn statement to a magistrate that you recognized this man?"

"Yes, of course, I have no problem with that. I never said I wouldn't make a statement. The facts are the facts."

"And what do you say about the woman?"

"Yes, I think she's the one I saw with them."

"You think?"

"Yes, it was her. That man's wife."

"Are you sure she didn't come with Valdés?"

"No, no, it was the other one she came with: I remember that very well."

"You may be lucky, but don't count on it. If I were you, I'd be ready to make that statement. I'm saying it for your own good."

"Yes, I will. I always intended to make a statement."

If that was not a clear case of police intimidation of a witness, I don't know what was. I left the bar feeling disgusted with myself.

"If that man decides to tell anyone about what has just happened, we'll be skinned alive, Garzón."

"He won't, he was too scared. Besides, he doesn't have the faintest idea of the difference between us and a magistrate. Did you hear what he said about the fines? To him, all law is the law."

"I feel a little ashamed of myself."

"Don't! In the end, it's always me who gets to do the rough stuff."

"That doesn't make me feel any less guilty."

"Don't talk to me about feeling guilty, inspector. Guilt has to be proven—that's why we're getting our hands dirty like this, isn't it?"

"That's police logic, all right. I must remember to apply it."

Garzón arranged for all the police surveillance team to turn their attention to protecting our witness. The way things stood, all we needed was for him to be our next stiff.

We called Coronas and explained our dirty work. He seemed quite happy with it.

"Sir, the witness has said he will make a statement."

"Fine, Petra, fine. What's your next move?"

"First thing tomorrow we interview Nogales, and this time we'll be less polite."

"I'll call you beforehand. I've been promised the autopsy report by eight. It might help."

So we had given reality a little push, and it had responded by offering us a couple of small, unexplained facts. Marta Merchán knew Nogales. Nothing more than that, but all we could expect from the clumsy work we had done. The internal workings of the machine had to be examined using more precise methods.

I went to bed still feeling anxious and uncertain. I was sure the phone would waken me in the middle of the night, but it didn't ring. I slept as soundly as a pair of old shoes in the bottom of a wardrobe. When I woke up, I had the impression I was late for my own funeral, yet there was no need to be alarmed, everything was going along perfectly normally. It was seven in the morning and nobody had even enquired after my health. I could have died and gone to heaven for all anyone cared.

Garzón's calm at breakfast drove these dark thoughts from my mind. He dunked his *churros* into his coffee with the same devotion as a pious Muslim saying his first prayers of the day.

"Did you sleep well?" I asked him.

"Like a log," he confessed. "There's not much in this world that can keep me awake. I always sleep like a baby. How about you?"

"Flat out."

"I don't believe you. You still look tired: I bet you spent the entire night going over the case in your mind. You're not always the most sensible person. At least make sure you get a good breakfast—these *churros* are fabulous. Would you like me to sprinkle a bit more sugar on them?"

I smiled.

"Are you trying to look after me?"

"Lonely people like you and me have to look after each other. You know what, Petra? I think you should get married again."

I laughed so loud that the other early-morning breakfasters all looked in our direction.

"Any idea to whom?"

"No, that's up to you!"

"I'll wait for you to get married first."

"It'll be a long wait."

"Do you only recommend marriage for other people?"

"I'm too old to try anything new."

There we were back talking about personal matters again, and I didn't want to continue in that vein. My cell phone was on the table in front of me. I looked down at it and said:

"Bet you the phone rings in the next minute? The chief inspector said he would call at eight on the dot."

"There's another one who should get married!"

"But he's been married for years! He and his wife have four children. How come you didn't know that?"

"We men don't share that kind of thing."

"But you tell women."

He looked surprised.

"Perhaps you're right."

At one minute to eight, the phone rang. Cool and collected from the minute he opens his eyes, Coronas snapped:

"Petra, I'll give you a summary of the autopsy report on Marta Merchán. Seven stab wounds pretty much at random. Only one of them was mortal. Not a hired killer. The attack took place at eight o'clock in the evening. The forensic expert says there was not much force behind the blows. None of them is any higher than the top of the thorax. His conclusion is that either the killer was a slender, small man or a woman. The victim put up a fight, but was obviously taken by surprise, and so had little time to react. The forensic team found a hair apparently not belonging to Marta Merchán, but it could be from her daughter, the maid, or anyone else. It is in the lab being analyzed. None of the neighbors heard any car pull up, or any other strange noise. No surprise there, because each house is surrounded by a large garden. That is all so far. Did you get all that?"

"Yes. Where are we up to with the interrogation of the daughter and the maid?"

"Moliner will make a start this morning. Raquel Valdés collapsed when she came back from school yesterday and saw what had happened. She spent the night sedated under medical supervision. When do you see Nogales?"

"Not until nine, Chief Inspector."

"Give it all you've got."

"Count on us, sir."

I told the sergeant the news and we set off for the *El Universal* building. Before we went in, I told my colleague:

"For the moment, I'm not going to mention Marta Merchán's death. We'll see if it's a good move to spring it on him at some point in the interview."

"It's up to you, inspector. I've no idea how best to approach this guy."

"We'll put our trust in intuition and improvisation."

"I'm not sure you've eaten enough *churros* for your intuition to be working properly."

"In that case, pay close attention. If it seems to you I'm floundering, I'll pass the interrogation to you. If it's all a question of how many *churros* one has eaten, you should have no problem."

"The editor has not arrived yet," the receptionist told us. "In that case we'll wait for him here," I told her. And that is what we did. For more than an hour we watched the morning activity in a busy newspaper office, with constant phone calls, and employees coming in and using their swipe cards, while visitors were thoroughly checked. When we had become utterly absorbed in all this, Nogales walked in. He saw us at once, and walked over. We stood up, and spoke before he had a chance to say anything.

"Señor Nogales, we've been waiting for you. We want you to come to the station for questioning."

"Am I being arrested?"

"No, but there is a sworn statement concerning you, and we would like to clarify the situation."

"All right, tell me which police station, and I'll get my lawyer to meet us there."

There was a taxi rank right outside the newspaper building, but when he saw that was where we were headed, Nogales said:

"If you don't mind, I prefer to take my own car."

For a moment we instinctively hesitated, but I knew he was not going to escape, and his cell phone was being tapped, so I nodded in agreement.

The interview room was ready for us. Nogales arrived five minutes later, and his lawyer half an hour after that. It was only then that we could start.

"Señor Nogales, behind the mirror is the manager of La Gloria bar. He is certain you are the man whom he saw having breakfast and talking to Ernesto Valdés on many occasions. Today he will give a statement to that effect and sign it."

Nogales's lawyer butted in immediately.

"We will not accept that as a fact until we see the signed statement."

"All right," I said. I got up and left the room. The witness was behind the two-way mirror with several policemen. I said hello, and then asked him point-blank: "Is that the man you saw with Valdés?"

Adolfo was so nervous his face was covered in a thin film of sweat. He nodded.

"Say yes or no."

"Yes, yes, it's him. I'm completely sure of it."

I breathed out heavily. I was mightily relieved.

"Fine, sign the statement here and add your ID details. The magistrate may well ask you to attend a police line-up."

He signed the prepared statement with a trembling, untutored hand.

I took a copy and went back into the interview room. I passed the piece of paper to Nogales, but his lawyer darted forward and intercepted it.

"I want to see the original."

I made no comment and did not allow my impatience to show. I picked up the paper and went back into the adjacent room. A minute later, I was back with the original.

"Here it is."

Garzón was shifting his weight from foot to foot, as if he was uneasy about something. I raised my eyebrows at him to get him to sit down, and he understood at once.

"All right, you can see how things are. What do you have to say in response to this statement?"

"My client will respond officially when he is legally required to do so by a magistrate on a specific charge. Until then, he continues to assert that he has never been to the La Gloria bar, and has never talked there to the deceased señor Valdés, whom he in fact never knew."

I kept my calm and replied.

"Very well. I should like to add, for your information and consideration, that the same witness states that on one occasion he saw señora Marta Merchán, Ernesto Valdés's former wife, go into the bar with him and señor Nogales. He furthermore states that this lady came not with her ex-husband, but with señor Nogales."

For a split second, the lawyer looked completely lost, but he soon recovered and answered like some legal robot:

"Your witness states as much when he saw the lady only on one occasion? He must be a very observant person! Did anyone else see them by any chance?"

I shrugged.

"I can only tell you about the legal evidence I have at my disposal," I said as neutrally as possible.

All of a sudden the lawyer seemed in a hurry to leave.

Nogales sat impassively throughout, not a muscle in his face moving.

"All right, then, if there is nothing more you require from my client, we will withdraw and wait for the appropriate legal order. Good morning to you."

They both got up and headed for the door. The lawyer walked behind his client, as if afraid he might be stabbed in the back. That is precisely what I intended to do. When they were almost at the door, I said in a loud, steady voice:

"Señor Nogales, you might be interested to hear some news. And your lawyer might be interested in learning the seriousness of the events in which you are allegedly implicated."

Their little procession came to a halt, although neither of them turned towards me. I went on in a chatty way:

"Marta Merchán was found yesterday in her Barcelona house. She was dead. Somebody killed her: we don't know who, as yet."

There was a tense silence. I saw Nogales raise a hand to his face. When he turned round, his glasses had been knocked crooked, which somehow destroyed the stern harmony of his features. He stared at me intently, his eyes full of loathing. Then his mouth tightened, and his lips started to tremble. His lawyer could not understand what was going on, and was obviously alarmed. He took his client by the arm and pushed him towards the door.

"Come on, Andres, let's go. This is nothing to do with you. Wait until you get the legal summons."

By now he was almost bundling Nogales out of the door. Still obviously affected, Nogales let himself be dragged away.

Once they were outside, I said to Garzón:

"Did you see that?"

"Yes, it's the first time that bastard showed any reaction, although he hid it well."

"He didn't hide a thing. The lawyer forced him out, but he didn't know where he was."

"It's obvious he knew her, and probably very well. For some reason, Marta Merchán is a link in this chain."

My cell phone began to ring. I picked it up anxiously. It was Moliner.

"Petra? Somebody called Marta Merchán's cell number a couple of minutes ago. They traced the call to Nogales."

"Who had the phone?"

"I was carrying it in my briefcase."

"Did you say anything to him?"

"I didn't answer."

"Maybe I should arrest him at once."

"I think you should. There's something more. Raquel Valdés told me her mother and Nogales had been a couple for the last two years or more."

"You mean they were lovers?"

"Yes."

"What else did she say?"

"Don't press me too hard at the moment. I'm still questioning her and she's very nervous. I can't rush things. As soon as I've finished I'll give you a call."

I didn't need to pass any of this on to the sergeant: he had understood everything.

"Do you think Nogales went back to the newspaper?"

"I'm not sure. But you go and find the magistrate on duty and get him to sign an arrest warrant. Tell him the legal authority in charge of the case in Barcelona is the 11th circuit court."

"What about you?"

"I'll wait for the lying bastard at the newspaper."

"What if he doesn't show up?"

"He will. His lawyer will have told him to carry on as if everything were completely normal."

"He also must have told him not to ring Marta Merchán's cell phone, but he did."

"That's true. Perhaps we've hit on his weak spot."

Garzón rushed off, and so did I, in another direction. As it turned out, there was no need to hurry. Nogales was in his office at *El Universal* and this time he didn't keep me waiting a minute: as soon as his secretary announced me, he had me shown in. He was not on his own. His lawyer was with him, and as soon as he caught sight of me, he went on the offensive:

"Inspector, not twenty minutes ago I told you . . . "

I turned on him almost gleefully.

"You may be interested to know that my colleague Sergeant Garzón is at this moment asking for an arrest warrant for your client."

"On what charge?"

"Raquel Valdés has just made a statement in Barcelona in which she affirms that her mother, Marta Merchán, has been your client's lover for the past two years, and still was when she died."

"What is my client accused of?"

"Murder."

"Whose murder?"

"Of Marta Merchán herself."

"But that's absurd, inspector. My client has not moved from Madrid."

"From the way that Marta Merchán was murdered, we are sure it is the work of a professional killer. The same professional who was hired to kill Ernesto Valdés; the same person who later murdered Higinio Fuentes, a convicted criminal and Barcelona police informer. He also killed Fuentes's wife."

I could see from the look of horror on the lawyer's face that he had no idea of the mess his client was in. To his credit he did not give in, although his doubts were growing more obvious by the minute.

"Inspector, you are going to have to prove all this. You can't simply burst in here and . . . "

At this point Nogales, who until now had been sitting stiffly at his desk, raised his voice.

"Agustín, leave me alone with the inspector, would you?"

When he heard this suggestion from his client, the lawyer grew more desperate still.

"Please, Andres, I don't think it's a good idea. You're not obliged to . . . "

Nogales cut him short.

"Agustín, leave, would you?"

"But this is madness. I'm your lawyer and I think that . . . "

Nogales leapt up and his swivel chair shot across the room until it hit the wall.

"Get out!" he said with a ferocity that curdled my blood.

I don't know how the lawyer responded, because my eyes were still fixed on Nogales. All I heard was the door closing behind him. We were on our own. I had made my play and achieved a result, but this was a dangerous game and I could not afford to make the slightest mistake.

Nogales took off his glasses and left them on the desk. He rubbed his eyes and then looked across at me. Without those lenses he seemed completely different. He looked naked. Yet I understood at once that he was not defeated and that he wasn't going to cave in during my questioning. He was as solid as a rock. I had to continue along the tortuous path I had ventured on. Then he put his glasses back on, and the moment of defenselessness was over. As he was the one in control, he began to question me.

"How can I be sure that Marta Merchán is really dead?"

"Do you seriously think that cops lay traps like they do in novels?"

"Answer me."

I took out my cell phone and passed it to him.

"Dial Marta Merchán's number. You're on a special police line. When you get an answer, give it back to me."

He dialed the number, waited a moment, then handed the phone back. I heard Moliner's voice on the other end.

"Is that you, Petra? At this precise moment I can't . . . "

"Moliner, I want you to tell someone who is here with me what your name and rank is, and which police station you belong to."

"But Petra . . . "

"Just do it."

I gave the phone back to Nogales and watched his face for a reaction. His eyes narrowed slightly, then he nodded.

"Thanks, Moliner, I'll call you later."

I spoke to him calmly.

"Would you like us to phone her house as well? We've left a guard there."

He shook his head. He had taken a heavy blow to the chin, but he soon recovered, even though his voice had lost its authority.

"How was she killed?"

"A shot to the forehead from a nine-millimeter semiautomatic. After that, they cut her jugular: they slit her throat."

This time the blow had him reeling. He sat in deep silence, until he stirred and said:

"Why?"

I realized that he was asking himself the question. He had suddenly broken out into a cold sweat that covered his entire face.

"Tell me who was responsible, Nogales, so we can catch him. There's still time." I was sweating as well, and my heart was beating so hard I could scarcely breathe. "Who killed her so brutally, Andres? You have to tell me. It was the same professional you hired, wasn't it? Because you are Lesgano, aren't you? Where can we find the hit man? Tell me now, time is running out if we want to catch him."

Nogales opened his mouth. I pushed a piece of paper across to him.

"Write it down: name, address . . . "

"I only know his alias and his contact phone number."

"Write them down, quickly!"

He knew them by heart, and wrote them down without hesitating. I picked up the piece of paper. I knew that was the moment to stop. I knew that was my best strategy. I rose theatrically from my chair and almost ran out of the room. I did not look back.

Outside the newspaper office I called for a patrol car immediately, and waited for it to arrive. Five minutes later, Garzón appeared with the arrest warrant. The patrolmen took rather longer. I gave them my orders.

"Go in and arrest Andres Nogales. Try not to make too much fuss. He won't put up a fight, he's the editor-in-chief here. Take him to the Tetuán station; they're expecting him."

At that moment I would have given anything in the world to be able to go to a bar and gulp down a whole glass of beer. But it was not yet time to relax; the race had only just begun.

I looked at Garzón with madly whirling eyes.

"Do you like action and danger?"

"More the first than the second."

"Then I think you're going to have fun."

"Tell me how on earth you got him to confess."

"I used a very personal method. I told him that Marta Merchán was murdered in the same way and with the same weapon as Valdés."

Garzón thought this over for a second.

"You mean you tricked him in a completely underhand way! I hope you went to confession afterwards."

"He gave me the details of the hit man he employed. Do you need any more proof than that?"

"He collapsed, in other words."

"No, he's a cool customer, but he realizes that the noose has tightened around him. He's done for."

"And the death of his lover has hit him hard."

"He wants to know why the hit man killed her, and so he wants us to catch him."

"What's the killer's name?"

"His alias is Toribio. I have his phone number. What do you think we should do?"

"Find out where he lives and go there. But avoid calling him."

We asked the Tetuán station to get his address, and while we were waiting, Garzón suggested we go to a bar. I hesitated, but then agreed to accompany him. I drank my beer with my mind focused on what had happened and what was still to come. All of a sudden, Garzón started waving his arms frantically in front of my face:

"Come back, come back, Inspector! Your brain will explode from thinking so hard!"

"I can't stop thinking. Our case is held together with pins, and I'm afraid it will all fall apart."

"We've got our man."

"We've got a man: but can one person have committed all those murders?"

"It seems as though he didn't kill Marta Merchán, at least."

"That's for sure. I'll call Moliner again; that girl might have said something more."

"Don't do it, Inspector, let time run its course. Interrupting him again could do more harm than good."

"You're right; you're always right."

"That's because I'm a calm, reasonable person."

I smiled indulgently. We'd need his calm, because I was feeling anything but. My jaw was aching from being clenched so tight.

Half an hour later we had the information we required. The telephone number was registered to a woman: Concepción Argentera. We had it tapped at once. The address did not mean much to us. We asked for a patrol car and two plain-clothes policemen as backup. It left before us, and we followed.

It was a nondescript, middle-class neighborhood, as was the apartment block we pulled up in front of. We had to drive around the block three times until we found somewhere to park. Our lead car double-parked about ten meters from the entrance.

We decided not to use the lift, but walked up the stairs. The apartment was on the sixth floor. I could hear Garzón wheezing and saw his chest heaving as he struggled for breath. I came to a halt on the landing.

"How are we going to do this, Sergeant?"

"With your permission, I'll go first."

I nodded.

"Would you like me to go in alone, Inspector?"

"Of course not."

He rang the bell. My stomach was churning as though I had swallowed a snake. From inside we heard a woman's voice.

"Who's there?"

"We want to talk to Toribio," said Garzón.

Complete silence. The door did not open.

"Open up, will you?"

"There's no Toribio here."

"This is the police: open up at once!"

We heard a bolt being drawn back and the childish face of a young woman appeared in the crack. She was wearing a flowery dress, with a bow in her hair. I could tell at once how frightened she was.

"I think you've got the wrong address," she said, almost in a whisper.

Garzón pushed hard against the door and it burst wide open. The terrified girl jumped back into the room. We followed her, and Garzón shut the door behind us. He took her by the arm and pushed her along the corridor. We came out into a living room full of tobacco smoke. The TV was on. Garzón pushed his captive down onto the sofa with a violence that shocked even me.

"Sit down, we're going to have a little talk."

Now that I could see her properly, I noticed her eyes were heavily made-up and her mouth caked in bright red lipstick, making a brutal contrast with her infantile features. Despite her fear, she looked at me with great curiosity.

"Where is he?" shouted the sergeant.

"I live on my own here."

Furious, Garzón started looking all round him. Then he left the room and I could hear him crashing around the rest of the apartment. The girl did not protest, but sat as though she had been pinned to her seat. She stared at the ashtray brimming with cigarette butts and waited. I did not move either, fascinated as I was by the mixture of frailty and vulgarity she demonstrated. High heels, the black bra I could see at her neckline . . . she was like a girl dressed up as a prostitute for a performance.

The sergeant came back carrying an armful of clothes. He shouted:

"Who do all these belong to then? The dog?"

In the jumble of clothes on the bed I could make out men's shirts and trousers. Garzón was still holding a pair of big heavy shoes. He threw them on the floor in front of the girl. His movements were very theatrical: it was a ballet he had rehearsed many times.

"Tell us where he is!"

Terrified, the young girl merely shook her head.

"O.K., we'll wait here then."

Were we really going to wait there as long as it took? I felt the desperate urge to get out. I felt claustrophobic and uncomfortable, but the sergeant seemed determined to carry out his threat. When I glanced across at him as though expecting instructions, he sat opposite the girl as calm as could be. He took out a cigarette and lit it. I looked for a way of staying on top of things without giving in to my nerves. I moved a chair to the window and sat gazing down into the street. For everyone else, this was a normal day. Buses stopped to pick up passengers. A young man was out walking three tiny pedigree dogs. I could hear the noise of children playing in a school playground. I envied ordinary people going to work or coming back from it, going into shops, meeting in a bar. But I had no reason to feel sorry for myself: it had been to avoid all that routine that I had become a policewoman in the first place. To end up in this depressing place opposite a poor young girl in a state of panic. I had a strange identity crisis: who was I, and what was I doing here? Who was that big, threatening man who seemed so determined to psychologically abuse a girl who could have been his daughter? Perhaps to avoid this sense of horror, I dozed off. I leaned on the windowsill and shut my eyes. Some time later, the girl's voice woke me. What had she said? I saw Garzón grasp her arm roughly, and leave the room with her. Shortly afterwards, he came back.

"She went to the bathroom," he said.

"How long are we going to stay here?"

"Until our man appears."

"What if he doesn't?"

"He will. Otherwise, she would have said something. She wouldn't have been able to bear us being here forever. Besides, she's dressed to go out."

"I'm the one who can't bear it."

"Leave, then, I can do this on my own."

"No, I'll stay."

"Keep an eye on her, then. I'm going to have a look around the apartment. I don't reckon I'll find anything, but just in case . . . "

The girl was already behind us, looking as fragile as a piece of crumpled-up paper. She sat down again and looked at me. I offered her a cigarette and lit it for her. All of a sudden the phone on the side table started to ring. She bit her lip.

"Don't answer that!" Garzón shouted again.

The girl started to cry softly. The tears flowed from her eyes down her cheeks and nostrils.

"Can I go and get a handkerchief?" she asked.

Garzón gestured his refusal. The phone went quiet. Two minutes later, it started to ring again. The same scene was repeated three times. Then the calls stopped. It occurred to me that by not answering we were alerting the killer to our presence, but I had to trust Garzón. He seemed very confident about what he was doing. The girl was wiping her face with the tip of her skirt. I fished for a paper handkerchief in my bag and gave it her.

So we waited. And waited. And waited. Garzón picked up the TV remote control and changed channels. He picked a sports program showing highlights from football matches. He became completely absorbed in it. It was incredible: every so often he would protest when a player made a mistake, or grunt with pleasure when somebody scored a goal. Is he doing it for real, or just pretending? I wondered innocently, until he raised his voice and said, as if we were in La Jarra de Oro:

"Of course it was a penalty! Did you see that, Inspector?"

I could have killed him there and then, but since there was a witness and he was in charge, I settled for glaring at him.

Another hour went by. Garzón had got a can of beer from the fridge, and just as I thought I was going completely mad we heard the sound of a key in the lock. The girl stiffened, her eyes came out on stalks. We heard the front door open, but it did not close. A man's voice called out:

"Patricia! Patricia, are you there?"

By the time I realized what was going on Garzón had pulled out his gun and was holding it to the girl's head. He whispered to her:

"Reply. Easy does it!"

The girl tried, but seemed to find it impossible to produce any kind of sound. The sergeant pressed his gun barrel against her cheek.

"Answer, you bitch!"

She uttered a strangled, eerie "Hello!" Nobody answered. Nobody came into the room. Garzón rushed out, shouting.

"Stop! Stop! Police!"

I ran after him. He was hurtling down the staircase, still shouting at a fleeing shadow I could not clearly make out. I heard a shot. I crouched down and peered through the rails of the banister, but the light's timer went off and everything was plunged into darkness.

"Garzón!" I shouted. "Garzón!"

No reply. Cursing to myself, I went back upstairs and into the apartment. I ran over to the window and forced it open. I fired a shot in the air. The two policemen in the patrol car leapt out and ran towards the building entrance. I paused for a second and took a deep breath. The girl was sitting on the floor, head in hands, weeping.

Trying to stay calm, I started back down the stairs. I found Garzón on the second floor. He was bent over, clutching his stomach. I knelt beside him.

"What's wrong, Fermín? Are you hit?"

He raised his sweaty, pained face.

"Don't worry, Inspector, it's only my arm. Don't worry."

I heard doors banging open, and an old woman shrieking:

"Who's there? What's going on?"

From the ground floor came the sound of the voice of one of our colleagues:

"We've got him, Inspector!"

I sank to the floor next to Garzón. I could have killed for a cigarette.

"Why don't you all just shut up for once!" I muttered to myself. Against all expectation and logic, Garzón burst out laughing.

9

Agustín Orensal. I did not want to interrogate him myself: he stank of death like a fox after a kill. A real professional. He denied everything, but he was carrying the semiautomatic used to commit the murders, and he had used the same ammunition. We did not need any further evidence. Apparently, he was part of an organized network of killers, but he refused to talk.

Arm in a sling, Garzón did go to the interrogation, together with two inspectors from Madrid. They must have been tough: by the third day he had confessed. Nogales had hired him to kill Ernesto Valdés. He had killed the informer on his own account, because he had made the mistake of telling him his secrets when he was drunk one night. He told him he had shot Ernesto Valdés and that Valdés knew Rosario Campos. Higinio Fuentes was obviously trying to sell these two nuggets to both me and Moliner, and to charge double. Moliner's intuition had been correct.

Somebody told Orensal that Fuentes's wife had spoken to me. He had to do something. There was no room for slipups in his profession, and he had committed one. It was a mistake he had to rectify. But he swore he had nothing to do with the deaths of Rosario Campos or Marta Merchán. My colleagues had not been able to make him budge on that.

"Aren't you even curious to talk to him?" asked the sergeant.

"Not in the slightest."

"They're going to carry on questioning him to see if they can get anything more out of him, apart from the names of this possible network of killers."

"Did they rough him up?"

Garzón showed me his splendid bandage.

"I'm a war invalid, don't look at me."

"What about the girl we found at the apartment?"

"They lived together. She's just some little slut."

"Does she know anything?"

"She's only spoken to the magistrate. I suppose she knew what line of business her lover was in, but not much more than that."

"He's a lot older than her."

"Love is blind, Petra."

"So they say. What will happen to her?"

Garzón turned towards me, shaking his head with weary resignation.

"You're really a piece of work, aren't you, Inspector? A guy shoots me and nearly sends me into the next world; we don't know how many people he has killed altogether, and what do you do? You worry if we roughed him up a little, you worry about his lover's future . . . Petra, you should have become a social worker, or a nun, even!"

"Don't bug me, Fermín, you know that deep down I really have no feelings."

He stared at me, then laughed.

"The sad thing is, you mean it."

I don't know if I meant it or not, but the truth is that I've never liked hurting a captured animal; perhaps we are all that really, and it's dreadful to know we can't escape. But Nogales was different: I intended to squeeze him out like a mop full of dirty water. We only had evidence that linked the hired killer to two murders, so somebody else must have given in to the absurd temptation of killing.

"How did Nogales find him?"

"One of the investigative journalists on *El Universal* had his details."

"Tell the magistrate that, in case it's a crime."

"They'll claim they have to protect their sources."

"That's not our problem; do it anyway."

"I don't like to insist, but I think you should question the hit man, too."

"Will I get any further than three tough cops willing and able to beat him up?"

"That's going too far."

But my mind and inclination were elsewhere. We had everything prepared to charge our prime suspect: formal indictments, ballistic studies, sworn statements . . . but I was still curious, and was desperate to question him before he appeared in front of the magistrate. I had a right to do so: there were still two unsolved murders—the first and the last, like some sort of parlor game people play to help an empty Sunday afternoon go by.

I had him brought to the police station. His tedious lawyer came with him. I was quite calm, and in no hurry whatsoever. I could afford to let him get nervous: all I needed was for his statement to have holes large enough in it to contain two dead bodies.

I had spoken to Moliner at length, and knew what the situation was in Barcelona. Raquel Valdés had said nothing more of interest. My colleague was convinced she didn't know many details of her mother's life, but she did know Nogales. She knew him and liked him. He had spent weekends in their house, they sometimes spoke on the phone . . . once she had even been to Madrid, where the three of them had enjoyed seeing the sights. All this was important for me to know before I went in to the interrogation. This time I had lots of information and was sure it would not take me long to get at the truth.

The first thing that struck me was Nogales's appearance. A few nights in jail had blurred his features, but he still looked like a distinguished gentleman keeping an appointment. I again noted the way his eyes narrowed behind his glasses: it seemed as though he was curious to talk to me again. He was not agitated or defeated; he did not even look depressed. He even allowed himself a small, wry smile. The lawyer leapt at once on my poor tired mind.

"Inspector, my client has been informed that . . . "

Garzón was shutting the door. I waved a hand to shut the lawyer up. Then I sat down and said to him in a completely relaxed manner:

"You have the right to be present during this interview. You may also indicate to your client, as briefly as possible, whatever you consider the law does not oblige him to answer. You know all of that perfectly well. What perhaps you do not know is that at the first interruption which I consider unnecessary, I intend to have you removed, and you won't come back. You can go and protest to a magistrate, tell your story to the press, or curse me to high heaven, but rest assured that as my name is Petra Delicado I will do it."

He was so surprised he could not even properly show his anger. His jaw dropped, then his mouth shut in a tight, furious line. Garzón enjoyed my outburst so much that he could not keep back a smile. I turned to Nogales.

"Señor Nogales, first, I'm going to outline everything that you cannot possibly deny by now. Then I'm going to ask you some questions, and you are going to answer them. That's all there is to it."

"Just a minute, Inspector. Thanks to my lawyer I have learned that you arrested a man, and that he has confessed. But I have no idea what his confession consisted of."

"What would you like to know?"

"Why did he kill Marta?"

"He swears he didn't. He says he has not left Madrid recently."

"So . . . ?"

"That's being checked, but it seems true."

"How can it be, then, that Marta was killed with the same weapon as Valdés, and in the same way?"

"I don't know. We'll find out."

He raised his voice.

"Is that all the police can do, say they'll 'find out'?"

"Señor Nogales, you may not have noticed, but I'm the one who asks the questions around here."

"I have the right to know . . . "

The lawyer interrupted him.

"Be quiet, Andres, please."

I cast him a sarcastic glance.

"Well said, sir, well said. I think we're all finally beginning to understand what our roles here are."

I was on my best behavior, and felt good. I was proud of the way I had begun this difficult session. Yet things soon got out of hand. I had not calculated the emotional impact the lack of information about what the hit man had said would have on Nogales. He became agitated, got up, and started pacing the room. I should have guessed: he was affected not only by the loss of someone he loved but by his loss of power. Nogales must have been accustomed to finding out what he wanted to know in a matter of seconds. All he needed to do was call in one of his editors. But now being left in the dark was putting him under pressure. He suddenly stopped pacing and confronted me:

"Inspector Delicado, you can go back wherever you came from. Accuse me of whatever you like, but I'm not saying another word. You're keeping vital information from me."

"What right do you have to know any of our information? You're not here as a journalist, you're the accused!"

"I don't care, there's no way I'm going to talk! You're not going to use me like one of those poor wretches you arrest every day."

His lawyer tried to calm him down, taking him by the arm and leading him back to his chair. He was obviously taken aback by his client's attitude. I on the other hand was delighted to see the cracks appearing in his character. I looked at Garzón, who was still standing there stiff and inexpressive. Perhaps it was time to try another unorthodox move.

"Nogales, would you like to do a deal?"

Garzón and the lawyer both nearly jumped out of their skin. Then they looked on tensely as Nogales raised his eyes. He had come back to his senses.

"What kind of a deal?"

The lawyer tried to interrupt, but Nogales silenced him. I still had my eyes fixed on him.

"You tell me everything from the beginning, and I'll tell what the killer confessed to."

"'Confessed' means that . . . ?"

"Listen to me, please. You have nothing to lose. All I'm asking is for you to help me work out the details: all the basic facts are there already, and you will be charged with the murder of Valdés."

"All right," was his only answer.

"Inspector, I have to tell you that . . . " piped up the lawyer.

"And your lawyer has to leave the room—that's part of the deal too," I said.

"He has to go as well," said Nogales, pointing at Garzón.

There was no reason for me to accept this demand, but I did. I did not have to order Garzón to leave: as soon as he saw me thinking about it, he went out without a word. Nogales had to stare more intently and threateningly at his lawyer to get him to do the same. Eventually, he complied, although fear and alarm were clearly etched on his face.

"You can start," Nogales said, giving me permission. I smiled.

"Do you still not get it? You start, Nogales, and remember that, in here, I give the orders."

"I would have confessed all I know anyway, because my statement will go a long way to ward exonerating me."

"I can't wait to hear how."

He pursed his lips at my irony, then went on.

"I met Marta Merchán at a reception in the French Embassy. She had come from Barcelona to represent the firm she worked for. We fell in love almost overnight. I'm almost fifty, and I'm not married. I had never been in love before. But when I found out she was Valdés's ex-wife I was annoyed: that was ideal ammunition for my enemies. We decided to let some time go by before we appeared together in public. During that period, Marta began to get to know me as I really am."

"And how is that?"

"An ambitious man, Inspector: surely you'd noticed that?"

"I suppose I had."

"Marta dreamt up a plan to help me professionally. Her former husband dealt with a lot of dirty gossip. She thought that possibly some information on the private lives of our politicians might be useful to me, so she put me in touch with him."

"And you paid him for each bit of information."

"Whether I used it or not."

"Were the people involved blackmailed?"

He said nothing. I insisted.

"As a last resort, yes."

"Can you explain that?"

"I wanted the information for professional purposes only, but if I decided not to publish it, then Valdés tried to get money out of them. If we used the stuff in the paper, I was the only one who paid him."

"With money from *El Universal*?"

At first he did not reply, but after a prolonged silence, he admitted:

"Yes."

"In any case, you had already got what you wanted, hadn't you? You could control those people who had something to hide. You became all-powerful in the shadows. You had endless possibilities to use your influence: appointments, alliances, even bringing down governments . . . it's been said that the real aim of your journalism was to launch you into politics."

"That goes beyond the scope of this interrogation, and I have no intention of answering it."

"Let's just say it wasn't money you were interested in."

"Basically, my interest in the good of this country. I wanted to stop corrupt politicians from getting into power or perpetuating themselves in it. I've sacrificed many hours and gone to an awful lot of trouble . . . "

I interrupted him without the slightest trace of sympathy:

"As you rightly said before, your possible motives fall outside the scope of this statement."

"You're right. I doubt that the police are interested in anyone's reasons for doing things."

"Go on, please."

"Valdés told me we could put pressure on the Minister of Health. He had been in contact with Rosario Campos and she had even offered to collaborate—for money, of course, someone like her was not interested in ideologies. Then something went wrong between them, and she threatened to expose the whole thing. When he told me, I said he should just offer her more money, but, without a word to me, that idiot, that son of a bitch, decided to get rid of her. I could have died when I heard!"

"How did he get rid of her? Did he hire someone?"

"I've no idea!"

"Think about it, please; it's very important."

"I think an associate of his whom he could trust did it, but he never told me who. It didn't matter; the damage was done. I had to stop Valdés: he was a murderer, a danger, he had set a terrible precedent. I had not planned on killing Valdés, but he was out of control."

"So in order not to become a murderer, you murdered him. You had one of your investigative reporters poke around in the world of professional killers, and when he had gathered enough information you yourself got in touch with one of them and hired him to kill Valdés. The end of your accomplice; he couldn't give the game away anymore, almost everything was dead and buried. All that was left was to find out who the real killer of Rosario Campos had been—for some reason, Valdés had refused to tell you that. That became your sword of Damocles, didn't it? Whoever it was, they didn't say anything. Everything nice and tidy, with only that one loose end. It was a risk you could take."

"The fact that I killed someone who was on a murder spree should stand me in good stead, don't you think?"

"Yes, I bet you will get a medal for bravery. But, tell me, what part did Marta Merchán play in all this?"

"None at all, apart from putting me in contact with her ex-husband at the start."

"I can hardly believe it, my friend! Perhaps you really are an idealist who is blind to the truth."

"What are you insinuating?"

"Has it ever occurred to you that your dear lover was also making money out of the deals you were doing with Valdés?"

"That's not true!"

"We have proof of an agreement between the two of them. Marta Merchán has been making strange investments with sums of money that are far in excess of her earnings."

"I don't believe you."

"I don't care whether you believe me or not. We suspect she

has more money hidden somewhere. I'm convinced it will turn up before too long."

"But that's ridiculous: she would never have done anything like that."

"Let's get this over with, Nogales. I want to keep my side of the bargain, so listen to what I have to say. I think it's unlikely that the hit man we've arrested was the person who killed Marta Merchán."

A worried frown appeared on his face.

"Why?"

"Your man killed our informer and his wife, but there is no evidence linking him to Marta's death."

"What do you mean, no evidence? What about the method, the weapon? You told me . . . "

"I was wrong. Marta Merchán was stabbed to death by someone much smaller than the professional killer. I'm sorry, but I was wrong."

His face flushed. His reddened eyes began to water. He clenched his teeth and threw himself on me. I tried to push him off, but could not get his hands off my neck. Then a policeman and Garzón stormed in. They grabbed hold of him and seized his arms, but it was not until a third officer came in that they managed to prise his fingers from my throat. They held him tight, and I scrambled away from him, but nothing could prevent him spitting in my face and hissing:

"Vixen! You vixen!"

Garzón made as though to punch him with his unharmed hand, but I stopped him:

"Don't be crazy, Fermín! Don't touch him! Take him away!"

The two policemen stood on either side of him. All at once, Nogales's anger subsided. He lost his composure, and almost begged me:

"Inspector, take care of the girl Raquel, she could be

killed too. Anything is possible, I don't understand a thing anymore . . . "

"That's because things have got out of your hands and there's nothing you can do about it. That's one of the risks that a manipulator like you runs."

I told the men to take him away. Garzón had been offering me a paper handkerchief for some time. I was still beside myself, gasping for breath, unable to get back to normal.

"Here, wipe your face, inspector. And come with me."

He led me along the corridor to the women's restroom.

"Go in there and wash your face, Petra. It'll make you feel a lot better."

I did as I was told. I bent over the washbasin with the faucet turned on. I let it splash on my face for a good while. My sense of disgust lessened somewhat. I straightened up. In the mirror I could see a woman with deep wrinkles, a tense face as pale as death, and with red marks all round her throat. It was not me: that deranged face, those eyes bordering on madness could not have anything to do with me. The real me must be somewhere else, attractive, serene, in control.

Garzón and I drank liters of tea as a precaution, before we got started on anything, before our neurons had time to react in any way. Green tea, Russian tea, mint tea . . . the waiter in this specialized tea emporium thought he ought to warn us about the enervating properties of caffeine, but a bit of a kick was what we both needed. After I had made my report to Coronas, I felt as limp as a dish cloth. Instead of congratulating us for our good work, our beloved boss reminded us that the case was still not closed. "All that's left are the loose threads," I ventured in reply. He flew into a rage: "Loose threads, you say? You call two dead bodies a matter of loose threads? Plenty of people would use those loose threads to make a fine patchwork."

"For Rosario Campos, we need only to find the person who pulled the trigger," I argued. I don't remember exactly what he said to that, apart from him asking what our plans were, or more exactly what our fucking plans were. Then, reaching new heights of poor taste and ingratitude, he went on to complain how expensive it was keeping us on in Madrid. I asked him to give us the afternoon to decide on our strategy. We had already spent two hours of it aimlessly drinking tea.

"What are we going to do, Fermín?"

"Are you able to think straight again?"

"Don't worry, I'm fine."

"If your mind isn't right, nothing else will be."

"Since when have you become a guru?"

"I'm doing a class in meditation."

"Well then, meditate on who Valdés could have hired to get rid of the minister's lover."

"Nogales claimed it was one of his associates."

"Who knows: Valdés could have told him anything! He may even have killed her himself."

"I don't think he would have had the guts. No, her killer was someone closer to the street, someone who could find a gun easily and who knew how to use it."

"Does that take us back to the hypothesis of another hired killer?"

"If that's the case, you can kiss him goodbye. We'll never discover who did it."

Garzón asked for an Arab tea, and watched the cardamom pods swirling round. My cell phone rang.

"Petra? Moliner here. The maid confessed when we questioned her last night. She says Merchán paid her to hide money in her house."

"That money has dirtied everyone's hands."

"Money always does."

"Anything else?"

"I'll interrogate Raquel again, but I honestly think she had nothing to do with it."

"Keep an eye on her, won't you? Nogales suggested she might be in danger."

"I'll mention it to the chief, but he's in a bad mood."

"I know."

"For the moment, she's at her aunt's place. I don't think anything will happen to her there."

"That depends on who killed her mother, and why."

"Are you coming back soon? I'd like you to have a look at everything on this end."

"We'll be back soon, Moliner, that's for sure. We don't want to stay in Madrid all our lives. We miss Barcelona, but there are a few things to tie up here."

Garzón was still fascinated by the cardamom pods.

"If you want to know what I think, Inspector . . . "

I knew that opening phrase well. It was the start of Garzón's great reasoning process, of conclusions reached against all the odds, of a pronouncement set to go down in history.

"What I think is, well . . . what I mean to say is that we know an associate of Valdés, perhaps the only one he had. And she knew all about street life."

"Maggy?"

"She was his only close associate. According to her boss at the TV company, Maggy was his right-hand woman, the person he could trust, the one who did everything for him. He put her where she is now."

"But was Maggy so faithful that she killed for him?"

"I don't think she had any other job opportunities besides the one Valdés had given her, apart from going back to waitressing or being a night cleaner. He could have threatened to sack her."

"But Maggy helped us catch Nogales."

"That doesn't prove a thing. Nogales was no threat to her. It may even be that she wanted her boss's murderer caught."

We stared at each other thoughtfully.

"We've got no evidence against her, except for that vague mention of an associate," I said, trying not to build up any false hopes.

"As I see it, Inspector, you're very good at lying; why not try it once more?"

"It's not very ethical to lie."

"No."

"I'm not even sure it will work."

"You could always try."

"What do you think of a trap?"

"Big enough to catch someone?"

"Maggy has never seen Moliner, and she doesn't know that the hit man who killed Valdés has been arrested."

"I see what you're driving at. Wouldn't someone from the station here in Madrid do just as well?"

"Are you crazy, Garzón? It's not the kind of thing we want anyone we don't have the utmost faith in to go anywhere near."

"What if Coronas won't allow him to leave Barcelona?"

"He will accept it. We're doing our best to solve a very complex case, there's no need to make life difficult for each other."

"He may accept, but he'll be in an even worse temper."

"That's all the same to me: bad temper is like love: it knows no bounds be measured."

My line of thinking was correct, but, even so, when it came to describing bad temper, there were several degrees of it: bad temper, extremely bad temper, hellishly bad temper, and the mother of all bad tempers. Coronas's bad temper was way off even this scale. If it had been an earthquake, it would have razed all the buildings in a medium-sized town. What was the exact epicenter of this devastation? I could not have said exactly: bosses tend to get nervous when any parts of their organization escape their direct control. We had obviously not been spending so much time in Madrid because we were so taken with its charm; we could even show positive results that showed we had put the resources spent on us to good use. But that did not matter; we weren't there, we couldn't be seen coming in and out of the Barcelona police station; we weren't lining up with the others by the coffee machine at eleven every morning. This gave us an air of independence, a theoretical possibility of freedom that did not fit in with the chief inspector's idea of a cohesive team.

In addition to that, we did not tell him exactly what we wanted Moliner to do for us in Madrid, promising only that we would fill in the details at a later stage. Coronas came out with all the typical excuses of an angry boss: he was short of staff, of money, we did not keep him informed of our investigation, we shirked work as other people went angling, and, from what he could tell, we sowed dead bodies all around us like others sow cabbages. If Coronas had said anything like that to me the day after I had joined the force, I would have handed in my resignation immediately. But by now I had developed the defenses that come with knowledge, and so I went along with the role assigned to me in this comedy, which was to withstand the onslaught, deny things briefly, repeat the same routine explanation a hundred times, and, when Coronas had finally finished his diatribe, add an "at your service, sir" that I once would have thought the height of embarrassment.

We went to the airport to collect Moliner at three that afternoon. He looked happy. I guessed that getting away from Barcelona meant he was getting away from his personal drama, his lonely house.

"So you want me to pretend to be a hit man. Shit, just like in the good old days! I haven't seen action like this for years."

"I'm afraid it's not what you may be imagining. We're not asking you to infiltrate a network of hired killers or to run any great risks. We simply want you to intimidate a young girl."

"To make her confess?"

"What we really need as evidence is for her to show you the money she got."

"Do I have to do anything?"

"Just be careful. We're not covered in this, and we're not even sure that she's guilty. If you touch her, there could be trouble. You simply need to put the fear of God in her."

He nodded, trying to work out what possibilities there were for him to shine or to enjoy himself. I admired him: he was the complete cop, an all-weather vehicle incapable of thinking without his police badge stuck in his brain. We needed more men like him in the force. He would probably forget about his wife leaving him in no time: his life was full enough with the joys of digging around in death. Was I all that different from him? Perhaps I was on the way to becoming a member of the same family. I was not consciously allowing work to take over my life, and it did not show in my daily behavior; but there was no doubt it was eating away inside me like an insidious cancer.

I became well aware of the danger (or was it good fortune) when my cell phone rang and I heard Amanda's voice greeting me from the far end of the line.

"Petra, since you've gone off and left no indication of when you'll be back, I'm calling to say I'm leaving Barcelona."

I had completely forgotten my sister. I had forgotten her problem, her existence, her call for help and for affection, the clumsy way I had reacted . . . everything. I didn't even know how to hide my surprise.

"Where are you going?"

She laughed briefly.

"I'm going home. I live in Gerona, remember?"

"But why are you going?"

She laughed again.

"Petra, have you got a mirror there? Take a look at yourself, and if your eyes are bulging and your face has a green tinge, that's because you need a good few days' rest."

"Yes, I'm sure you're right, but apart from that, are you going back for any particular reason?"

"I suppose I have to face things. Enrique will leave, and I'll be left with the kids, and at that point I'll have to decide what to do with my life: that's how they put it, isn't it?"

"Something like that. Do you mind if I say I think this is the best way?"

"Is there any other way?"

"Well, facing up to things is always better than . . . "

"Going around fucking cops?"

"I didn't say . . . "

"I know, I know, I'm only joking. And asking you to forgive me. I think I reacted far too hastily, but I was distraught: you know what these marriage break-ups are like."

"I never had much luck with them. But listen, I'm just about to finish my work here in Madrid."

"Case solved?"

"Solved or not, I'm going to have to come back to Barcelona the day after tomorrow at the latest. Why don't you wait a couple of days so that we can say a proper goodbye?"

"Do you think that will give me time to go to bed with another pig?"

"Do me a favor and have a go at the chief inspector. He's been in a foul mood recently."

This time she laughed out loud. It was good to hear it.

"All right, I'll wait for you. But if something goes wrong and you have to stay on, make sure you don't forget me this time."

"I hadn't forgotten you! I was only trying not to interfere."

Of course, she didn't believe me. I had not made my lie sound sufficiently convincing. As it was not trying to get a confession out of a murderer, it was probably not important enough for me. But what was I doing reproaching myself for my attitude: did I really feel that guilty for my lack of family feelings? Perhaps it was true, and I needed a mirror to see the green lines under my eyes, the clear sign that I was on the verge of madness. Did I feel bad for having neglected my sister? Would it not have been worse to neglect a case involving so many terrible deaths? I felt the kind of deep, absurd tiredness that always comes over me when I try to adjust my behavior to someone else's rules. Family and a sense of duty were two things that made me feel nauseous, and yet there I was, up to my neck in them.

I had dinner that evening with my two colleagues. I did not feel like talking, not that this was a problem: the two of them more than made up for it. They were delighted to be able to plan a strategy for tripping Maggy up. To get her to confess. Threatening a twenty-two-year-old girl: what a feat of detection! Though the punky, squalid-looking girl in question could have killed someone. Killed a woman she did not even know in cold blood, for money. By this stage in my police career, I had already reached a clear conclusion: whatever the context, nearly all crimes were committed out of self-interest. Dirty money was the universal motive. It was obvious that to solve a case you did not need the whole gamut of Shakespearean emotion: just one or two would do. Perhaps that was why Nogales's case was original. He had been driven by a desire for power, even if that had been complicated somewhat by the fact that he thought he was doing things for the good of his country. I would have preferred him to become aware of his massive paranoia.

I realized that Moliner and Garzón were looking anxiously at me. I had nodded off. Moliner asked very discreetly:

"Aren't you feeling well, Petra?"

Garzón was much more direct.

"Why don't you go to bed? There's not much more to do here."

"I want to know what your strategy is."

"But that's what we've just been explaining!"

"That's all right, Garzón. I'm sure Inspector Moliner won't mind going over it again."

Moliner smiled. I think he was rather surprised at the particular kind of banter between the sergeant and me. He probably did not approve. He must be more used to a rough-and-ready kind of comradeship, whereas sometimes Garzón and I behaved like a couple of married pensioners. We must have made a funny sight, to say the least.

Moliner briefly outlined what I had already imagined, and what could not really be planned step by step. Moliner would turn up at Maggy's apartment and demand part of the money she had been paid for killing Rosario Campos. Naturally, she would insist she did not know what he was talking about. Then things would get hot, as Moliner liked to put it. He would tell her he was the hit man who had killed Valdés, and that he had been ordered to murder her by Nogales, the man who gave him his instructions. He would remove any of the doubt still tormenting her: before he died, Valdés had confessed to him the name of his murderous accomplice. At that point, Moliner would show what a real professional he was, and say that since his boss was in the slammer, he would save Maggy's life if she gave him more dough.

The key to the plan was her reaction. I was afraid that she might be terrified, and that this would lead Moliner to spice up his performance with a bit of violence. Better for me to heed Garzón's advice and go to bed. Maggy may have been a murderer, but I could not help feeling sorry for her.

"Are you sure you don't need me?" I was really asking for permission to leave.

The sergeant fussed over me like a concerned mother:

"Leave it to the two of us. There's no need for you to worry. As soon as Inspector Moliner is done, we'll call you."

"Even if it's three in the morning?"

"Word of honor."

I struggled up. I would not have stayed for anything in the world. Garzón had given me full permission with that phrase "leave it to the two of us." Of course, we were here in Madrid and there was still some time before the "action" started. As soon as I was out of the restaurant door, my two male colleagues would be off to drink whisky in a topless bar. The poor sergeant really had not had much luck getting me as a work partner. I promised myself I would make it up to him one day by going with him to the most outrageous striptease on offer in the city. As I left the restaurant, I waved to them. Freedom beckoned them.

The hotel receptionist stared at me as though he had seen a ghost. He must have had his reasons. At all costs, I had to avoid looking at myself in a mirror. But we live in a profoundly narcissistic civilization, which meant there were a lot of them to avoid: one in the elevator, another in the corridor, one in the entrance to my room, another in the wardrobe door, and another in the bathroom. But my mind was made up, and I kept my eyes fixed on the floor. As in legends about vampires and the living dead, my image had vanished from the earth.

Moliner and Garzón were feeling protective towards me and let me sleep in. I reproached them for it when they finally came down to breakfast. They paid me absolutely no attention. They were very pleased with themselves: Maggy had confessed almost at once. She had been terrified. She tried to give Moliner two hundred thousand pesetas, and when he grabbed her by the throat and said she must have a lot more than that stashed away, she completely caved in. She didn't have any, she said, she had spent the rest renting a decent place to live. Anyway, there wasn't that much more. That miserable louse Valdés had only given her a million pesetas to shoot Rosario

Campos. What had really turned her into a killer was the promise that she could stay in her job. It was that easy: a banal, everyday motive for murder. Anyone can become a professional killer.

"She said it's very hard to find a proper job these days," Moliner said ironically.

"That's right, to get a decent position you have to kill for it."

The two of them laughed as though they found the whole thing hilarious. Wonderful: thanks to a gross deception and perhaps a bit of violence they neglected to mention, the two tough-guy detectives had succeeded in unmasking the blood-thirsty assassin, a girl, poor devil, who had completely lost her moral bearings.

"What did she say when she found out you were cops?"

"You should have heard her language! She gave me an earful of pure Madrid curses. I could barely understand her. But you can imagine what she said: that all cops are bastards, and so on and so forth. I had to restrain myself not to slap her one."

"Did you?"

"Did I what?"

"Restrain yourself?"

"Petra, believe me, there was no violence."

Garzón spotted an ideal opportunity to indulge in one of the ironic quips he normally has to suppress.

"You may not know it, Inspector Moliner, but Inspector Delicado is a dedicated defender of crooks. You could almost say she's the criminals' Mother Teresa."

I gave him a pitying look.

"Oh, poor Fermín: how much you must suffer having to work with me!"

He halted, but then decided to take it as a joke.

"Not at all, Inspector, most of the time it's not that bad."

I sighed. There was no doubt that Garzón and I formed an odd couple as far as police reality was concerned, and he must have regretted it on more than one occasion. But, as he had just said, it was not always that unpleasant. For example, now we could head back to Barcelona, reoccupy our abandoned apartments, get back to our comfortable routine, and no longer have to sleep in cold hotel rooms. What more could we ask? Indeed, all the tiny threads of optimism I had been gathering up to that point unravelled faced with this question. We could ask for a stamp reading "case closed," that's what! Sadly, nothing seemed to suggest that this was imminent. We still had to resolve Marta Merchán's mysterious death.

10

Amanda's things were ready in the living room. Her plan was to have dinner with me, then head back immediately to her devastated home. As soon as she saw me come in with my bag, she gave a stifled cry and led me to a mirror.

"Take a good look."

I looked. My hair was bedraggled, my face showed how tired I was. The unremarkable black jersey I was wearing was full of creases on the shoulders. I had no make-up on.

"What do you see?"

"I . . . I don't know."

"Do you think the way you look does you proud?"

"Listen, Amanda, when you're on the trail of a murderer you don't have much time to think of anything else."

"You mean it's like being in love?"

"A bit like that, without the magic."

"But you should never let yourself go this way."

"When I'm on a case, I lose all sense of myself. I live in another reality."

"That's sounds good. Could you find a case for me?"

"Your reality isn't that catastrophic."

"I'll tell you once I've faced up to it."

"I think if you tell me all you've been up to in the past few days I'll have more than enough."

She laughed.

"Yes, I'd better tell someone, because I'm sure that a few

months from now, I won't even believe it myself. Listen, do you know what we should be doing? Come on, have a shower and I'll take you to dinner in the best restaurant in town."

I hadn't expected to find my sister in such a festive mood. I was pleased for her. Perhaps she had found the way to deal with her situation.

I took a shower, washed my hair, and then smeared a perfumed cream all over me. Amanda wanted to make up my eyes, but I wouldn't let her. It might have seemed unfriendly of me, but I was not really looking forward to having dinner with her. What I had told her was true: when my mind was focused on a case, I hated any kind of distraction. At that moment, I could think of nothing else apart from the question beating over and over again in my brain: Who killed Marta Merchán, and why?

We had dinner in the Olympic Village. Fish. Amanda observed me, satisfied.

"You look much better now."

"And you look much better than when you first arrived in Barcelona."

"You're right. A few madcap adventures have done me a world of good."

"What are you going to do now?"

"What I can't avoid any longer. I'll go home, talk to Enrique, come to an arrangement with him over custody and money matters, and . . . watch him leave."

"None of that's exactly pleasant, but even so . . . "

"Even so . . . ?"

"Even so, try to stay friends with him. There's not much point making an enemy of him."

"I suppose you're right, but I'm really tempted to send him to hell."

"Funnily enough, in the case I'm on, I've found a couple who stayed friends after they split up."

"The criminal world always sets a good example."

"That world is closer than you might think. As I've discovered, everybody has it in them to become a crook."

"Yes, in the end I may even decide to bump Enrique off. A real crime of passion to make your hair stand on end."

"With all the new friends you've made in the police force, you might get away with it. You'll always find someone to help with a cover-up."

She burst out laughing.

"But seriously, Amanda, tell me what you're going to do."

"You're so funny, Petra! All of a sudden you remember you're my sister, so you say what you think you have to say, but deep down inside you couldn't give a damn."

"I care enough not to want you to become a nymphomaniac, or to do the opposite and bury yourself alive . . . "

"You really don't have to worry! I'll do as my common sense tells me to. But to set your mind at rest, I can tell you that my adventures with policemen are over and done with."

"That's a relief. Was the experience useful?"

"Yes. I felt so humiliated, so put down . . . those few crazy days when I lost all control were like getting my youth back."

I smiled at her, but I was still worried. She still had to face the worst, the moment when he really left her, and she found herself with an empty house and an empty bed . . . I remembered what Moliner told me the day it happened to him.

"Go back to work, Amanda. That could be important for you."

"Don't worry, I will."

Once Amanda had left, I also felt that my apartment was empty, but that was more because I had not been there much in recent days. All there was in the fridge was a sad bit of Camembert and a soggy apple. All the same, I could pour myself a slug of whisky and listen to some Beethoven. Which is what I did before I went to bed, remembering the days when I was civilized, worked on cases with only one murder victim, and did not have to spend my time hopping on and off the air shuttle between Barcelona and Madrid. In bed I was not able to relax either, because those same, unanswered questions kept on at me: Who and why?

Our first interview with Coronas was a disaster. We had not had time to prepare anything, and we arrived at his office clutching armfuls of papers and reports that obviously needed classifying. To add to the confusion, Moliner came along as well. The overall effect was like a police collage, with each of us bringing our own little piece of a painting that seemed to have nothing to do with anybody else's.

Given the bad temper the chief inspector had shown recently, I was afraid he would tell us all to go to hell at any moment. But he didn't. For some mysterious reason, the chief's state of mind had changed dramatically. He was as beatific as a prior, as patient as a kindergarten teacher. He sat there looking relaxed, and did not grow impatient even once while we explained our doubts. He repeated each question as often as was necessary, and waited patiently for our replies. We scrabbled through all the reports we had just printed off our computers and tried to piece together all the different bits of this complicated affair.

He ended by asking:

"So, do you have the faintest idea who killed Marta Merchán?"

This was exactly what I had most feared. Trying to avoid his curses, I ventured:

"Well, sir, the case apparently stops there. All the information is here, there's nothing that has not been explained. It all fits; there are no loose threads left over for this particular murder."

"Have you gone through everything as carefully as possible?"

"We need to sort the information and coordinate it properly," said Moliner.

"O.K., then get on with it. Sort out the statements, classify them, do the same with the interviews, the ballistic and financial reports, the results of all the searches. Put it all together, then shut yourselves in with everything. You seem to be looking for a needle in a haystack. I'm not at all sure you'll find anything that will help."

The three of us filed quietly out of the chief's office, wondering whether Coronas's mood could really have improved that much. I said as much out loud, and Garzón told me:

"The word is that he was having problems at home, but that things have improved now."

"How can people possibly think they know things like that?"

Moliner shrugged fatalistically.

"In here, everybody's secrets come out. You can imagine what's being said about me. Good God, he let his wife abandon him!"

"Do you care?"

He bristled far too much for us to be able to believe his one word answer:

"No."

"It's like we've all got some matrimonial virus," said Garzón.

"You shouldn't have to worry then."

"One of these fine days I'll get married again, Inspector, just to flummox you."

"She won't be flummoxed for long, Garzón. The station gossip would soon fill her in on every detail," Moliner said.

We split up. The work we had to do meant we needed to spend several hours shut up in our own offices.

The fact that the chief inspector had ordered us to do filing at a time when we were engrossed in our investigation might have seemed surprising, but just looking at the piles on my desk made me inclined to agree with him. Apart from all the files and bits of paper, there were the computer print-outs.

And that was only the start of it: once I had gotten all my stuff in order, the three of us had to meet up again to compare notes.

I began my task in low spirits, knowing how hard it is to find any jewel on a path one has trodden so many times before. But feeling that way is a luxury no policeman or woman can allow themselves. However hard one looks, nobody ever really finds a jewel. The most one can hope for is to see the reflection of a jewel in a puddle as one passes by. When a good cop sees that, she stops to take a look. A bad one carries on, hoping to find the treasure.

A good while later, Garzón called me from his office.

"Inspector, how about a coffee in La Jarra de Oro? This office work is getting me down."

"I'll answer with just one word: no. And that goes for you, too."

"I'll remember not to ask you next time!"

"Work, sergeant, work. I've just reached the conclusion that the tiny traces hidden in the undergrowth are what separate good cops from bad ones."

"That sounds like Confucius for the fuzz."

I hung up. I was not sufficiently convinced by my own maxim to go into details.

Two hours later it was me who phoned Garzón.

"I've more or less got everything ready; what about you?"

"I finished an hour ago, but I didn't want to tell you in case you got me to mop the floors so as not to waste time."

"Have you heard anything from Inspector Moliner?"

"I'll call him right now."

Half an hour later, we gathered in the meeting room. All three of us had finished our filing. We began comparing notes and trying to construct an objective view of events. It was hard going: we went off track, doubled back, inched forward. The

sheer amount of information on hand made it even more difficult to see clearly. We made three copies of all the relevant
information and postponed our meeting until the next day. It
was impossible to make any more progress until each of us had
studied one another's material.

Coronas observed all this from a distance, doubtless wondering how much of it was sheer incompetence on our part,
and how much was in fact hard work.

Our meetings went on throughout the next day, without us
being able to reach any conclusion that had not occurred to us
when we first started the investigation. The wonderful jewel
remained stubbornly invisible, and there weren't even any puddles to see reflections in. There was only one tiny loose end left:
had Valdés been paid recently for his "work" with the minister? There was no trace of it in Valdés's accounts, but that was
nothing new. Was whether he had been paid or not relevant?
This affair was what had triggered the whole series of murders,
after all. Did it cast any kind of shadow over the case? That did
not seem likely, but, all the same, it was something that needed
clearing up. I doubted whether my relationship with Nogales,
after the way I had deceived him, was sufficiently friendly for
him to want to tell us whether the minister had paid the blackmail money or not. Would it change anything at all if that
money had existed? Probably not. Did it matter whether
Valdés had kept a little more loot stashed in his sock, or that
Marta Merchán's maid had hidden it in her wardrobe?

Yet by mentioning the matter out loud, I found myself
becoming curious about the answer.

"Where do you think Valdés hid the money before he trans-
ferred it to Switzerland?"

My companions stared at me as if convinced I had been
working so hard that my mental faculties had collapsed.

"Well, either at his own home, or in Marta Merchán's
maid's place, or at his lover's apartment," said Moliner.

"O.K., given the pressure he was under all the time, he would probably have been too scared to keep it in his own place. Somebody could have checked, or brought in a detective. Besides, he didn't have a safe or anything else that was properly secure. It's possible his ex-wife's maid could have stored it. I don't think Pepita Lizarrán would have got mixed up in that kind of thing."

"That's what we thought when we questioned her. There was nothing unusual in her accounts, but we could go and search her apartment if you like," Garzón offered politely.

Moliner was more skeptical.

"Petra," he said after a pause. "Don't you think that finding out who kept the money temporarily is a bit irrelevant? And if any of them did have money stashed away, don't you think they would have gotten rid of it by now?"

I could only agree. He clearly seemed to be saying that he thought I was going off course. Garzón must have picked something of this up, because he looked at me slightly embarrassed, and insisted:

"If it will make you happy, I'll go and see Pepita. It's no trouble."

I was grateful that he was so punctilious in his loyalty to me, but I shook my head.

"No, forget about it. It may well be irrelevant. Although . . . Marta Merchán's murderer did start searching her house. Perhaps he thought the money was there because he didn't know that the maid usually stored it."

Moliner jumped like a jack-in-the-box.

"Look, Petra, I can see you're not convinced, and I think we should question all the suspects again. I'm the only one to have questioned them thus far, and that's too much weight on my shoulders. What would we be doing if this were the start of a case? We'd question everyone involved several times! We have to do the rounds again."

I sighed and wrinkled up my nose in distaste.

"Just hearing you say it's the start of a case gives me goose-flesh."

"Well, if what you've just said is right, that's what it might be. If Marta Merchán let something slip to a friend whom we don't even know about, we're done for. We'd have to start again almost from zero. That really would be another case."

"Do you really think the world is full of murderers?"

"I think that the world all these people moved in was full of individuals who try to live beyond their means. And that can lead to killing for money."

I scratched my head like a vulgar monkey who had never heard about evolution. I didn't have to show my disgust, I was full of it.

"My God! Can I resign and leave it to you? I'll lend you sergeant Garzón here."

"Don't even think it! And don't go to Coronas! I might ask him if Rodríguez can give us a hand."

I nodded several times in exhausted silence.

"All right. Let's start this damned case all over again, dammit!"

"What's the difference between one dead body and another? We still have to investigate."

"I like a bit of a change."

"Don't try to be funny. I'm going to ask for a report on all the people Marta Merchán worked with. Rodríguez and I will look into her friends. We'll investigate her family. While we're doing that, you question the people I talked to on my own. I'll be right back."

He left the office. I looked across at Garzón.

"He's already started giving orders."

Garzón shrugged offhandedly.

"It's all the same to me. I'm like a Hoover that can be lent to a neighbor."

It was only then I realized he had been offended by me offering his assistance to Moliner.

"Don't you see I was being funny? Don't be such a stuffed shirt, Fermín! I thought we were more of a team than that!"

I guess I must have convinced him, because after complaining a thousand times about how long it had been since he'd had even a cup of coffee, he offered to buy me one, and we left the station. Just because Moliner seemed anxious to speed up the investigation into the "new case" did not mean we had to follow his orders as if he were Napoleon. This supposed new case could wait another half hour.

And it was not merely because I was being frivolous or lazy that I refused to see Marta Merchán's death as a new case. Deep down I was convinced it was directly linked to Valdés. What was all that if not a cheap movie where everybody settled their scores with a beating or a bullet to the heart? We might all agree that money often led to murder, but that did not mean that in Wall Street people had to wade to work through rivers of blood. All of which meant that I approached the work at hand in a different light from my colleague Moliner.

Of course, Coronas approved our plan with his usual stream of invective. He had no alternative. Yet, if after a sufficient period of time we had got no results, he said he would take Moliner or me off the case and separate the two investigations.

Since Garzón and I had to interview everyone again, we decided to start with Raquel Valdés. We needed a court order to be able to see her. She was a minor, and under the protection of the court. We were denied permission to bring her to the station, so we had to travel to the house of her aunt, Marta's elder sister.

The reception she gave us was icy. Margarita Merchán came out with the long list of recommendations and protests we had been expecting: we were to treat the girl gently, she had just been through a very difficult, traumatic experience, we shouldn't stir up images that would upset her, or disturb her with too emotive questions. We agreed to everything with the same cold politeness as she showed us. But our soft approach simply meant that she started to explain the conditions for our interview all over again. As soon as she began, I interrupted her:

"Tell me, what are you most interested in, saving your niece from a possible trauma, or discovering who killed your sister?"

She was a refined, well-brought up lady and such a direct question left her nonplussed. But when she answered, her voice was clear and composed.

"Inspector Delicado, I never approved of the way my sister lived, nor of her unfortunate marriage, which was what possibly led to her death. That girl is the only good thing Marta ever did, and I will not allow her to be ruined."

After this warning, she informed us that a psychologist appointed by the Board of Minors would sit in on our interview, which was to take place in the living room. Great. Depending on what the psychologist was like, this might turn into play school. At least one thing was clear, though: the murdered woman's sister agreed with me in thinking that whoever killed her came from Valdés's world, so there was no point in looking into her work connections.

The psychologist who sat in on Raquel's interview was a young man who looked like a 1950s crooner. He did not open his mouth once. We could have done Raquel irreparable damage and he would not even have noticed. Not that it mattered: Raquel did not have much to say either. She knew nothing, and if there was something on her mind she had plainly decided to forget it. She constantly referred us back to the conversation she had had with Moliner. I decided it was useless, and to call it a day.

So there we were, empty-handed again, and with little urge to continue. We both still felt weary from all the time we had spent traveling between Barcelona and Madrid, and from the stresses of a case so full of complications and suspects.

Garzón said:

"O.K., all that's left is for us to talk to the maid. If she's as talkative as the girl, that shouldn't take too long!"

"Has she been arrested?"

"No, but the magistrate ruled that she is involved in the case and she will have to make a sworn statement."

I gave a deep sigh.

"Have you lost interest in who killed Marta Merchán?"

"What I've lost is the strength to go on, sergeant. I need a holiday! But don't let anyone say we don't do our duty! Ever onwards! I think the photos of the dead body could help us with the maid. They'll have a big impact on her."

"Let's go and get the file back at the station then. The only problem is . . . "

"Is what?"

"Is that Coronas might see us there and think we're jerking off again."

"Jerking off! Who on earth suspects us of doing that? You have to believe in yourself, Fermín!"

"Yes, but what's going to happen is that Moliner and Rodríguez will get all the credit for the case if they come up with the answer before us."

"Would you like me to tell you just how much I care about that?"

"Yes, I know, Inspector, I know. You couldn't give a damn about it, could you?"

"Exactly right, my friend. What about you, do you care?"

"Well . . . I . . . well, we've put an awful lot of work into this case, too much to be screwed over . . . "

"Keep calm, Fermín! What do the glories of this world matter to good cops like us?"

He raised his eyebrows indignantly and gave a resigned sigh.

The photos our people had taken of Marta Merchán's body were really shocking. The blood stood out in stark contrast against the white skin of that beautiful woman. It was particularly striking to see that all the blows were concentrated around the chest and neck. All the rest of her body was intact. In death, she did not seem to be in pain, but in a deep sleep. Her fists were clenched and, as she had fallen, she had hit her forehead, which was covered in a purple bruise. I studied her at length.

"An absurd death," my colleague ruled.

"All deaths are. But we have to assume she had done something which provoked her murder. What can that have been?"

We both stood silently for some time.

"Perhaps she wanted to talk, to tell the truth?"

I shook my head, unconvinced.

"Shall we go?"

"Yes, before the chief inspector sees us. What about the photos?"

"Take them with you. I don't care whether they're supposed to stay in the station or not."

Encarnación Bermúdez, the maid and cashier, was not surprised to see two cops visiting her again. She knew very well that her freedom was only conditional. Not that she received us with open arms. On the contrary, her first look at us would have stripped a tree of its leaves.

I have to say that in the end I could excuse her attitude. The life she led did not exactly predispose anyone to politeness. Her apartment was dark, cold, tiny, and claustrophobic. We knew something about her life from our files. Living alone and working more than ten hours every day, all she needed was the threat of a prison sentence hanging over her.

In fact, I did not know how to approach her: whether to

start off aggressively or to try the soft touch. If it had been up to me, I would have left as soon as I had come.

"Encarnación, we need your help."

"I'm the one who needs help, Inspector."

"That might be possible," I said, amazed at my own lack of resolve.

She showed us into a small sitting room cluttered with furniture. We could hear heavy rock music booming out from one of the bedrooms at full blast. She shut the door to reduce the noise, and we all sat on a plastic three-piece suite.

"How can you help me?"

"I can make a report stating that you gave us your full cooperation, and make sure the magistrate gets to see it."

"And that would help?"

"More than if we didn't do it."

She stared forlornly down at her hands in her lap.

"The best for me would be to never have been born," she said with the melodramatic emphasis that simple people use to express their despair.

"Encarnación, we'd like to know what happened with a final amount of money that Marta Merchán received. Did she bring it to you to keep for her?"

This upset her. She raised her hands in entreaty.

"Your colleagues wouldn't believe me and searched the whole place looking for money. They turned everything upside down, but couldn't find anything. What more could you possibly do?"

"Nothing, don't worry. We believe what you're saying. What we need to know is whether Marta talked about bringing you another sum of money to keep—if she mentioned it in any way."

At first she did not respond, and kept her eyes on her lap. Finally she almost whispered:

"If I say she did, you'll immediately suspect me of hiding it. Do you want me to bring more trouble on my own head?"

"Yes, Encarnación, that's exactly what we want, because someone who brings trouble on themselves shows she is not lying. Finding out if she said she would bring you more money is crucial to discovering who killed her."

"All right, yes: that is what happened. A few days before she died, my mistress told me she would be coming to see me again. That was what she always said when she was going to bring money. But I swear that she never brought it."

"Did she say there was some delay or problem, that she would be bringing it later?"

"She didn't say a thing, and I didn't ask her, either. Usually she would say she was coming, and then a few days later tell me, 'Don't go out this evening, I'll be dropping round.' She would also ask me not to have anyone at home, not even my children. This last time she just said she would be coming, and nothing more. I assumed she would turn up at some point, but didn't think too much about it. And she never mentioned it again."

"Perhaps because she was killed?"

"I've no idea."

She burst into tears. She sobbed:

"Sometimes I wake up in the middle of the night and think all this has been a bad dream, that my mistress is still alive."

"I'm afraid that's not the case, Encarnación."

"Will you put in a good word for me with the magistrate?"

"I promise I will."

"I don't think it will help. They'll send me to jail and put my youngest kids in an institution. And all because I wanted to earn a bit more money."

Out in the street, which was as cramped and dark as her apartment, I said to Garzón:

"We didn't even need to show her the photos."

"Do you think she's telling the truth?"

"I would bet on it. She's a trustworthy person, otherwise Marta Merchán would not have used her."

"But someone who's really trustworthy would have thought that money was illegal and told the police."

I gave him a scornful look.

"What percentage of the public do you think would react in that way?"

He was equally scornful in his reply.

"I don't know. What do you reckon? Around eighty per cent would react like that?"

"Don't you have any faith in the Spanish people, Fermín? Why didn't you say one hundred per cent?"

"That seems a bit exaggerated."

"Perhaps."

"Well, Inspector, you got what you wanted. There was another bundle of money somewhere. What happened to it?"

"It may never have reached Marta Merchán, or even Valdés. Or the maid could have been lying—or it may even still be in Marta Merchán's house. How about us paying another visit there?"

"But the villa has already been searched!" Garzón protested.

I did not care; above all, I wanted to avoid bumping into Moliner and Rodríguez after what had probably been a fruitless day for them.

The first problem we had was that the villa had been sealed off as a crime scene. We had to talk to Coronas, even though this was precisely what the sergeant wanted to avoid. The chief seemed to have run out of insults to heap on us. I argued that we were going over all the ground that Moliner had covered in our absence. Coronas was inclined to send us to hell, but he restrained himself. He talked to the magistrate in charge of the murder enquiry, who authorized us to visit the villa, but would not allow another search. Which meant we had been warned that nothing could be taken from there, or added to the files on the case without the magistrate examining it on the spot.

"That's fine," I said, staring him wearily in the face. Then I added: "Thank you, sir: you really know how to handle these magistrates."

I think that when he saw how exhausted and at the end of my tether I was, Coronas took pity on me for the first time in all this messy business. Garzón tugged at my sleeve to get us out of there before he changed his mind and came down on us like a ton of bricks.

It had gotten very late, and I was exhausted. I fell asleep in the car, my head lolling against the backrest. My companion saw how deep in slumber I was and didn't wake me until we reached San Cugat. I opened my eyes in complete darkness and did not recognize the gardens of the estate where we had pulled up.

"Would you like me to go in on my own, inspector? If it's only to have a look round, you could continue your nap."

"No thanks, we'll both go in."

The damp got right inside me even in the time it took us to reach Marta Merchán's front door. The sound of music came from somewhere in the vicinity. We went through a small, unlit garden and stopped at the tapes our colleagues had placed around the house. Garzón pushed his way through, but then had difficulty finding the keys. When we finally got in, he had another battle looking for the light switch. As we went through the rooms, he turned on all the lights: the living room emerged from the darkness, and the corridors beyond it. A faintly sweet, indefinable smell hung in the air.

I was taken aback by the crime scene. By the blood stains on the armchair and the carpet, by the layer of dust quietly covering everything. A standard lamp still lay across the sofa. The disorder caused by the murderer's search also hung suspended in time: magazines lying open, empty envelopes . . .

Garzón was prowling round the room as stealthily as a cat. We did not speak to each other. It was as if the spirit of the dead woman were still in the air, and also, perhaps, that of her killer. A book lay on the centre table, with a bookmark somewhere in the middle of its pages. It was an American thriller. Marta never got to find out who the murderer was. It was plain to see that Marta Merchán lived a refined, sophisticated life. For her, safeguarding this way of life was her highest priority; even more important than the peace of mind that came from not getting mixed up in any shady business.

I was curious about the rest of the house.

"What's upstairs?" I asked Garzón.

"The bedrooms, but Moliner's report says there's nothing to suggest the murderer even went up there. He only went into the study."

I said nothing, but climbed the staircase, leaving the sergeant investigating a concertina file on the study desk. The staircase walls were lined with paintings made from dried flowers.

I came to a halt on the landing, which gave onto three closed doors. I went into the nearest, and switched the light on. This was Raquel Valdés's bedroom: it was full of books, teenage posters, a few dolls . . . a child's world she would have to bid goodbye to. All of a sudden I really wanted to see Marta Merchán's bedroom. I was embarrassed to realize it was simply out of curiosity. I turned round and went into the second bedroom. I switched on the light, and a big double bed showed me I was in the right room. I took everything in at a rapid glance. Then I looked again more closely, trying to convince myself that what I was seeing was true. I was so excited I found it impossible to speak. Slowly, trying hard to control my feelings, I went to the top of the stairs and called down:

"Come up here at once, Fermín!"

In two seconds flat the sergeant was beside me, puffing and panting, gun in hand.

"What's wrong?"

"Take a look at this," I said, gesturing towards the room.

"What am I supposed to be looking at?" he said, totally bemused.

I glided around the furniture as if this were a dance number I had previously rehearsed, touching the tassels that hung everywhere: on the edge of the bed, the reading chair, the dressing table, the drapes, the cushions on the bedspread.

"Don't you see, Fermín? All these dreadful cinnamon-colored tassels everywhere. I bet that Marta Merchán changed her bedroom décor over the past year. Did you discover any bills like that in her accounts?"

"I'm not sure, I don't think I even paid any attention to it."

We went quickly downstairs, and I began to search through the household files the sergeant had been looking through earlier. All the bills began to pile up on the floor. I finally came across one that interested me.

"Look at this: a bill for drapes. Let's see the date: six months ago! Do you realize what this means?" I asked, overjoyed by my discovery. My colleague was still staring at me slack-jawed and with an empty expression in his eyes. I put both my hands on his shoulders and said, proud of my perspicacity: "I think that the *entente cordiale* between this divorced couple was much closer than we thought, sergeant! In fact, I think they were a real couple!"

We had to think clearly and carefully: we would pay dearly for any false move. There was no way we could rush off to meet Pepita Lizarrán and use the tassels as evidence to arrest her. If I did anything of the kind, Coronas would eat me alive, and dip his bread in the sauce. We had to work out a plan—and that did not include informing Moliner of something we were almost sure of. In all honesty, I saw no point in going to an experienced cop like him and telling him the history of the decorative arts. And if I had my doubts on that score, the sergeant was absolutely adamant. He still thought the whole business of the tassels was a huge risk for us. However much I insisted how right I had been last time, Garzón was horrified to think we were going to confront Pepita Lizarrán with nothing more than a few bundles of threads in our hands. I explained patiently why everything fit perfectly, and in the end I either convinced or exhausted him, because he covered his face in his hands and said:

"All right, inspector, all right. Let's start from this theory of yours and work out a plan if that is at all possible. But please, whatever you do, don't breathe a word about tassels unless it's absolutely unavoidable."

I suppose I understood his position: men have a scale of values that always tries to exclude being made to seem ridiculous, even if only in appearance. So I said nothing to Coronas about tassels, merely informing him about my well-founded suspicions that Pepita Lizarrán had decorated Marta Merchán's bedroom. Coronas was about to question the importance of the discovery, but I cut him short:

"If she decorated it, that means they knew each other, sir, and that's something we never counted on. And if they knew each other, she could have killed her. The physical profile of the murderer coincides with that of Pepita Lizarrán."

"What would her motive been?"

"The money. She thought the last bribe paid to Valdés belonged to her. She must have known how the whole network ran, even though she denied it."

To arrest Pepita Lizarrán on the basis of her taste in décor was bordering on a legal impossibility, but Garzón and I decided to go to her home and question her anyway. Her hands were trembling as she denied all our accusations, but nobody can be charged because of the impression they give while being questioned. A much more definite clue came from the fact that she steadfastly refused to have a DNA test carried out. This was enough for the magistrate to take our arguments seriously. Finally, with this threat hanging over her, she agreed to the medical test. Perhaps she thought it was a trap to get her to confess.

A few days later, the DNA sample clearly showed that the hair found with blood on it in Marta Merchán's house was one of hers. It was only then, when she was convinced we were not trying to set her another trap, that she laconically confessed to having killed Marta Merchán.

Like everything else seen in hindsight, her guilt now seemed obvious. It was the only piece in the huge mosaic we had completely overlooked. It never crossed any of our minds that her initial statement was a lie. Why would we have doubted that a man would seek to protect the woman he loved from all the shady deals he was involved in? Why should it even occur to us that his new love would know his ex-wife? How could we imagine that ex-wives and new lovers would be such great friends? After all, this was Spain, and we were not used to such levels of promiscuity. Pepita Lizarrán had met Marta Merchán several times, and knew what her role was in the criminal chain. There was only one little thing she did not know: where she hid the ill-gotten gains. That was what cost Marta Merchán her life, even though Lizarrán stressed in her declaration that she had killed Marta because she had always thought she was involved in Valdés's death, that it was she who had led him astray, that she hated her and would never forgive any of those who had taken the only man she had ever loved from her.

"It's possible she killed her more out of revenge than self-interest," the sergeant conceded. "Apparently she and Valdés were deeply in love."

"That is of absolutely no consequence. The fact is that, trying to get her hands on the last wad of money that Nogales had paid Marta Merchán, this Lizarrán killed her," Coronas said brutally.

"Loving the same man did not make them enemies, but money did."

"Do you mind leaving your soap-opera philosophy out of this, Garzón?"

"I'm sorry, I thought it was quite a good description."

I had to suppress a desire to burst out laughing. The chief had not finished.

"Well, it isn't. Forget about your billing and cooing, this case has been a nightmare, what with all its ramifications, so many dead bodies, all those suspects, and political implications at the highest levels that are still giving me a headache . . . "

"But everything has been wrapped up, chief . . . " I said.

"So what do you want? You want me to go down on my knees and say how much I admire you?"

"I don't think there's any need to be so foul to us."

This seemed to have the desired effect. The chief inspector backpedalled.

"I'm sorry, I admit I do tend to shout. It's just that I've got so much work and the stress is terrible. Truth is, both you two and Inspector Moliner have done a great job."

"Thanks," said the sergeant.

"Oh, and by the way, Petra, I'd like you to tell me how on earth you came to suspect that Lizarrán woman and what all the decoration stuff was about."

I glanced at Garzón. Before I could mention the tassels, he butted in:

"Female intuition, Chief."

"One more thing, Chief Inspector. I'm afraid we were obliged to make a small deal with Encarnación, Marta Merchán's maid. It would be a real help if you could talk to the magistrate and tell him that she cooperated fully with us. Basically, she's just an unfortunate woman."

"I knew it! Petra Delicado, sometimes I think you're only happy if you get me into hot water!"

"Talking of hot water, don't forget you have the whole of the press outside, ready to hang on your every word."

Coronas looked as though he would like to throttle me with his bare hands, while next to me Garzón held his breath. Then the chief inspector walked off, muttering curses he must have thought were too obscene for a woman to hear. Relieved, Garzón let out his breath.

"Thank God for that! I couldn't have stood to listen to you tell him about the tassels! Just imagine how he might have reacted. The chief inspector is always very patient with you, but one of these days he's going to blow his top."

"I hope you'll be on my side when he does."

"I'll think about it."

"I'm truly grateful."

The sergeant left me in a hurry. As I learned later on, this was to try to prevent Moliner taking all the credit for our investigation. Garzón felt I was not competitive enough in this area, and perhaps he was right. Fighting over who wins the laurels for a case you have given your all to has always seemed to me a step too far. I don't think I'm being humble, simply practical.

As for me, I went straight to the hairdresser's, not even pausing to look at myself in any mirror. What was the point? I already knew I looked ghastly, and had no desire to check just how ghastly.

I really enjoyed my time in the beauty salon. I let myself go. When the shampoo girl asked if I'd like a head massage, I told her I'd prefer three. It was pure pleasure. I let her skilled hands explore my scalp, and could feel the effect of her rhythmic movements sinking deep into my brain. I forgot all about Valdés, Rosario Campos, the minister, Marta Merchán, about all the dead people who had once been on this earth. And I felt at peace, because when you feel comfortable in your own skin, what do you care about what is happening beyond you? That has always been the guiding principle behind the search for beauty and personal satisfaction: the desire to be pleased with yourself, the need to feel you are worth it. "Would you like a magazine?" the girl asked. "No!" I replied, perhaps a little more vigorously than required. She shrugged and said: "Good for you, they're full of rubbish anyway."

They made me up, did my eyes for me, gave me a manicure, and then put my hands in a steam bath. With every passing minute I felt better, more sure of myself. But the hairdresser's was only my first stop.

When I came out of there, I visited a couple of boutiques. And bought things—determinedly, delightedly: a sweater, skirt, black stockings, a pair of high-heeled shoes. They were all elegant, impressive additions to my wardrobe which I was sure I would look good in. I eventually arrived home, threw my packages on the sofa, and ran a bath. I lay back in it for a while, then anointed myself with body cream and sprayed on an expensive perfume. Then I got dressed. I was admiring the sheer stockings up against the light when the phone rang. It was Moliner.

"Petra, we didn't even have a moment to talk."

"If you've called about work, it's better that way. I'm desperately trying to get away from it."

"Oh, I'm sorry, I'll call you back tomorrow. On the other hand, if you're trying to get away . . . I'm on my own this evening. How about going out for dinner?"

"Being on your own is never a bad thing, Moliner. I can tell you from experience."

"I suppose we men aren't very good at solitude."

"Believe me, it's something even you can learn!"

He understood. To go out with him that evening would have been stupid of me. It was so nice just to feel pampered! It increased my self-confidence and the possibility of saying no without agonizing over it. I poured myself a whisky to celebrate.

The last touch was to put on my new shoes. Black velvet: elegant, comfortable, lovely. They helped lift me just that necessary little bit out of the ordinary.

When I was satisfied with my appearance, I sat down and picked up the phone.

"Amanda?"

"Petra, I thought you were never going to call me again."

"Why?"

"Because of all the trouble I gave you."

"Forget it! Oh, by the way, we've solved the case!"

"Good, then you'll be able to rest."

"Not for long, I'm sure. But I'd like you to know something: I spent the entire afternoon in a beauty salon, then I went out and bought some new clothes. I feel like a new woman."

"This is new for you! Are you going out to dinner?"

"What do you think? I don't know whether to go out alone or to ask someone along, but I'm determined to go."

"I'm so pleased you're in such a good mood."

"And what kind of mood are you in?"

At that, my sister fell silent. After a while, she said:

"I'm fine. Enrique has left. It was hard seeing him take all his things, but . . . well, I'll get over it. I'm looking for a job."

"That's a great idea."

"I only hope the work isn't as absorbing as yours."

"Of course it won't be, it'll be something normal! Police work isn't normal, it's an abomination, it's . . . you've seen what it's like."

"I didn't think some cops were all that bad."

"I know . . . don't remind me!"

Amanda burst out laughing. I was glad of that—it was the best thing she could do. Why cloud our lives with tragedy when in the end everything becomes routine?

My next phone call was to Fermín Garzón. As I had thought, he was still at the police station.

"What on earth are you still doing in the office? It's almost nine o'clock!"

"Still working, of course! Trying to write a final report on the case before Inspector Moliner puts his own slant on it."

"Don't worry so much, Fermín: it's our case, even if we have to lynch the guilty ourselves to prove it."

"Now there's a good idea! Why did you call?"

"To invite you to dinner. What do you say?"

"Yes, of course, what else can I say?"

"If it's such a sacrifice . . . "

"As you know, making a sacrifice now and then is good for the character, it strengthens the spirit, helps one be a better person."

"In that case, make the sacrifice, you obviously need it."

I could hear him trying to stifle a husky laugh.

"I'll pick you up in half an hour," I said, and hung up.

So had I gone to all this trouble just to take out a work colleague I would never in a million years feel attracted to? No. I had needed to dress up so elegantly in order to remove the last traces of crime, death, suspicion and guilt. And I needed to smell good.

The fact of dining with the sergeant was no coincidence. Both of us lived alone, and we had known each other a long while. We had, however, developed the civilized habit of keeping our own lives to ourselves. Doubtless that evening we were going to talk about how complicated human relationships are. We would comment on divorced couples who get together to collaborate, lovers and crimes of passion, abandoned husbands, desperate housewives on the path to recovery. With all this to talk about, we would probably not come to any conclusions, apart from the fact that there are more and more lonely people in the world. Of course, neither the sergeant nor I were forced to face loneliness like a lot of people are. Not everyone could become a member of our select club. No way! To do that you need a certain background, a good dose of *savoir faire*, even a bit of *numerus clausus*. Not everybody has what it takes to be one of the lonely.

Anyway, in the end, it was an entertaining evening. Garzón praised my beauty, and I stressed how impressed I was by his sense of duty. On his recommendation, we ended up eating ham off the bone in a bar down by the port in Barceloneta. He said that if he had met anyone from the jet-set crowd the food would have disagreed with him, but that there was no risk of that in a dive like this. Even so, the wine was good, the people in the bar unassuming, and the ham was delicious. We had solved a case, and I had saved my skin. It was a mild night, and the Mediterranean was right outside. I could smell the attractive smell of the perfume on my wrists mixed with the aroma of wine and coffee. Who could ask for anything more?

Barcelona, November 19, 1999

ABOUT THE AUTHOR

Alicia Giménez-Bartlett was born in Almansa, Spain, in 1951 and has lived in Barcelona since 1975. After the enormous success of her first novels, she decided to leave her work as a teacher of Spanish literature to dedicate herself full-time to writing. In 1997, she was awarded the Feminino Lumen prize for the best female writer in Spain. She subsequently launched her Petra Delicado series (*Dog Day*, *Prime Time Suspect*), whose success rapidly made her one of Spain's most popular and best-loved crime writers.

About Europa Editions

"To insist that if work is good, no matter what, people will read it? Crazy! But perhaps that's why I like Europa . . . They believe in what they are doing above everything. Viva Europa Editions!"
—ALICE SEBOLD, author of *The Lovely Bones*

"A new and, on first evidence, excellent source for European fiction for English-speaking readers."—JANET MASLIN, *The New York Times*

"Europa Editions has its first indie bestseller, Elena Ferrante's *The Days of Abandonment*."—*Publishers Weekly*

"We certainly like what we've seen so far."—*The Complete Review*

"A distinctly different brand of literary pleasure, thoughtfulness and, yes, even entertainment."—*The Ruminator*

"You could consider Europa Editions, the sprightly new publishing venture [...] based in New York, as a kind of book club for Americans who thirst after exciting foreign fiction."—*LA Weekly*

"Europa Editions invites English-speaking readers to 'experience all the color, the exuberance, the violence, the sounds and smells of the Mediterranean,' with an intriguing selection of the crème de la crème of continental noir."—*Murder by the Bye*

"Readers with a taste—even a need—for an occasional inky cup of bitter honesty should lap up *The Goodbye Kiss* . . . the first book of Carlotto's to be published in the United States by the increasingly impressive new Europa Editions."—*Chicago Tribune*

www.europaeditions.com

www.europaeditions.com

The Days of Abandonment
Elena Ferrante
Fiction - 192 pp - $14.95 - isbn 978-1-933372-00-6

"Stunning . . . The raging, torrential voice of the author is something rare."—*The New York Times*

"I could not put this novel down. Elena Ferrante will blow you away."
—ALICE SEBOLD, author of *The Lovely Bones*

The gripping story of a woman's descent into devastating emptiness after being abandoned by her husband with two young children to care for.

www.europaeditions.com

Troubling Love
Elena Ferrante
Fiction - 144 pp - $14.95 - isbn 978-1-933372-16-7

"In tactile, beautifully restrained prose, Ferrante makes the domestic violence that tore [the protagonist's] household apart evident."—*Publishers Weekly*

"Ferrante has written the 'Great Neapolitan Novel.'"
—*Il Corriere della Sera*

Delia's voyage of discovery through the chaotic streets and claustrophobic sitting rooms of contemporary Naples in search of the truth about her mother's untimely death.

www.europaeditions.com

Cooking with Fernet Branca
James Hamilton-Paterson
Fiction - 288 pp - $14.95 - isbn 978-1-933372-01-3

"Provokes the sort of indecorous involuntary laughter that has more in common with sneezing than chuckling. Imagine a British John Waters crossed with David Sedaris."—*The New York Times*

Gerald Samper has his own private Tuscan hilltop where he wiles away his time working as a ghostwriter for celebrities and inventing wholly original culinary concoctions. His idyll is shattered by the arrival of Marta. A series of hilarious misunderstandings brings this odd couple into ever-closer proximity.

www.europaeditions.com

Old Filth
Jane Gardam
Fiction - 256 pp - $14.95 - isbn 978-1-933372-13-6

"This remarkable novel [...] will bring immense pleasure to readers who treasure fiction that is intelligent, witty, sophisticated and— a quality encountered all too rarely in contemporary culture— adult."—*The Washington Post*

The engrossing and moving account of the life of Sir Edward Feathers, from birth in colonial Malaya, to Wales, where he is sent as a "Raj orphan," to Oxford, his career and marriage, parallels much of the twentieth century's dramatic history.

www.europaeditions.com

Total Chaos
Jean-Claude Izzo
Fiction/Noir - 256 pp - $14.95 - isbn 978-1-933372-04-4

"Rich, ambitious and passionate . . . his sad, loving portrait of his native city is amazing."—*The Washington Post*

"Full of fascinating characters, tersely brought to life in a prose style that is (thanks to Howard Curtis's shrewd translation) traditionally dark and completely original."—*The Chicago Tribune*

The first installment in the Marseilles Trilogy.

www.europaeditions.com

Chourmo
Jean-Claude Izzo
Fiction/Noir - 256 pp - $14.95 - isbn 978-1-933372-17-4

"Like the best noir writers—and he is among the best—Izzo not only has a keen eye for detail but also digs deep into what makes men weep."—*Time Out New York*

Fabio Montale is dragged back into the mean streets of a violent, crime-infested Marseilles after the disappearance of his long-lost cousin's teenage son.

www.europaeditions.com

The Goodbye Kiss
Massimo Carlotto
Fiction/Noir - 192 pp - $14.95 - isbn 978-1-933372-05-1

"A nasty, explosive little tome warmly recommended to fans of
James M. Cain for its casual amorality and truly astonishing .
speed."—*Kirkus Reviews*

An unscrupulous womanizer, as devoid of morals now as he once
was full of idealistic fervor, returns to Italy, where he is wanted for a
series of crimes. To avoid prison he sells out his old friends, turns
his back on his former ideals, and cuts deals with crooked cops. To
earn himself the guise of respectability he is willing to go even further, maybe even as far as murder.

www.europaeditions.com

Death's Dark Abyss
Massimo Carlotto
Fiction/Noir - 192 pp - $14.95 - isbn 978-1-933372-18-1

"A narrative voice that in Lawrence Venuti's translation is cold and heartless—but, in a creepy way, fascinating."—*The New York Times*

A riveting drama of guilt, revenge, and justice, Massimo Carlotto's *Death's Dark Abyss* tells the story of two men and the savage crime that binds them. During a robbery, Raffaello Beggiato takes a young woman and her child hostage and later murders them. Beggiato is arrested, tried, and sentenced to life. The victims' father and husband, Silvano, plunges into a deepening abyss until the day the murderer seeks his pardon and he begins to plot his revenge.

www.europaeditions.com

Hangover Square
Patrick Hamilton
Fiction/Noir - 280 pp - $14.95 - isbn 978-1-933372-06-8

"Hamilton is a sort of urban Thomas Hardy: always a pleasure to read, and as social historian he is unparalleled."—NICK HORNBY

Adrift in the grimy pubs of London at the outbreak of World War II, George Harvey Bone is hopelessly infatuated with Netta, a cold, contemptuous small-time actress. George also suffers from occasional blackouts. During these moments one thing is horribly clear: he must murder Netta.

www.europaeditions.com

Boot Tracks
Matthew F. Jones
Fiction/Noir - 208 pp - $14.95 - isbn 978-1-933372-11-2

"More than just a very good crime thriller, this dark but illuminating novel shows us the psychopathology of the criminal mind . . . A nightmare thriller with the power to haunt."
—*Kirkus Reviews* (starred)

A commanding, stylishly written novel that tells the harrowing story of an assassination gone terribly wrong and the man and woman who are taking their last chance to find a safe place in a hostile world.

www.europaeditions.com

Love Burns
Edna Mazya
Fiction/Noir - 192 pp - $14.95 - isbn 978-1-933372-08-2

"This book, which has Woody Allen overtones, should be of great interest to readers of black humor and psychological thrillers."
—*Library Journal* (starred)

Ilan, a middle-aged professor of astrophysics, discovers that his young wife is having an affair. Terrified of losing her, he decides to confront her lover instead. Their meeting ends in the latter's murder—the unlikely murder weapon being Ilan's pipe—and in desperation, Ilan disposes of the body in the fresh grave of his kindergarten teacher. But when the body is discovered, the mayhem begins.

www.europaeditions.com

Departure Lounge
Chad Taylor
Fiction/Noir - 176 pp - $14.95 - isbn 978-1-933372-09-9

"Smart, original, surprising and just about as cool as a novel can get . . . Taylor can flat out write."—*The Washington Post*

A young woman mysteriously disappears. The lives of those she has left behind—family, acquaintances, and strangers intrigued by her disappearance—intersect to form a captivating latticework of coincidences and surprising twists of fate. Urban noir at its stylish and intelligent best.

www.europaeditions.com

The Big Question
Wolf Erlbruch
Children's Illustrated Fiction - 52 pp - $14.95 - isbn 978-1-933372-03-7

Named Best Book at the 2004 Children's Book Fair in Bologna.

"[*The Big Question*] offers more open-ended answers than the likes of Shel Silverstein's *Giving Tree* (1964) and is certain to leave even younger readers in a reflective mood."—*Kirkus Reviews*

A stunningly beautiful and poetic illustrated book for children that poses the biggest of all big questions: Why am I here?

www.europaeditions.com

The Butterfly Workshop
Wolf Erlbruch
Children's Illustrated Fiction - 40 pp - $14.95 - isbn 978-1-933372-12-9

Illustrated by the winner of the 2006 Hans Christian Andersen Award

For children and adults alike: Odair, one of the Designers of All Things and grandson of the esteemed inventor of the rainbow, has been banished to the insect laboratory as punishment for his over-active imagination. But he still dreams of one day creating a cross between a bird and a flower.

www.europaeditions.com

Carte Blanche
Carlo Lucarelli
Fiction/Noir - 120 pp - $14.95 - isbn 978-1-933372-15-0

"This is Alan Furst country, to be sure."—*Booklist*

The house of cards built by Mussolini in the last months of World War II is collapsing and Commissario De Luca faces a world mired in sadistic sex, dirty money, drugs and murder.

JUL -- 2007 PCR

www.europaeditions.com

Dog Day
Alicia Giménez-Bartlett
Fiction/Noir - 208 pp - $14.95 - isbn 978-1-933372-14-3

"In Nicholas Caistor's smooth translation from the Spanish, Giménez-Bartlett evokes pity, horror and laughter with equal adeptness. No wonder she won the Femenino Lumen prize in 1997 as the best female writer in Spain."—*The Washington Post*

Delicado and her maladroit sidekick, Garzón, investigate the murder of a tramp whose only friend is a mongrel dog named Freaky.